ADAM BENDER

The characters and events portrayed in this book are fictitious. Any similarity to real persons, living or dead, is coincidental and not intended by the author.

Text copyright © 2014 by Adam Bender

Cover design by Belinda Pepper

Edited by Coraline Denhart

First paperback edition 2014

All rights reserved.

No part of this book may be reproduced, or stored in a retrieval system, or transmitted in any form or by any means, electronic, mechanical, photocopying, recording, or otherwise, without express written permission of the publisher.

Print typesetting and e-book formatting by BookCoverCafe.com

www.WeTheDivided.com

978-1-4954921-2-9 (pbk)

978-0-9924629-0-1 (ebk)

Dedication

For Mallika, a true love who I could never forget.

Table of Contents

Part One: Divided — 9
Fallen Apart — 11
At First Sight — 17
Panic — 23
Blockade — 31
Missionary — 39
Loganville — 49
First Date — 59
Heresy! — 67
Lost & Found — 79
The Prisoner — 85
The Promise — 93
Allies — 99
Surprise — 111
Reunion — 115
Plans — 121
Doors — 131
Bridge — 141
Engine Valley — 147
At Second Sight — 155
Division — 161
Facility B — 171
Seven v. Jon — 175
The Return — 181
Until Death… — 191

Part Two: United	197
Last Days	199
Regrets	209
Politics	215
Alone, Together	227
Heretics & Saints	235
Evidence	243
V-H Day	249
Commitment	259
The Debate	267
Life Support	277
Once & Future	289
Attack!	299
Faith	307
A New Day	317
Ever After	321

—PART ONE—
Divided

CHAPTER ONE
Fallen Apart

The entire limousine shook as another squadron of jets rocketed into the smoking Capital. Eve did her best to keep a glass of red wine from spilling onto the plush white seats.

"I'm starting to suspect drinking was a bad idea," she lilted to her chauffeur through the partition. "And yet it seemed like such a good idea at the time."

With a wry smile, he released the brake and caught up with the traffic jam.

Lifting a free hand, Eve pulled several fugitive blond hairs from her eyes. Now she could see why the evacuation was proceeding at such a trickle pace–the Guard had formed a blockade at the Tunnel. They were stopping everyone.

Eve counted three lanes open for the evacuation, with a fourth reserved for Guard vehicles coming into the Capital. Two soldiers stood in front of each entrance.

Fascinating, she thought. This was the kind of thing the Guard did before sports events or big parades downtown. But Eve couldn't quite wrap her head around why the president would have ordered a roadblock during a national emergency, when the priority should be moving people along.

"This all seems a bit excessive, don't you think?" she asked the driver.

He didn't reply.

Frowning at her Pinot Noir, Eve remarked, "You give me no choice," and tossed it back.

She caught a glimpse of the chauffeur's critical eyes in the rear-view mirror. She moaned slightly and covered her face.

"Sir?" the driver tried.

Following the advice of her psychologist, Eve took a deep breath. Then, she disregarded it and poured herself more wine.

Eventually, the limo pulled up alongside one of the soldiers. He looked like all the Guard did: tall, stiff, midnight blue uniform. This one had tan skin and a mat of black dots for hair.

"Driver's license," the soldier commanded.

The driver handed him a card and the Guard swiped it though a black, handheld terminal. He studied the device's screen for a few seconds before handing the card back.

Without warning, the soldier popped his head through the window. The driver reeled back and coughed at the intrusion. Eve raised her eyebrows.

"How's everyone doing in here?" the Guard asked with a bit too much mirth for Eve's liking.

She tilted her head just slightly. "We're fine."

"Oh, just one in the back," the soldier mumbled. He studied her, and added, "Have you been crying?"

Her mouth dropped. "Excuse me?"

"Your eyes are red."

She couldn't believe it–not only were the Guard stopping cars, they were wasting people's time! Didn't he have any idea who she was, where they were going?

"This is an evacuation!" Eve finally exclaimed. "We're being attacked!"

He nodded. "Don't worry, it's all under control. Please roll down your window. I need to see your ID as well."

Mumbling curses, Eve followed instructions.

The Guard swiped the card. What appeared on the screen turned his face white. "Oh," he whimpered.

"Is there a problem?" Eve asked. "Does it say I'm a *Heretic*?"

"No, I just–I didn't realize," he stuttered. Still shaking, he attempted a salute. "I'm sorry, sir–I mean, madam? Um, ma'am?"

FALLEN APART

"You can call me 'sir,'" she snapped. "What's your name, soldier?"

"Rodriguez, m–sir!"

"Rodriguez, don't ask people so many questions," Eve sneered. "We're under attack, for God's sake! Do you see that line of cars back there? They don't want to talk. They want to get out."

"Yes, sir!" he said. "Sorry, sir!"

"Well?" she said. It wasn't really a question. "Can we get on our way now?"

Rodriguez's face took on the complexion of a tomato. He saluted, stumbled away from the car, and saluted again.

The chauffeur rolled up the windows and shifted into drive. "Sorry about the inconvenience, sir."

Eve squeezed drops into her eyes and blinked at her reflection in a pocket mirror. Her eyes really were red, and the veins were showing. With a look of disgust, she tossed the glass aside and pressed her hands across her face.

The light from Eve's tablet provided some familiar warmth in the mountain underpass known as the Tunnel. She had a word processing app open. In a previous attempt to type out her emotions, she had managed the word *Journal* and today's date. Biting her lip, she tapped return and wrote:

So, the War's come home.

Eve groaned. She deleted the line and started over again.

Last night, the Enemy arrived on our shores and bombed the Capital. They destroyed the Tower.

Suddenly, her typing turned frantic.

I had Jon. But he ran away, and I don't know where he's gone.

She clenched her teeth.

> *No, that's wrong. That wasn't Jonathan Wyle who ran away; it was "Seven." He didn't know what he was doing. He doesn't remember who he really is. He doesn't remember me.*
>
> *I can still get my Jon back. I will get him back.*
>
> *I tried, God. I really tried! I did everything I was supposed to. I go to church every day! I joined the Guard! My job is to remove Heretics, for God's sake! What have I done wrong to deserve this punishment?!*

Eve took a few seconds to roll the kinks out of her neck.

> *I'm sorry. I didn't mean to speak out of turn, my Lord. Please forgive me. It's just…this war, it was never supposed to come home. We worked so hard to prevent this from happening. How could this be happening? Have we failed You? I know the Headmaster always said You would become vengeful if we couldn't curb the Heretic problem.*

Eve read over the entry and shook her head in disgust. She considered deleting it all but couldn't bring herself to do it. Instead, she hit the return key until the text scrolled up off the screen. Composing herself, she typed anew.

> *Last night's attack proves one thing: we are still so weak. After all the government's efforts to purify the nation, we are still so weak. We should have been ready for the Enemy. But all that doesn't matter anymore. This is the situation, and we're all just going to have to deal. For now, I've just got to sit back in this stupid car*

> *and try to relax. Sure, I don't know who I'm supposed to report to anymore, or even what I'll be doing...*

She hit return again.

> *This isn't productive at all, is it? Why do I even keep a diary?*

Light peeked into the limo and soon the Tunnel was behind them. Eve tossed the tablet into the seat next to her and gazed at the tan blur outside. It was spotted here and there by brown tumbleweed and dull green cacti.

"You know, I really hate the desert," she told the driver.

He grunted.

"This is why I never leave the Capital," she continued, undeterred. "How can one side of a mountain be so much greener than the other?"

The driver pulled his cap up by the brim to scratch a spot on his forehead, and tugged it back down. "I think because the other side has an ocean," he said finally. "It's a geological phenom–"

"That was rhetorical," Eve sneered. "But your answer brings up another point. Why did we have to abandon the ocean for this dry shit? Don't answer that."

The driver took a sip from his bottled water instead. Eve felt sick. They must have waited for hours in traffic trying to get past the Guard's blockade. She wanted to get out and stretch–have a jog maybe, followed by a hot bubble bath.

She shivered. "Can you turn down the A/C, please?"

Everything felt wrong without Jon. She'd managed without him–barely–during his last mission. She had his ring, so she never doubted for a second he'd come back to her. But now he was calling himself by a different name, and wanted nothing to do with her.

Again she stared at the handheld screen. "This is shit," she whimpered. Then, to the driver, "I thought I told you to turn down the A/C."

"It's off, sir."

The diamond on her finger sparkled. Suddenly she was hyperventilating.

The driver half-turned in concern. "Is everything all right?"

"I–I need some air," she choked. Then, screaming, "Please! Just let me out of this goddamned car!"

The limo stopped abruptly on the side of the road. Eve tore open the door and pushed her way into the desert. At last she crumpled over and vomited into the desert sand.

CHAPTER TWO
At First Sight

His eyes swept the café like a security camera, pausing occasionally on tables with ladies and empty seats. Agent Eve Parker watched him carefully. When she felt certain that he was her contact, she called out over the caffeine-enhanced chatter. "Jonathan Wyle!"

The tall man smiled and strolled toward her table. Everything about Wyle exuded youthful energy, from his dark brown sideburns to his clothing, which looked like something between business and business-casual. He was much more dashing than his profile let on, thought Eve, tucking her golden hair behind one ear.

"Call me Jon," he said with a steady gaze into her eyes. "I take it you're Eve?"

"Right-o." She glanced down at her drink and was surprised to hear herself stammer, "I bought a cup already–just two minutes ago–if you want to get some, I'll–"

"No worries, I'm okay," replied Jon, dropping into the wooden chair across from her. "So have you found the hidden camera in here yet?"

"Excuse me?"

He grinned. "A little game I like to play when I come to a new place. The Guard must be monitoring a popular coffeehouse like this, right?"

"Oh, definitely." Eve laughed. She looked up and scanned the ceiling. "My guess," she said, pointing past him, "is that smoke detector over there by the window."

Jon looked over his shoulder. "Maybe."

"No, it has to be. There's another fire alarm by the coffee machines. The Guard can't possibly need two, and anyway, the battery light isn't even blinking."

Jon clapped. "Impressive…So how long have you been an Elite, anyway?"

"Just started," she said. Then, reconsidering, "Well I guess it's been a little more than a year."

"Me too–funny how fast it's gone, huh? The only thing that makes me feel like less of a newbie is all the actual newbies."

"Is that so?"

He leaned forward and explained. "I was introduced to this kid the other day–just started training. He asked me if I'd ever shot anyone."

"Oh no, that's precious," Eve cackled, eyes flashing into his. "So have you?"

"I–I mean…"

"Sorry, you don't have to answer that." She downed the rest of her coffee, slammed it on the table, and got to the point. "I asked you to meet me because I think one of my Watched has been talking to one of yours. Joanna Phelps is one of your targets, right?"

Jon leaned back into his chair and grinned. "You mean Shaan is on the Watched list, too?"

Eve smiled back. "He's one of mine."

"And you think they're conspiring?"

"Well, they've been meeting–"

"–like every other day!" Jon finished for her. "What do you propose we do about it?"

"Well," she said. "I guess we could start with the facts. First thing's first–I intercepted a text message today from Shaan. Maybe you saw it, too?"

"Luna Coast," he recited. "8 p.m. Come alone."

"That's the one."

"What do you think it is? Information exchange?"

AT FIRST SIGHT

"Might be more serious than that," she said. "My guy Shaan is into explosives."

He leaned forward and whispered, "That's why he's on the List?"

"A couple years ago, he built a cherry bomb and blew up a mailbox."

Jon's eyes widened. "And they let him live?"

She shrugged. "No one got hurt. He said it was a test gone awry, and no one could prove otherwise. Also, he works on special effects for movies, and it was *his* mailbox that he destroyed."

He laughed. "Perfect."

"All that aside," said Eve with a wave of her coffee mug, "I've been building a case on him for the past six months. Don't have enough to prove it yet, but I think he's connected to the Underground. Radical group like that could use a good engineer."

"Interesting," Jon mused, "though I'm not sure how that fits with Joanna's story. She's just a reporter—wrote an editorial on the *National News* blog a little while back that was a little controversial."

"What did it say?"

"Um, I haven't read it, actually," he said, clearing his throat. "The Guard caught it before it went to press, and I'm not aware of any copies floating around. I started watching her a few days later." He swatted the air and continued. "But that's beside the point. Sounds to me like we need to get a bit more information on these people. I was planning to head to the Luna Coast tonight and check up on Joanna anyway. You wanna come along? Eve?"

She lifted her eyes quickly from Jon's biceps. "Yes! Sure."

From the Elites' perch atop the lighthouse, Eve watched the last embers of sun sink slowly into the sea. They had a 360-degree view of the precipitous Luna Coast. A sculpture garden stretched several hundred feet from the edge of the cliff to a twisted highway. The marble statues cast long shadows of knights and horses on the grassy field.

"You know, I don't think I've seen a real sunset since I was a little girl," Eve remarked. "Amazing how you can stare right into it–"

"–without going blind?" Jon finished. "Yeah, we Elite Guard don't really get out much, do we?"

As they laughed, a car came up the highway from the direction of the city and pulled into an empty parking lot. Jon lifted his binoculars. "Looks like Joanna."

The target stepped out wearing a blue denim jacket and tall black boots. She retrieved a cigarette from her jacket pocket and lit it. Holding the fag tightly in her mouth, Joanna bent into her car's side mirror and teased her silvery hair with both hands.

Eve glanced at her watch. "Just like a man to be late," she said. Jon gave her a look like he had something to say, but that was the end of it.

A bumblebee buzz developed slowly into the roar of a lion, and a biker appeared on the horizon. "That's Shaan," said Eve.

"He's a motorcycle man, huh?" commented Jon. "Well, you've got an easy job."

She rolled her eyes. "Whatever–I could track a man driving a sedan with tinted windows."

"Touchy."

"I think you mean 'touché.'"

"What, you mean that was supposed to be a comeback?"

Eve stuck out her tongue. Then she swiveled and focused her binoculars upon Shaan, who was busy dusting off his leather jacket and tight jeans. He pulled off his helmet, revealing dark brown skin and wavy black hair.

"He's slick," Jon remarked.

"Your type?" she replied.

"No, I'm allergic to Y chromosomes, unfortunately."

Chuckling, Eve donned a pair of headphones and switched on the audio feed. After some static and a few high-frequency squeals, the scene below amplified into full stereo.

AT FIRST SIGHT

"Sound okay?" asked Jon, slipping on a pair of his own.

"Loud and clear. Let's find out what they're up to."

Joanna looked shakily at her feet as Shaan approached.

"Hey, Jo," said Shaan, reaching into his coat. "Got something for you."

"Oh no," she replied with a tremor.

Eve fiddled with the visual focus. "We getting this?"

Jon pressed his headphones tighter against his ears. "Yeah, camera is rolling and tape is recording."

Shaan pulled out a white and gold cardboard package. Gasping, Joanna snapped it out of his hands. With great exuberance she popped the box open.

Eve's binoculars fell limply to her chest. "Oh no," she groaned. "It can't be."

"Chocolate...cherries, I think," Jon said with a smirk. "Hey, why'd you stop looking? You're missing them kiss."

"Jon, I am so sorry," Eve said meekly at the bottom of the lighthouse. She couldn't believe she'd managed to embarrass herself so much on their first stakeout together. "I just had this hunch, and I was so sure..."

"Hey," he tried, "I mean, it seemed reasonable at the time they might be trading weaponry, or illegally obtained data..."

His rationality didn't make her feel better. "They were trading spit!"

Jon smiled. "Honestly, I think the fact we didn't suspect a date just proves once more how little either of us gets out."

She giggled. "Yeah, I guess so."

They walked to their cars. Eve turned once for a last glimpse at the darkening vista. Somehow the statues seemed to glow more vividly than before.

She breached the silence. "Well, it was nice working with you, Jon."

"Yeah, it was fun," Jon said. He stopped and looked at her.

Eve started to speak, but decided there was no need to manufacture additional humiliation tonight.

"Well…uh…it's still pretty early," said Jon, breaking the silence. "Do you maybe—I mean, do you have any dinner plans…currently?"

CHAPTER THREE
Panic

He saw but could not hear the evacuees as they hurried past the electronic eye of a DAY cash machine. Closed-circuit TV screens inside the bank's basement flashed live images of mothers wrenching children's arms forward and grown men plowing through human gaps. Sometimes someone would trip and disappear into the swarm.

The Heretic known as Seven rubbed a fresh thatch of stubble on his chin. There were bags under his eyes and he had to use his elbows to support his head over the computer desk. Glancing downward, he realized that an idle right hand had carved the name *Eve* into the pinewood with a ballpoint pen. Cursing under his breath, he tossed the writing tool across the room. It bounced across the unfinished concrete floor and disappeared beneath a tangle of gray computer cords.

"...just received confirmation of another church demolished," buzzed the radio news. "The 12th Avenue Cathedral is the sixth major church, and–including the Capitol Tower–the seventh national landmark destroyed since the Enemy began its air strike on the city last night. President Drake has directed the Guard to manage an evacuation of the Capital. We have been asked to remind our listeners to do so in an orderly fashion so as to..."

Up on one of the screens, a guy with a baseball bat took a big hack at the glass door of the car rental place across the street. The smash diverted a stream of evacuees into the opening. Meanwhile, in the foreground, a crumpled woman latched onto the midnight blue leg of a policeman of the Guard. When she refused to let go, the Guard pulled a pistol from his holster and pushed it into her forehead.

Seven forced his attention away from the monitor to the far wall, where there was painted a jet-black face with fiery red eyes. The visage was the sign of the Underground.

He wondered if it was right to hide down here in one of the rebels' nests. Not after everything that had happened, not after everything that he'd done. But where else could he go?

"...are exploring possible communications between the Enemy and the Heretic group known as the Underground in the days leading up to the attack..."

His eyes fell blearily upon a silver thumb drive sticking out of the dusty computer tower by his feet. The red-blinking box contained information that–he hoped–was powerful enough to turn things around in this country, or at least start moving them in the right direction. It had already been an hour since Seven had attached everything to an e-mail and clicked send. The Underground should now have all the evidence.

Seven groaned. He had betrayed the Underground before he helped them, and the guilt lingered like a bad hangover. The past stalked and hounded him at every turn, but the Enemy's attack provided a grand distraction. If he just ran fast enough, he thought, maybe he could leave it all behind.

The lens flared as late-morning sun bled into the streets. A single surveillance monitor was the only source of natural light in the secret basement beneath the DAY Bank, but still the change finally roused Seven from slumber.

He awoke in a fit of profanity. If the clock on the wall was correct, he'd been asleep for almost two hours. After a couple deep breaths, he tugged the memory stick out of the computer and moved for the exit.

PANIC

It was a struggle keeping his gaze high as he crossed the street toward the car rental store. Eventually, avoiding the millions of glass splinters forced his eyes down to the trampled dead and dying. He shivered but pressed on.

Finally, Seven came upon the entrance of the car rental shop. A small sign lying on the ground exclaimed in big red letters: *COME ON IN, WE'RE OPEN!*

He shrugged and shuffled inside.

A CCTV screen hanging in the corner of the room immediately caught his attention. The image was grainy but instantly recognizable. Seven waved his hands and the short-haired man on the screen mimicked the motion on a half-second delay.

The floor of the shop was smothered with torn yellow brochures. The papers, rustling gently under a slow-rotating fan, piled up to swallow the counter in the back. Seven looked left and right, and then clambered over the top. On the other side, he pulled open a drawer and scavenged. Finding nothing, he slammed the drawer shut and yanked at another. After this and a third drawer also proved unfruitful, he let loose an agonized scream.

There must be keys in here somewhere, he told himself. There must be at least one car left.

A deep rumble rattled the counter, shaking loose a brochure. It shimmied out from the pile and floated to the ground. Tracing its fall, Seven's eyes landed upon something else entirely. Poking out from beneath the yellow trash on the floor, a bronze object glinted in the sunlight.

He picked up the key and rushed through the back door labeled *Garage*.

The parking lot was smaller than he had anticipated, and there was only one vehicle left—a slightly beatup looking purple minivan. After some hesitation, he tried his key in the door and it fit. Seven climbed inside and sunk into the driver's seat. He left the door open as he considered where to drive. He couldn't think of a single destination.

It didn't matter, he decided eventually. He would do what he always did–keep moving and let things sort themselves out. The strategy hadn't exactly turned up great results so far, but at least he was still alive and a free man.

Seven reached out to shut the door. To his surprise, his hand met something round and covered with soft cotton. He was swatted away with painful force.

"Hands off!" shot the newcomer, a sharp-eyed girl with a red bandanna wrapped tightly around her hair. She pressed a blunt metal object into his side. "And, like, get your butt out of the van!"

The words "Don't shoot!" came spluttering from his mouth and he flailed his hands wildly in the air. "I'm unarmed. What do you want?"

"What do I want?" the young stranger protested, pointing at the sky. She was short, but stood like a giant. "Didn't you hear the bombs? This city is turning into a war zone! I want to get the hell out!"

"Well, I guess that makes two of us," he said. Suddenly, a strange idea surfaced from the ether and he waved manically at the backseat. "But look, this van has got to be big enough for eight!"

"What?" she seethed, lowering her gun. "Are you suggesting that we…*car pool?*" She said the last two words as if it described a shockingly immoral act.

"Um," he said, "yes?"

The stranger's jaw dropped. "But–but, what do I need you for?"

"I mean," he replied, sounding a little surprised at his success up to this point, "it's pretty easy to steal a car from someone when they're on their own, isn't it? I think you just proved that."

"But you–" she gasped, eyes smoldering. "Fine! But I'm driving–"

He shrugged and slid into the passenger seat. "Then I guess I call shotgun."

PANIC

"And we go where I say, and I drop you off where I want—"

"I'm Seven, by the way."

"—and you—what?"

"Seven. It's my name. Do you have one as well?"

"Talia," she grumbled, swinging her small frame inside. Her ponytail hit him in the face.

A sign at the garage exit asked Seven and Talia to stop to pay the attendant. But the station was empty and the gate was smashed to pieces. Talia sped up and the minivan shot out into the morning light.

The radio, which had been nothing but a hiss of static in the garage, came suddenly alive. "…state of emergency is still in effect, and Patriots living within the Capital have been instructed to evacuate. No word yet on whether the Guard anticipate further attacks from the Enemy, and if so, when and where they might occur. But if you are still in the city, you must evacuate immediately."

The intersection ahead was a sea of pigeons. Most of the gray birds bobbed around an upturned pretzel cart; though some hadn't yet caught on to what all the excitement was about. The birds stiffened as the van neared. Then, like one great phoenix, they lifted off into the smoke-filled sky.

"So," said Talia over the broadcast. "You call yourself Seven, huh? That's an interesting name."

He looked at her blankly.

"Are you very lucky?"

"Not especially."

Talia rolled her eyes. "C'mon, there's no way your parents named you after a number."

"Oh, well, it's kind of a dumb story…"

"In that case, you can spare me the details."

Seven looked helplessly at the tuner. "Enemy fighters late last night appeared over the Luna Coast and launched a bombing campaign on the Capital," the radio said. "In the attack—wait, hold on a minute—we're receiving some new information. We're going to go to Alan Thomas for the latest."

"Thanks, Ethan," said a new voice. "We've just learned that the Enemy has a full navy fleet located about twenty miles off the Luna Coast, and the Guard believe that's where the fighters returned after the attack. An administration official told us the Guard has just sent its own jets into the Capital to engage them."

"Is there any word on the Enemy's next move?"

"Not at this time. But we should be getting more information shortly."

"Thanks for that report in our developing story. Just fifteen minutes ago, the president said this about the attack…"

"Make no mistake—we will get these guys! The Enemy will pay dearly for its aggression upon our great, peaceful nation. But as we strike outwards, we must also look inwards and consider how we might stop this from happening ever again. Although our nation remains strong, we must consider the damaging and divisive impact of heresy in our land."

Seven shook his head. Even when the country was getting attacked by another country, the Guard blamed alleged Heretics inside its own borders. Seven was not surprised. The so-called Heretics had been the Guard's default scapegoats for as long as he could remember.

"For the past year, we have been tracking a group of Heretic extremists known as the Underground," the president went on. "Their work has been to sabotage our fine nation, and their attacks have become increasingly vicious in recent months. Yesterday, we captured their leader. In the days to come, we will snuff out their faction entirely."

Seven felt a rush of guilt as he recalled the role he had played in the arrest. He anxiously fingered the memory stick in his pocket.

The anchor's warm vibrato returned. "The president, of course, was referring to yesterday's capture and execution of Daniel Alexander Young. The Guard learned that Young, president of

DAY Corporation, was secretly funding the Underground using company profits. Last night, just before the attack, Young's son and likely successor–Daniel Alexander Young, Jr.–released this statement about his father's arrest, which denies any DAY ties to the Underground."

Young's voice was tremulous. "Although DAY Corporation certainly signed my father's paychecks, the company was unaware of–and exercised no control over–how he spent his money after hours. One man's mistake should not–and will not–jeopardize the jobs of the thousands of flag-waving Patriots who work for DAY Corporation. The Board and I are currently reviewing our books to ensure that any and all lingering connections between the company and Heretic extremists are severed."

"Again, those were the words of Daniel Alexander Young, Jr.–or Danny Young, as he's better known in the tabloids."

The radio burst with drums and staccato synthesizer. "Coming up after these messages, we'll have more on what the attack means for citizens living *outside* the Capital. Stay with us."

Seven looked up and saw that Talia was running a red traffic light. He didn't flinch. "Well this certainly is disconcerting," he said instead.

Between the cavernous skyscrapers, the place was a ghost town. Newspapers and other garbage rolled by like tumbleweed. Here and there, bodies lay crumpled on the pavement. But there was no one else. Even the homeless seemed to have gone.

"You and I waited a long time to get out of the city," said Talia as if she could sense Seven's awe. "Most of the people who wanted to leave are out already or on the highway."

Seven considered. "So what are *you* still doing here?"

"You first," she returned.

Not wanting to divulge any details either, he asked, "Where are we going?"

"Like, duh, the only exit out of this city?" she said.

He looked at her blankly.

"Uh, the Tunnel?"

"Oh right," he said, trying to pass it off like a momentary lapse. "And after that?"

Talia gasped and slammed the brakes. The van stopped short a few feet from a garbage dump of twisted metal and crumbled concrete.

"Oh my God," she said, turning off the radio. "Is that…?"

"The Capitol Tower," Seven finished. "You didn't know?"

"I heard," Talia said with a hand on her forehead. "But I'd only seen the cathedral on Bell Street."

"The Enemy seems to have targeted national symbols," he replied.

"What's their game?" she cried. "They've got bombs so big they could wipe our whole country off the map, just like that! Why didn't they use them?"

"Maybe they were worried we'd nuke them back."

She shook her head condescendingly. "You say that like it's off the table."

Talia shifted into reverse and pressed the gas. The minivan did a backwards U-turn, raced forward a block and whipped around a corner. Someone on the street screamed–Talia ripped the steering wheel back and forth and the van squealed by a soot-covered woman. Seven spun around to watch the lone figure through the rear window. The lady dropped to her knees and appeared to cry out.

"If we pick one up," stated Talia, "we'll have to pick them all up."

CHAPTER FOUR
Blockade

Hawk-eyed agents of the Elite Guard filled the Desert Base's double-tiered auditorium to capacity. Conversation was kept to a hush, but Eve doubted it was out of respect to the lives lost in the Enemy's attack. The predators were silent by instinct.

A hook-nosed man with silver hair slid carefully into the seat next to Eve and stared. She returned his gaze with a polite smile and turned her attention to the stage.

"Hey, angel, what cloud in heaven did you come from?"

She looked at him for a few seconds to verify the question was directed her way. When he nodded she gritted her teeth, and without emotion replied, "The Capital."

"I'm from the Engine Valley."

Figures, she thought. "And what a *lovely* city that is. By the way, I'm engaged."

He frowned and muttered, "I don't appreciate the sarcasm."

Of course he didn't, reflected Eve. Very few Guard–and fewer Elite Guard–had a sense of humor–something to do with the overbearing alpha-male culture of the institution, she suspected. Still, it wouldn't stop her from trying. As a man wearing sunglasses approached the oak podium and tinkered with the microphone, she nudged her other neighbor, who looked younger and thus potentially still human.

"This is the third time that man has been on the stage," she whispered with a hint of mischief. "The government does more sound checks than a *rock* band."

The agent produced a smile, but seemed to have trouble holding it. "I wouldn't know," he said.

Eve nodded until he looked away, then she buried her head in her hands.

The house lights dimmed. President William Drake and his entourage strolled onstage to roaring applause. He was a distinguished looking gentleman with salt-and-pepper hair, and his every movement oozed charisma. Eve thought him attractive, but impossibly unattainable. Anyway, she had a man. Or did, anyway.

"Thank you," Drake purred with a sprinkle of country twang. "Thank you. Thank you. Thank you." He raised his hands gently for quiet, but the sign wasn't understood. "Please," he tried.

The applause continued.

"Please," he said again, tightening his navy blue tie. "Thank you…Thank you…Please…"

"Silence!" roared a black-cloaked figure, striding to the president's side. The cleric's face was barely visible beneath the shadow of his hood, but Eve knew it was the Headmaster. The appearance of the Church leader brought quick silence, leaving only the shallow cough of someone in the back. The dark figure glared it into submission.

"Thank you, Father," Drake said sheepishly. He looked out over the crowd. "And thank *all of you* for coming out here on such short notice. It's vital that you be here with us during the greatest crisis our nation has faced since the Great War."

Eve couldn't help but shiver. The president and the Headmaster rarely appeared together. President Drake tended to take on the more public duties of leadership—including speeches to the troops—while his counterpart in the Church kept to a largely background and administrative role in the nation's affairs. Certainly the Enemy's attack on the Capital was serious enough to justify a joint briefing, but for Eve the bombing somehow hadn't felt so real until now.

Drake took a deep breath and began. "As you know, the Enemy has arrived on our soil. In the initial attack, we lost the

Capitol Tower and some of our largest churches. But we have not lost the Capital, and we have not lost our great nation!"

The Elites cheered.

"We have taken a hit, but we will not sit idly by. No, we will face them and remove them from our land!"

Another roar of approval from the assembled Guard. Drake bared his teeth until it settled down.

"At this very moment," he continued, "the Enemy is planning a raid on Luna Coast. Already we have troops ready to meet them at the shore, and reinforcements will be sent from this base shortly. The Enemy will be stopped, and then killed."

"Nuke them to Hell!" shouted someone in the crowd.

Eve rolled her eyes and half turned in her seat to see who said it.

Drake forced a smile. "Now, now," he said shakily. "In terms of using atomic weaponry…we are at this time…considering our options. Although the Enemy *has* attacked us on our own shore, we do not want to be hasty in our response. We must focus now solely and completely on fighting them back and removing heresy from the Capital."

"Some kind of blockade," observed Talia.

"Uh huh," Seven replied listlessly. He was caught up in a scene about thirty feet down the road where a Guard wearing thin black shades was pulling a lanky kid out of his black sports car seemingly by the scruff of his neck. The soldier shoved the boy face-first into the asphalt, kicked him until he stopped moving, and shackled his wrists.

Talia shifted into park just as a different Guard rapped at her window.

"Good evening," the soldier stated through lowering glass. He had to bend slightly to make eye contact with Talia. "My apologies for the inconvenience. Just need to see both of your licenses."

Talia turned hers over as if on autopilot. Seven froze. An ID was one thing he never got around to faking.

The Guard swiped Talia's card through a black handheld. It blipped and the soldier's eyes widened. "Huh," he said.

"What?" asked Talia.

The soldier ignored her and looked to Seven. "Sir, I need your card, too."

"Uh, I left it at home," he lied. "There was a panic, and we had to get out quick, and so—"

The Guard turned and waved at the soldier with the sunglasses who seemed to be finished with the youthful offender in the other car. "Hagarton, come over here and help me with these two."

Hagarton marched over to the passenger side of the vehicle.

The Guard on Talia's side cleared his throat to regain her attention. "Could you please tell me where exactly you thought you were going?"

"Loganville," she said.

"Why?"

"My brother lives there," she said. "Wait, what do you mean, *thought we were* going?"

The Guard ignored the question. "Both of you are going to need to get out of the car and come with us."

"What?" Talia exploded. "What's going on?"

Now the soldier's expression turned severe. "By the order of the president, Watched are not permitted to leave the Capital."

Hagarton attempted to open Seven's door but it was locked. "Come out of the vehicle, please." As he growled, an aroma like coffee in an ashtray wafted through the minivan.

Seven's mind raced. This wasn't right, he thought. Even if Talia was Watched, that just made her a suspected Heretic. The Guard had always maintained a careful eye on Watched, but as far as he knew they couldn't legally arrest someone until proven Heretic.

He was about to air his grievances aloud when Talia floored the gas pedal.

BLOCKADE

"I would like to—" the president started, then stopped. "I would like to assure you that this attack does not mean that our defenses are inherently weak, or that the Guard is ill prepared to deal with surprise attacks from hostiles. The problem is, as it has always been, the frightening growth and purveyance of heresy amongst our citizens."

Perhaps realizing the crowd's eyes had fallen upon him, the Headmaster nodded gravely.

President Drake continued. "Mere hours before the attack, we made significant progress on this front. We arrested and killed the traitor Daniel Alexander Young. Young used his riches—riches that could only have been gained in this fine nation—to fund a militant rebel group called the Underground. For this, he paid the ultimate price. With his death we've cut the roots from the Underground, and soon its existence will be but a mere memory. But still, perhaps Young's execution was too little, too late. His treason divided the nation and left it vulnerable to the horrible attack we witnessed yesterday."

The president dropped his speech on the podium and continued. "You know, the other week I was visiting National University, speaking to students about what it means to be a Patriot. National, as you know, is my alma mater, and I give this speech every year around graduation time. Well, they put us in an auditorium much like this one, and they had microphones in the aisles for students to ask questions. At first, I got the usual questions—how's the First Dog, how do you manage the stress of running a country, and so on and so forth. But there was this one girl—I forget her name but I'll never forget what she said to me—she asked me, 'What gives you the authority...'"

The audience hooted.

"I'm not kidding!" Drake returned merrily. "She asked, 'What gives *you* the authority to decide who's a Patriot and who's a Heretic?' So I'm up there thinking, 'God almighty, where do I even begin?' I'm about to answer, when—thank God—a school official pulls her away from the mic and escorts her out the building!"

Drake waited for the cheers to subside. "But I don't want to go off on too long a tangent here. If you want to know more, ask Agent William Graves—he's assigned to watch her now." The president held a hand up to his forehead and squinted into the crowd. "You here, Willy?"

If Willy was around, he didn't respond. Eve figured he was probably drunk somewhere. She knew the asshole and didn't think much of him. On several occasions the agent made arrests based on what Eve considered rather flimsy evidence. It usually held up in court, but that wasn't the point.

"Look," said Drake, "the lesson here is that we must not merely exterminate the Enemy, but indeed all enemies to this country's welfare. We simply must ramp up our efforts to eliminate heresy. That is why today I have ordered the arrest of every Heretic on the Watched List."

Eve straightened in her seat. What did he just say?

"All of you should be commended for your brilliant work following these dangerous men and women, and sniffing out their deviance. But yesterday's attack proved that our policies have given the Watched too much slack. My friends, I tell you now that too many Heretics have slipped through our fingers. But we have learned. And now they will pay the price."

"But not all Watched are Heretics," mumbled Eve, shutting up as she became aware of her hook-nosed neighbor's suspicious gaze.

Drake shuffled through his papers. "Now," he said, scanning the page. "We have already begun arresting the Watched from the Capital. We set up a blockade at the Tunnel, and have so far captured hundreds of would-be escapees. But now we must extend our net to the rest of the nation. Those of you here from out of town will be given new orders upon your return home. You will arrest your current targets, and interrogate them. We will compile what information we learn and use it to wipe heresy from our fair land. Meanwhile, agents who were based in the Capital will stay here at the Desert Base until further notice."

The president took a step back from the podium and the Headmaster glided forward. The black-cloaked priest breathed slowly through his nostrils and then spoke. "Let us pray." The minister's head lifted skyward and he began to hum a low drone. The congregation soon followed. Eve closed her eyes and felt her shoulders relax.

Seven watched their interrogator fall flat on his back and shrink in the rear window. The other Guard, still standing, pulled a gun from his holster.

"What the hell do you think you're doing?!" he yelled at Talia.

A bullet dinged off the trunk.

"What the hell?!" he cried again.

Talia's hands tightened around the wheel. "Shut up, shut up, shut up!"

The Tunnel's darkness fell upon them. The dash glowed 65, 66 and then 67 miles per hour. Seven spun around and saw a Guard vehicle in hot pursuit. "I think their car is a little faster than ours," he griped.

"Oh, ye of little faith," she said, but a waver in her voice betrayed the show of confidence.

Another bullet smacked off of the minivan's bumper.

"That's it," Seven declared. He unbuckled and bent over Talia's lap.

"Um," she said. "What are you doing?"

He came up with Talia's gun in his hand.

"Hey!" she protested.

Ignoring her, Seven leaned out the window, took aim at the police car and pulled the trigger.

Nothing happened. He slid back into the car and gritted his teeth. "Has this been empty the whole time?"

Talia's eyes flitted in his direction. "Um…maybe?"

Ridiculous, he thought, glancing into the side mirror. One of the Guard was hanging out the passenger-side window, lining up another shot.

Seven had an idea. He buckled his seat belt and ordered Talia to slam the brakes.

"What?" she squawked.

"Remember what you did to the gas pedal just a minute ago? Do it to the brakes."

"Are you crazy?!"

"Now!"

The minivan screeched to a skidding stop. Talia and Seven shot forward, but the belts caught them.

The wheels of the police car squealed behind them. The soldier leaning out the window plunged forward, smashing his shoulder against the frame. His pistol skipped and rattled across the pavement. Talia braced for collision, but at the last minute the Guard car swerved and slammed into the right side of the Tunnel.

Talia opened her mouth to speak, but failed miserably.

Seven didn't give the accident a moment's notice. "Now, drive!"

CHAPTER FIVE
Missionary

"Eve heard a squeaky voice call out as she left the auditorium. She turned and saw a short, pudgy man in a crimson robe hustling in her direction. "Excuse me," he wheezed, clearly out of breath. "Are you Agent Eve Parker?"

She squinted at him. "Yes?"

"He wants to see you–immediately."

"Who?"

"*He*," the churchman repeated with more emphasis.

A chill ran down her spine. She bit her lip and followed the small man through three hallways and two security checkpoints. Eventually, they came upon a thick metal door and a fresh-faced soldier. The priest signaled to the Guard and he tugged the hatch open, revealing a black, empty room.

"I'm not to come any further, my child," the clergyman told Eve. "The Headmaster seeks you alone."

Before Eve could protest, the priest had scuttled back down the fluorescent tunnel from which they had come.

Eve gathered what courage she had and stepped inside. The door slammed shut behind her, leaving the Elite in bleak darkness. Suddenly a spotlight snapped on, revealing a single gray folding chair in the middle of the room. Eve stepped cautiously toward it, holding her hands out in front of her for protection. It felt like hours before she reached her destination and lowered herself into the seat.

"We have you on tape saying something we find quite disturbing," bellowed a deep voice that seemed to come from all directions.

Eve blinked. "I'm sorry, what–?"

There was a click and a whir, and then a buzzing playback of Jon's voice filled the room. "Why should I believe you?" he was demanding.

"Because I would never betray you," cried Eve with a touch of static. "Not even for the Guard!"

Something clicked and the sound cut out. "This was recorded in the Capitol Tower shortly after the bombing, before the building came down. The voices, as I'm sure you remember, belong to you and Agent Jonathan Wyle. We have reason to believe that Agent Wyle escaped the building's collapse, and that you assisted him in that escape."

Eve rubbed her arms for warmth. She knew what the Headmaster was getting at, and admittedly it looked bad. But she also knew she wasn't a traitor. She could explain all of this.

"Agent," the Headmaster growled. "Is there anything you would like to add?"

Eve's mouth opened before she found the words. "I think there's been a misunderstanding," she tried. "He had a gun to my head and–"

"But did you mean what you said? Does Agent Wyle come before God and country? Do not lie to us."

"I…" gasped Eve, shutting her eyes tightly. "All I meant was that I love my fiancé. I meant that I love him more than anything in this world, and yes, that includes my allegiance to the Guard. But Father, that's only because the Guard are but mere men. I promise you…I would never go against the will of God Himself."

The Headmaster sounded mollified by this answer. "But this man–your fiancé–he is not your Jon any longer. He refers to himself by another name, correct?"

"Yes…he calls himself Seven. We weren't able to restore his memory before the Enemy attacked. I tried to tell him who he was, but he wouldn't listen."

"How could he?" the Headmaster asked rhetorically. "Modern science has fashioned him into a blank slate, and the Heretics scrawled their demonic views all over him. Mr. Wyle has lost his way, and we suspect there is no return."

No, she wouldn't believe that. She would find a way. She had to.

"It is more than your words that concerns us," said the cleric, breathing deeply through his nostrils. "You gave him something. What was it?"

"A memory stick," she said.

"What information does it contain?"

"The stick itself doesn't contain much data at all. But we need it to access the surveillance chip in Jon's head."

Eve felt unnerved by the Headmaster's silence. Finally, he spoke. "So what you are saying is that you gave this Seven character access to everything that was recorded during Agent Wyle's mission, including your confession to him about the nature of his mission. And then, without restoring his identity, you let him get away. Is that correct?"

Eve's face plummeted. It all sounded much worse coming from the high priest. "Y-yes, Father."

"Do you see how that might create a problem for us?"

"We were being attacked—the building was going to collapse—he was going to shoot me!" She was whimpering. "I'm…I'm so sorry."

"Do not apologize to me. Apologize to God. Beg Him for Forgiveness."

Eve clasped her hands together and groveled.

"On your knees!"

She did as she was told. "I'm so sorry…"

"It is of *national importance*," said the Headmaster, pausing for emphasis, "that information about the technology in Mr. Wyle's head is not revealed to the public. You will find this Seven and bring him to us."

Eve opened her eyes. "What will you do to him?"

"Jonathan Wyle," he hissed, "will be Saved."

She bit her lip. "But Father, I'm sorry, but I don't even know where to look. He could be anywhere in the Capital right now…"

The Headmaster grunted with disgust. "He's not there. We have information from the blockade that he's crossed city lines and headed north. There's a woman with him named Talia. She told the Guard their destination is Loganville. You will prepare tonight and leave first thing tomorrow morning."

So Jon had made it out. More importantly, thought Eve, they knew where he was. It was a second chance and it felt like destiny. She would track him down, explain everything again, and maybe this time he'd listen to reason and let her help.

"Agent Parker, a reminder," the Headmaster hissed. "If you fail us again, we may no longer shield you from God's vengeance."

Eve zipped open her suitcase and sighed heavily. She bit one of her fingernails, and began to pace.

The Elite's room at the Desert Base wasn't large. Whoever designed the soldiers' quarter was obviously more interested in efficiency than comfort. The cabinets, chests and even TV were sunk into one wall, and everything but the blankets seemed to be made of polished steel. She had to read a clock to tell if it was light outside.

Not that there was a place for a window. The Desert Base was hidden deep underground, completely invisible to even the best spy satellites. Getting there required a driver with a good sense of direction, and–perhaps more importantly–great patience. The exit off the highway was visible only to the trained eye, and the dirt road stretched on for miles. During her journey here the only assurance Eve got that her driver was going the right way had been a series of Guard checkpoints. After three of those isolated shacks, the road sank dramatically into a sandy cave that was the entrance to the compound.

MISSIONARY

She wasn't looking forward to sleeping here tonight.

Eve reached into her pocket for her cell phone, but it slipped out of her fingers and slid beneath the bed. She fell onto all fours to get it. Just as she got a hand on the device, a thunderous knocking at the door jolted her head up against the bottom of the bed frame. Many expletives followed.

"Everything all right in there?" called a male voice behind the door.

Eve gritted her teeth, and seethed, "Yes, fine." She stared at the door, transfixed.

"Good to hear," the voice answered with some hesitation. "Um, could you open the door?"

"I told you I'm fine," she snapped. "I don't need a doctor, if that's what you are."

"What? I'm no doctor. Agent Rik Rodriguez reporting for duty, sir. I was sent down to meet you, to prepare for our mission."

Eve rubbed her bruise. "Excuse me? Our mission? I'm working alone."

There was a long pause. "Um, have you checked your messages recently?"

"Hold on," she grumbled, pulling out her phone. Indeed, she had three new messages. "Huh," she commented.

"May I come in now?"

"One minute," she said, thumbing through the first e-mail.

Eve,

We have decided to partner you with Mr. Rik Rodriguez, a rising young star we are considering for the Elite Guard. He is an expert marksman, but could use some more experience. We believe that you will make an excellent mentor.

"Great–they don't trust me," she muttered, sheathing the phone. She adjusted her hair with one hand and pulled open the door with the other.

The sight of the Elite-in-training made her gag. It was that fool from the blockade who'd asked her if she was crying!

His eyes widened as he, too, made the connection. "Oh!" he gasped.

"What are you doing here? Shouldn't you be out directing traffic?"

He grimaced. "I was promoted?"

Rodriguez looked horrified as Eve collected her suitcase and stomped out the door. Ten feet down the hall, she looked over her shoulder. "Planning to follow?" she fumed.

"Yes, ma'am–sir," stammered Rodriguez, jogging to catch up. "Where…where are we going?"

"To get some coffee," she said. "Or possibly hard liquor–I haven't decided yet."

The desire to rouse her brain eventually beat out the thirst to numb it, so they went to the base's coffee house. The only other person there was a cashier whose only responsibility seemed to be asking customers from which self-serve dispenser they poured their drink. Eve chose the extra dark variety, while Rodriguez opted for hazelnut light. The seasoned agent took her coffee black; the rookie dropped in two packets of white sugar and a dollop of heavy cream.

Eve picked a table that was as far away from the cashier as she could find. She dusted a scattering of sugar off the top and they sat down.

The coffee was awful, tasting staler than even the atmosphere. She put the drink down and slid her cell phone across the cold-steel table toward Rodriguez, who was smiling a bit timidly. "This is a photograph of the target," she said. "His name is Jonathan Wyle but lately he's been going by the alias Seven."

Rodriguez picked the phone up carefully, as if it might break in his hands. He squinted at the image on the screen, and choked a little bit on his drink.

MISSIONARY

Eve's eyes narrowed. "What?"

"Is that you in the back? Wearing the bikini?"

She turned red, leaned over the table, and snatched the device back. "We were at the beach, and it's not a bikini. It's a two-piece swimsuit."

"Wait, the target is your boyfriend?!" he exclaimed. "Oh my God, is that why you were crying earlier?"

This was exactly why she didn't want a partner on this mission. "You don't know the whole story," she seethed.

"With all due respect, sir, it might help if you told me."

"Fine." She leaned back in the wooden chair and sipped her hot drink. "So as I was saying, the target's real name is Jonathan Wyle. He was one of us–an Elite Guard–but recently he elected to take part in a top secret mission to infiltrate the Underground and expose their secrets."

"It didn't work?" Rodriguez asked.

"No, it *worked*," she answered. "It was actually because of this mission that we just nabbed Daniel Alexander Young–you know, industrial giant by day, secret leader of the Underground by night? But there were some…complications, I suppose, arising from the, shall we say, *experimental* nature of the mission."

Rodriguez nodded.

Eve scowled. "Don't act like you understand."

He blinked helplessly, like a fish caught on a line.

"See," she began, "it's not exactly an easy task to get into the Underground. If it was, we would have done it a long time ago. The thing is, for all the shit we give the rebels, they're actually kind of clever. And they're really good at sniffing out Guard."

"So you're saying the Underground is too smart for us to infiltrate by ordinary means?"

"Well, phrasing it like that would be borderline heresy," she snapped. "All I'm saying is that their ideology is so contrary to our own that we tend to stand out like a wolf in a flock of sheep. We needed a disguise."

"More than a sheepskin costume, I hope?"

"Science," she answered. "Our best engineers designed a microchip implant that could block out selected memories, essentially resetting a person's beliefs about the outside world, the government, and etcetera. His mind would be like a hunk of fresh clay, ready for sculpting. Am I getting too science fiction for you?"

"I love sci-fi."

"Good, that will help you in this line of work," she said. "Anyway, we saw the chip as an opportunity to finally carry out a successful undercover mission. The thinking was an Elite who doesn't think like one just might have a chance of monitoring the Underground without arousing suspicion. So we sent the chip back to the labs and asked our guys to add a few more functions, like the ability to record sound and relay it wirelessly to our computers. It would be our most advanced surveillance effort to date."

Rodriguez nodded. "And your boyfriend took the mission."

"Fiancé," she corrected. "It was a little over a week ago. We turned Jon into a blank slate, and with careful intervening nudged him toward the Underground. He joined up, made friends, and absorbed critical information. The mission was successful. Unfortunately, there were some unforeseen…um…"

"Side effects?"

She sighed. "Because the chip had rendered his mind so malleable, Jon couldn't defend himself against the Underground's poisonous influence—and they brainwashed him. That had kind of been the point, but what we didn't expect was that he'd put up so much resistance when we tried to bring the real Jon back."

Rodriguez furrowed his brow. "Even if he resisted, couldn't we have just knocked him out and removed the chip anyway? I mean, this Seven, it shouldn't be his choice, he's not real. The old him, buried inside, would want us to restore his memory, right?"

"Right," said Eve sadly. "And we *were* going to take the chip out, no matter what he said. But, see, this all happened last night."

His eyes widened. "Oh, you mean…"

"We were in the Capitol Tower. The bombs struck and Jon escaped. Worse, I gave–I mean–he got access to a memory stick providing access to all the recordings stored on the chip. Now the Headmaster is worried he'll use that evidence against us."

"Like blackmail?"

"Maybe, but…Jon is so brainwashed now…The truth is…I don't think he cares about making a deal with us. I think his plan might just be to pass it on to the Underground and let them deal with it. Maybe he's already done it."

Rodriguez released his breath in one whistling burst. "Is the chip still active?"

She raised her eyebrows. "The only way to turn it off is to remove it. But we can't track him that way. The memory stick is the only key, and Seven has it."

CHAPTER SIX
Loganville

The purple minivan got long stares as it cruised down Main Street in the small desert town of Loganville. "What are they looking at?" asked Seven, adjusting the air conditioner. "I know this clunker is ugly, but–"

"It's probably just me," Talia said. "I'm used to it. Even if I wasn't Watched I wouldn't fit into a secluded, hick town like this."

"But you said your brother lives here. Does he fit in?"

She cackled. "No, but he's stupid."

A painful swallow reminded Seven that he hadn't had a thing to drink since leaving the Underground's hideout in the city. There was no water in the car, and he could feel the dry heat coursing through the windows, even with the air conditioning on. Desperately, he sought distraction. He tried analyzing the architecture of the post office, general store, and other assorted buildings, but the maroon and adobe red only added to the overwhelming dryness.

"What do people do for fun in this town anyway?" he asked with a slight rasp.

"Um," Talia strained. "Like, get drunk, I guess. There's a tavern somewhere that's pretty popular."

Imbibing copious amounts of booze sounded like a pretty good idea at the moment, Seven thought. A tall, cold beer sounded particularly refreshing. But none of this was helping. "What do the kids do?"

"Probably they get wasted, too, only they do it in their parents' basements. Also, I guess there's a movie theater. I would imagine they do a lot of making out in both locations."

A smile crept onto Seven's face. Talia was rude and frequently insulting, but not entirely unenjoyable to talk to. He wondered how old she was, but pushed the thought aside almost as quickly as it had arrived.

They turned right at the next intersection and rode past a baseball diamond. Some boys were throwing a ball back and forth, pausing every few seconds to wipe their brows. Seven was appalled. "Are they crazy?"

"I told you!" said Talia. "Want another example of this town's insanity? Check out that cluster of town homes up ahead."

The construction of each two-story building looked identical, right down to the baby cactus on the porch. "Modern comfort, I guess?"

"No, that's exactly the problem. C'mon, how out of place are they? Did someone forget to tell the architect that his spaceship houses were gonna be planted in the middle of freaking nowhere? Those cactuses…"

"Cacti."

"Whatever. They were probably an afterthought. Ugly, ugly, ugly!" Flicking on the blinker, she added, "I can't believe my brother actually bought one."

The van seemed to float over the freshly paved driveway leading into the community. Upon closer inspection, Seven noticed subtle variations among the houses. The first featured a rather large and shiny gold ball propped up in the middle of the yard. At the second home, the ball was magenta. The third home had the biggest difference of all–a dead-brown lawn. Talia parked in front of it and announced, "This is his place."

She tapped the doorbell until the door cracked opened. A bug-eyed man squinted out at them.

"Wow, Shaan," Talia greeted. "You look like you haven't been outside for months. You trying to turn white or something?"

"Talia?" he choked, pulling the door wide to get a better look. "What are you doing here?"

"Haven't you been following the news?" she demanded. "The Capital was evacuated."

He looked annoyed. "That's not what I'm asking. I'm asking what you're doing *here at my house!*"

"Where the hell else was I supposed to go?"

They glared at each other. Seven eyed the bare concrete doorstep and then his shoes. Maybe this was a bad idea, he thought. He should have asked Talia to drop him off at a hotel or something. Not that he had any money to pay for a room, but perhaps he could work out some kind of deal and–

Talia punched Seven in the arm. "Stop being awkward."

Jostled by the impact, Seven looked up and extended his arm. "Hi," he said, "I'm Seven."

Talia explained. "I helped him get out of the city."

Seven looked at her. That wasn't how he remembered it.

Her brother considered Seven's hand for a few seconds, and then clasped it. "Shaan," he said.

"Now," said Talia, "are you going to keep us hostage on your porch, or are you going to let us in for some tea?"

He grumbled unintelligibly and waved them inside. They stepped into what appeared to be a living room, given the large-screen TV and sofa. But it seemed to Seven to really have more in common with a messy closet. Some stray dust tickled his nostrils and he sneezed.

Shaan whispered something to Talia that seemed to get a rise out of her. "He's not!" she sneered. "Look, I'll tell you everything in just a minute."

A sudden sleepiness overtook Seven, and he found himself looking longingly at Shaan's black leather sofa. "Have a seat!" Shaan burst with false enthusiasm. "Make yourself at home! Blah, blah, blah."

"Thanks. This is a nice house."

Talia shook her head and told Shaan sweetly, "I'm sure he's kidding."

Shaan ignored his sister and beamed at the compliment. "It looks expensive, but believe me, I paid more for my old studio in the city," he said. "Tea?"

"Just water would be great," answered Seven.

"Tea for me," said Talia, looking pleased by the rhyme. "Seven, why don't you stay here. Shaan and I need to talk in the kitchen."

Seven considered the clutter on the floor for a few seconds before snaking toward the couch. There were books and copies of *Computers Weekly* magazine in a variety of bad places, including the tops of lamps and millimeters from a fireplace. Finally, he fell into a milky soft cushion and yawned magnificently. He picked up the black remote control on the seat next to him, but quickly reconsidered. In all likelihood the news would be on, and Seven wasn't sure he was ready to hear more about death and destruction, let alone the Guard's likely diabolical response. No, he would just sit here and try to relax.

Closing his eyes, Seven couldn't help but overhear the raised voices of brother and sister in the kitchen.

"Why are you being such an asshole?" Talia cried. There was a metal clang, followed by the snap and whoosh of an igniting gas stove.

"I want to know how you got through the blockade," Shaan replied angrily. "Last time I checked, sister, you were still on the Watched list. The president was just on the news calling for the arrest of all Watched, and I heard they were stopping cars at the border. I'm glad you're safe, but the fact you're here in Loganville means you evaded arrest!"

"Yeah, well I guess it runs in the family," was the bitter response.

An unpleasant laugh shot from her brother's lips. "What if they followed you? Do you know how much work it took for me to start a new life here? You're going to undo everything!"

"They didn't follow us," whimpered Talia. "I'm sorry!"

Shaan sighed, clearly won over by his sister's display of sorrow. "It's okay," he said. "I'm sorry, too. I've been on edge since the attack. And it really is good to see you–I was worried."

For some time, they said nothing. Seven considered the remote control again, but couldn't bring himself to pick it up. A sharp whisper broke the silence. Seven leaned forward to hear.

"…not your boyfriend in my living room," said Shaan, "then who is he?"

"Shut up! He's just someone I met on the way out of the city. He forced me to share a car with him."

"And did he also make you bring him to my house?"

"No," she said. "But I got him in trouble with the stunt we pulled at the blockade, and he doesn't seem to have anywhere else to go."

"Well, that's uncharacteristically nice of you," Shaan deadpanned. "Should we order a pizza and have a party? You could invite your friends."

"Oh, go to Hell!"

He laughed merrily. "Ah, now there's the Talia I know and love!"

Something beeped.

"Is that a cell phone?" Shaan asked suspiciously.

"Text message," she said. "Just one of my girlfriends telling me—hey!"

There was a clamor of falling pots and pans.

Talia yelled, "What the hell do you think you're doing? Give that back!"

"Are you stupid?" Shaan snapped. "The Guard is probably looking for you, and you keep a cell phone? Don't you realize they can track your location on this?"

"I got the model without the GPS chip!" she snapped. "Give it!"

"It doesn't matter. If your phone's on, they can triangulate your location! All they need is three cell phone towers and your signal!"

"Yeah, as if this crappy town had three cell phone towers. You're just being paranoid."

"Can't take the risk," he grumbled.

"What are you doing with that? Shaan? No!"

There was a loud bang followed by another high-pitched scream. The kettle whistled. Talia, with lips twisted in malice, entered the living room and dropped a tall glass of water in front of the guest.

Seven gave a look of concern. "Everything okay?"

All he got in response was a growl, so Seven let the issue drop. He snapped up the glass of water and began gulping it down.

A minute later Shaan arrived with two mugs of tea.

"Seven," he asked, "do you have a phone by any chance?"

"No, why?"

"Good man," he replied. "Good man."

The siblings sat across from each other and sipped their tea in long, angry silence. Seven considered the ceiling.

Talia pointed at the window. "Are your curtains always closed, Shaan?" she sneered. "There's a sun out there you know."

Shaan scrutinized the thick white fabric as if for the very first time. "I guess I don't like the idea of people looking in."

"You're *such* a hermit."

He shrugged. After several more sips of tea, he turned to Seven. "So, my sister tells me you helped get her through the blockade. Have you always been such a nice guy?"

Seven laughed. "Well, you kind of have to be nice when someone's holding a gun to your head–"

"I didn't point it at your head!" protested Talia.

Shaan turned violently to his sister. "You carry a gun now? Do you even know how to use a gun?"

"Want to find out?" she sneered.

"I apologize for her foul mood," Shaan said without shifting his glare. "She's angry because I smashed her cell phone with a hammer."

Talia looked as if she was trying to singe her brother with her eyes.

"To be fair," offered Seven, "the gun didn't have any bullets in it. But she *was* quite convincing."

"Well," said Shaan, "it means a great deal to me that you

helped her, and I want you to know you're welcome to stay here for a while, provided you lay low and don't cause any trouble."

Seven nodded. "I appreciate that."

"But first I need you to pass me the remote control."

Seven tossed it to Shaan and the TV came to life. "For that extra-white clean, nothing beats Oxideen," sang a chorus.

"What are we watching?" Talia complained.

"It will be the news in a second," Shaan snapped.

Almost on cue, there was a pounding drum and an image of the Capitol Tower shining brightly against a dark red sky. "This was the terrifying scene one night ago," announced the TV, "presented in high definition, where available."

Giant block letters flashed onto the screen: *Yesterday*.

"Minutes before midnight," the narration went on, "the Enemy sent eight unmanned bombers into the city. Six targeted our Capital's cathedrals. The final two aimed for the Capitol Tower."

Two dark things shot out from the smoky clouds. They dropped a series of even darker eggs, and the top of the silver skyscraper blew to pieces. The image cut to a handheld camera's take on a busy thoroughfare, bouncing like an earthquake. People ran off-kilter, twisting around lamp posts and breaking through the arms of families.

Seven felt his legs starting to shake involuntarily and Talia flashed him a look of concern.

The TV now showed a room of intense light with flashing screens and people tapping away on computer keyboards. The camera panned right to reveal a frosty-haired man with narrow eyes and a square jaw. "Good evening, I'm Fox Reynolds. Welcome to Code Red."

The reporter paused for a five second snare drum fill. "Since the attack, President Drake has assembled the famed Guard, sending them to sea to stop the threat from the reviled Enemy! Let's bring you there now."

The word *LIVE* appeared in the corner of the screen as it faded to white. The fog hid all but the black railing of a boat and the first fifteen feet of choppy sea, giving the scene an unfinished look, as if an artist had spread deep-blue paint over the bottom third of canvas but completely neglected the top. That changed suddenly as a rush of orange refracted through the mist.

"The good fight carries on," said a windswept reporter strolling into the frame. "We are told the numbers are in our favor."

A boom burst from the television speakers. The war correspondent covered his head with his hands and fell off camera. There was another crash and the image went blurry.

"Oh, God," whispered Talia.

The newscast cut back to the Reynolds, whose face seemed a shade greener. "As you can see, we've got reporters quite close to the battle," the anchor said, glancing off screen. "Is Craig okay?"

The image of the sea returned, but now there was a flaming airplane nose-first in the water.

"Oh no," groaned Reynolds. "Is that–do we know whose fighter that was?"

Seven reached into his pocket and removed a thin piece of plastic, no bigger than a stick of gum. He flipped the memory stick around nervously in his fingers. After some time he shook his head and returned the item to its home.

"You know what's weird?" Shaan asked suddenly, putting the TV on mute. "It's almost as if I don't believe the attack happened–that it's still happening. I've been watching this for hours, but none of it seems–I don't know–real."

Talia raised her eyebrows. "Oh, it's happening. We were there."

"I know," Shaan said. "I just mean, you know, I was always anticipating some kind of attack, but not on this scale. Not a full-on war…" He shook his head. "You know what scared me the most when I lived in the city? The Metro during rush hour. There'd be all these people pushing down into the tunnel, practically crawling over each other like ants. And then, as soon as there was any sign that a train was coming, all these people would start freaking out and running, like their lives depended on it—even though nine times out of ten the next train was coming in less than five minutes."

He swallowed. "I used to have this dream where Joanna and I are running for the train. I tell her to slow down—tell her that we'll catch the next one—but she won't listen. We get separated. She gets on the train, but it's so packed I can't follow. The doors close and the train shoots off. Then there's this deafening boom. I look at the tunnel and see it glow orange, then red, then white."

"And then what?" inquired Talia. Her concern seemed genuine.

Shaan shrugged. "I wake up."

For a while they said nothing. Finally, Shaan put the sound back on.

"...the best thing we can do right now is support our boys in the Guard," said the woman on the screen. Her voice carried an inoffensive twang. She looked middle-aged but still attractive, with tan skin and reddish brown hair up in a tight bun.

"Who's that?" asked Seven.

Talia gave him a weird look. "Like, seriously? Were you born yesterday?"

"Well, not yesterday..." he replied.

"It's Susan Levi," said Shaan with a matter-of-fact tone. "She's the mayor of Loganville and a media darling."

Talia clicked her tongue. "More like a media whore."

The reporter interviewing Levi asked if there was anything she thought the government could have done to prevent the Enemy's attack.

"I don't think the problem is...I mean, the Guard—our boys—are doing everything they can to stop this kind of thing. But there's so much, um, heretical activity to deal with, and, you know, they're spread thin. If we could keep everyone in church, then I think we wouldn't have this. I think we'd be in a much better place. You know, this isn't a time for heresy. What we all need to do is focus on our faith in God, really concentrate on that, and of course support the troops—our boys who are working so hard to protect this country. And then I think everything will be okay."

Seven felt a headache coming on. He stared vacantly at the carpet, lost in a maze of sorrow and frustration.

"You know, Seven," said Talia, standing up and adjusting her bandanna. "That bar I was telling you about earlier is starting to sound like a pretty good idea."

CHAPTER SEVEN
First Date

Jon looked like he had something to say, but couldn't quite get the words out. He grabbed a second slice of pizza instead.

"It's better with some red pepper," Eve said. "Do you like spicy food?"

Jon glanced down at his slice as if it might provide some advice. "I think so."

"You think so?"

"I mean, yeah, let me try a little." He grabbed the red pepper and started shaking. "How much is best exactly?" He shook the bottle some more.

Eve failed to restrain a devilish smile as the red flakes piled up. Finally she couldn't take it anymore and kicked her date under the table. "I think that should do it."

Jon popped the bottle up with such force that an extra sprinkling of pepper puffed onto the table. With some hesitation, he took a bite of the pizza.

A giggle escaped Eve's lips as he smacked his lips. Whistling painfully, Jon snapped up his pint of beer and gulped down what remained.

"Yeah…that's tasty," he managed with a slight cough.

Okay, so he was a little goofy, but she liked him. There was no way she could have anticipated the night would turn out like this. "Sorry again about wasting your time tonight with Shaan and Joanna."

He waved her off. "Seriously, it's no big deal. I thought something was going down just as much as you did," he said. "And anyway, I'm glad it led to you and me…"

He couldn't finish the sentence. She looked into his sharp gray eyes and prodded, "To you and me…?"

"To you and me…getting pizza. Because, um, this is really good pizza. Don't you think?"

Eve raised her eyebrows and nodded. Maybe this wasn't going to work out, she thought, but at least she was having fun.

A small girl sitting at another table pointed at the Elites and loudly asked her mother, "Why are they dressed like that?"

The pair still had on the black, slim-fit garb they put on for their mission at Luna Coast. The clothes, designed for darting between shadows, ironically made them stand out in well-lit settings.

Glancing quickly, the mom gasped and shushed her daughter. She whispered fiercely, "Don't point, those are Elite Guard!"

Jon grinned. "So," he said to Eve, "are these uniforms what got you interested in the Guard? They were a big deal for me, let me tell you."

Eve burst out laughing. "No, no," she concluded. "I joined up because of my dad, probably."

"Was he an Elite, too?"

She shook her head. "My dad can't keep quiet long enough to do anything involving stealth," she said. "He's a priest."

Jon considered taking another bite, but, remembering the red pepper, let the piece drop onto his plate instead. "In that case, I better watch what I say, huh? I bet you've got a sharp ear for heresy."

"What?" she protested. Then, realizing she may have reacted a bit strongly, Eve attempted to explain. "Oh no, I don't think…I mean, I'm no more religious than the next girl…I just meant that Daddy talked a lot about morals–what's right and wrong–that kind of thing. So I think that made me…I don't know…For example, there was this one time he–"

"Another beer?" the waiter interrupted.

Jon started as if the server had materialized out of thin air. His eyes snapped to the empty glass mug in front of him. "Oh," he said, recovering. "Yes, thank you."

The waiter nodded and began to leave, but Jon hastily grabbed him by the arm. "You didn't ask if the lady wanted a refill, too," he explained.

Amused by Jon's neurosis, Eve raised her nearly three-quarter filled mojito. "No thanks," she said, jingling the ice around. "I'm a-okay."

The waiter raised his eyebrows slightly. "So just the beer?"

"Yes," said Jon. "Sorry. Thanks."

Jon looked embarrassed. Eve thought it was cute.

"Sorry," he stammered. "What were you saying before? About your dad?"

"Right. So, this was a long time ago. I think I was pretty little."

"You're not sure?"

"Well, I didn't feel little at the time." She smiled. "Anyway, whenever my mom took me to church we always walked by this strange man sitting on a bench by the courtyard. His clothes were rags, and his face was always covered with black dirt. Mom loved to scare me, so she told me that this man was in fact the Devil himself. She warned me not to look him in the eye when we passed. It was a weekly test of faith. If I looked, she said, I'd join him in Hell."

"Well, damn."

"Damned, actually, but I think you've got the idea. So, anyway, there was this one week when we didn't see him on his usual bench. I freaked out, of course. I guess I thought, 'How am I going to avoid eye contact with the Devil if I don't know where he is?'"

Jon grinned. "How indeed."

"I got so flustered looking for him on the grass I didn't watch where I was going, and I walked smack into a tree! Only it wasn't a tree, because when I looked up I saw this man who I thought was the Devil staring back down at me!"

"What did you do?"

"What do you think I did? I ran as fast as I could! The rest of the morning I was inconsolable. My mom got so mad at me because I wouldn't shut up about it, not even during mass! At my quietest I was whimpering...worse than you after that hot pepper! I mean, I thought I was going to Hell!"

Jon attempted to dust off his pizza. "I could see how that might be upsetting."

"Upset is an understatement!" exclaimed Eve, eyes wide. "My mom told my dad later how crazy I'd been all morning. I told him everything–that I'd made eye contact with the Devil, that I wouldn't be Saved...the whole thing. And you know what he did? He just nodded, took it all in and took me outside for a stroll. Well, just being in the sun made me feel a little better, but all too suddenly it became apparent where we were going. I looked up and saw the Devil himself sitting on his bench–we were heading straight for him! So of course I start crying again. Dad patted my shoulder and called out to the Devil, 'Hello, Bill!'"

Jon chuckled. "The Devil's name is Bill?"

"As you've probably surmised, Bill wasn't the Devil," she sighed. "He was just homeless."

"And he was friends with your dad?"

"Well, my father had an agreement with him–Dad would let Bill stay in the church at night, and in exchange, Bill tended to the garden and did some repairs around the building. Turned out he was actually a really nice guy–and truly a man of God–who just happened to be down on his luck and facing hard times. It taught me that Heretics aren't so easily picked from a crowd. Before you can make any judgment, you have to watch people carefully and really get to know them."

"And that's why you decided to be an Elite Guard."

"That's why exactly."

FIRST DATE

"Wow," said Jon, leaning back in his seat. "Well, my story isn't nearly as interesting."

"Tell me anyway."

He held up his hands. "Are you ready?"

Her eyes widened. "Ready."

"Okay, so get this: my high school counselor recommended that I enlist in the Guard." He paused for dramatic effect. "And so I *did*."

She laughed. "Wow, you must have had top grades."

"Yeah, they were okay. But I'll tell you a secret. I think it actually was my outstanding dodge ball skills that put me over the top."

She giggled. "Oh, I miss dodge ball."

"Me, too. Hey, maybe we should get the Elites together for a game."

"Think the captain would play?"

"Oh, God," Jon gasped. "That old fart can be on your team."

They laughed loudly, attracting angry glances from the mother who up until then had avoided eye contact.

"I could totally take you," Eve snarled, "even with the captain on my team *and* your so called skills."

"Sounds like a challenge!"

Unable to contain her smile, Eve tossed back the mojito and gazed out across the boardwalk to the ocean. Electric light bounced over the black water. "You come here much?" she asked.

"Not really, what with work and everything," sighed Jon. "But I always like it when I'm here."

"I used to come here all the time. Daddy liked to pull me pretty far into the water, even when I was only like eight. Really, it's a wonder I didn't get eaten by a shark."

"I'm glad you didn't," Jon remarked.

The things this man said, thought Eve. She leaned back and tilted her head curiously. "Why's that?"

"Um," he stammered, derailed. "Because, I mean, if a shark had eaten you, then…um…we wouldn't get to eat this delicious pizza together."

"You know, Mr. Wyle," she said with a flip of her hair. "I'm beginning to think you're flirting with that pizza."

A series of three ear-piercing cracks snapped Jon's and Eve's eyes to the window. "That was a gun," they said in unison.

Eve flashed her badge at the waiter, who had just returned with Jon's beer. "We're Guard," she said. "Be right back." And they darted for the door.

Within minutes, the Elites found a trail of blood smeared along the boardwalk, snaking around the corner of a popcorn stand. On the other side, a crumpled body in midnight blue uniform.

"It's a Guard," gasped Eve. "I'll call for help."

Jon kneeled over the body. "He's breathing."

The soldier gurgled, and then spoke: "Goddamned Heretic… found him under the boardwalk…wasn't even going to arrest him…"

Jon nodded. "Which way did he go?"

"Oh, God," exhaled the Guard, face whitening.

Jon shook him. "*Which way?*"

He chuckled absentmindedly. "The…the restrooms."

Jon followed the soldier's gaze toward a shack on the beach, and then turned to Eve, who had just finished her phone call.

"Go," she said, stroking the fallen Guard's forehead. "I'll stay with him until the ambulance gets here."

Pulling a pistol from his jacket, Jon sprang up and swooped toward the shack. Eve watched him take cover against the wall by the door. Then the Elite burst into the building. The door shut behind him.

After a minute, Eve heard something like the howling of a wounded dog. "Jon!" she screamed. Leaving the fallen Guard behind, she careened toward the source of the cry. A few feet from the restroom, she planted her feet in the sand and drew her automatic. The door opened and Jon popped out. He looked completely unscathed.

"I heard yelling. What happened?" she burst out, dropping her weapon.

FIRST DATE

"He's tied up and waiting inside for the cavalry to arrive."

"But how did you get him so quickly? I didn't even hear any shots."

"I think he got freaked out after he shot that Guard. When I went in, he was splashing water on his face, and getting it all over his gun." Jon rolled his eyes. "He tried to use it on me, but it stuck, of course. So, I tackled him."

Eve liked the way his voice sounded. His nervousness from earlier had completely vanished. "Well then," she said, edging toward him, "I guess you ended up getting a little action tonight anyway."

Two police cars and an ambulance screeched into the parking lot. Agent Parker was too involved with Agent Wyle's lips to notice.

Later, on the way home, it occurred to Eve that no one had paid for the pizza.

CHAPTER EIGHT
Heresy!

The two agents of the Elite Guard didn't reach the Loganville police station until just before lunchtime the next day. Eve gawked at the sluggish ceiling fan and groaned. Rodriguez snatched a wet patch of shirt plastered to his belly and shook it vigorously.

Across the big wooden table, the town sheriff tweaked his salt-and-pepper mustache. "Based on the buckets of sweat pourin' down your face," he drawled, "I would conjecture you're not from around these parts."

Eve pulled her hair back. "It's cooler in the Capital," she muttered.

"This station's got history, as a matter of fact," the old man went on. "Dates back to the Great War, yes sir! You know what they used this place for?"

Rodriguez shrugged. "What?"

"Ammo-nition!" he replied excitedly. "This where our good men in the Guard stashed their weaponry, yes sir, they did. When the war ended—when we won—they were thinkin' about tearing the old girl down, on account of how torn up with bullets she got. But our good townspeople came together, fixed the place up nice and tidy, and I reckon we've been using it as police headquarters ever since!"

The Loganville man took a gulp from a clear plastic bottle. He hadn't offered any water to the Elites. "All this, of course, is just a long way of explaining why we got no A/C. But as much as I hate to cut through this de-lightful treacle, would you mind telling me what two Elites are doing in my town? We ain't got no Watched here. Just real good patriots. *Real* good."

"I'm actually not an Elite yet," Rodriguez piped up. "Just training."

The sheriff responded with a vacant stare. Rodriguez turned to the window and busied himself by squinting at the morning sun.

"We're looking for someone, an out-of-towner," said Eve. "He goes by 'Seven,' and was last seen traveling with a Watched named Talia. They broke through the blockade yesterday and came here."

The old man cracked a smile. "I'll need more than that."

She pulled out her phone and scrolled through the photos. Two pics past Jon and Eve's day at the beach was an image of Jon giving a double thumbs up. Sighing slightly, she leaned over the desk and showed the sheriff.

The sheriff gazed at Eve's chest, and then the picture. "Oh," he said.

"Familiar?"

"I reckon that's the one gave us some *fine* trouble last night. In fact, I'm sure of it. This is the reprobate that last night took to fightin' in the tavern!"

A large glass mug clapped down on the bar, jerking Seven's attention from the buxom gal with the jogging shorts and gunslinger hat. For a split second he watched the black-and-tan fluid foam over the top. Then reflexes took over. He caught the pint, pulled it to his lips, and cleaned off the suds.

"Put that one on my tab, too," called Talia, who was sitting next to him.

She had been buying him drinks all night. "Why are you paying for me?" Seven asked suspiciously.

"To celebrate!" she exclaimed, taking a sip from the red potion in her hand. "It's not every day you get chased by the Guard and live to tell about it."

Seven thought it was somewhat remarkable they could actually hear each other above the drunken din. A smarmy band in the corner played some noisy old ditty that half the tavern's patrons knew well enough to sing along with.

"Anyway," she continued, "you don't have any money, so it's not like you were going to buy your own drinks."

"How do you know I'm broke?"

"Your pockets aren't exactly bulging. Do you even *have* a wallet?"

He smiled slightly. "I lost it during the attack."

She scoffed. "Yeah...right."

Seven picked up his mug and studied the throw-away coaster. The bright red background now featured a circular brown stain. His eyes floated back to the cowgirl who was now bouncing to the country music.

He was feeling a bit more himself. Seven was still wearing the same clothes from the previous night but at least he'd finally had a chance to shave at Shaan's house.

"Do you have a girlfriend?" asked Talia.

He gaped alternately at his companion and the coaster. How could he explain his relationship with Eve, exactly? Not even Seven was quite sure what was going on there. She had told him they were engaged to be married, but he didn't remember any of that. Something about it felt true– and well, she was hot–but Eve had also deceived him about a lot of other things.

"It's complicated," Seven concluded.

"Well I could have found out that much from your Internet profile," replied Talia. "What, did she dump you or something?"

Seven squinted hard at his pint, as if the answer might be floating within. "No, not exactly. Look, um, no offense, but I really don't want to talk about it."

"At least tell me if she's *pretty*." Talia pronounced the last word like she was talking to a baby.

"Um..."

"What, she's ugly?"

"No! I mean, she's not—you know—she's very—" He rowed his hand out from his chest in a circular motion.

Talia squinted at the gesture. "Large breasted?"

He looked mortified and emitted a series of short, incoherent gasps.

Grinning, Talia threw up her hands in surrender. "Okay, okay, I'll stop!"

Seven took another gulp of beer and tried to segue into a new subject. "Shaan seems nice…"

Now it was Talia who took a vigorous sip of her booze. "My brother is a fool."

"What do you mean?"

"Well for one thing, he lives in this shit hole town."

"I dunno," he said, marveling at the rough-and-tumble gal by the entrance. "It's not all bad."

"He moved here because of that girl, Joanna," Talia continued, sprinkling a little contempt over the name. "You may remember her from his weird dream about the subway."

Seven was confused. "Couldn't they just commute? This place isn't that far from the city."

"What?" she yelped in outrage. "No, I said he moved here *because* of a girl, not to *pursue* one. Joanna was dropped."

His eyes widened. "What, they hanged her? Why?"

Talia seemed alarmed by Seven's sudden focus on the conversation. "Promise you won't tell Shaan I told you?"

He nodded.

"She'd been on the Watched list from the start of their relationship. Years ago she was like this famous journalist, but her career was destroyed when she tried breaking a story the Guard didn't like."

"What was it about?"

"Um," she struggled. "I read it, but it was a while ago so I don't exactly remember. But the Guard said it threatened national security, so they put her on the Watched list. She was dating my brother when all this happened. And they continued to go out long after that, and like everything was fine, until one day she started writing something else on the newspaper blog that the Guard *really* didn't like. A week later, they dropped her for heresy and treason."

"God," he managed.

"But like the worst part for Shaan was how he found out. He had this whole date planned out, where he was going to propose and everything. When she didn't show, he thought she'd stood him up. Then of course he goes home and turns on the TV, and there she is waiting to be dropped. I...I think he may have seen the telecast."

Seven shuddered. He remembered the first time he'd stumbled upon a live TV execution of an alleged Heretic. It was like a game show with smiley hosts and brass fanfare. But rather than dunk the contestant in a pool of water, or slime him with green goo, they put a rope around his neck and dropped him through a trap door.

"So Shaan left the Capital?"

"More or less," she said cryptically. "Point is, he ended up in this shit hole. The really sad thing, though, is he still talks about her like she's alive."

"So why are you on the Watched list?" Seven asked out of the blue.

"Racial profiling," Talia replied without hesitation.

"What? That can't be true."

She shrugged. "It certainly didn't help."

A shadow fell over Talia. She gaped at the hulking bartender whose eyes now burned into hers. The man's choice in clothing–red short-sleeved shirt, faded jeans, and big, thick glasses–only served to accentuate his size.

"Are you Shaan's sister?" the beast rumbled.

Talia breathed a sigh of relief. "Yes...how did you know?"

"Um," he said dumbly.

Talia glanced around the room, and shook her head knowingly. "See? This town is so white," she muttered. Then, speaking up, she said, "Never mind. How do you know my brother? Regular customer I expect?"

A heavy hand landed on Seven's shoulder, jerking his attention to the boar in the stool next to his. Yellow stains spread from the man's armpits down the sides of his white T-shirt, which depicted a scantily clad woman draped over the hood of a red pickup truck. "Hey you," the stranger grunted.

Seven cringed. "Hi?"

The pig licked some BBQ sauce off his chops. "Where you from?"

"The city."

"You there when it all went to Hell?" the stranger prodded.

Seven looked at his beer.

"Well?"

"No."

The pig downed a shot of something that smelled like rubbing alcohol. "Goddamned Heretics," he whined.

Seven turned. "Who, the Enemy?"

"No, the *Heretics*," he emphasized. "There is no Enemy," he replied gravely. "The attack was just God's vengeance against the Heretics."

"Wait, what?" Seven laughed. "You're saying that, if more people went to church, we wouldn't have been attacked?"

He felt a sudden, sharp nudge from Talia, whose conversation was apparently over. "Hey, Seven?" she said.

The stranger bore his teeth. "Everyone goes to church," he growled. "But some don't believe."

"Right…" said Seven, continuing to ignore Talia's tapping.

"You go to church, don't you?" said the barfly.

"Everyone goes to church," mimicked Seven, taking another gulp of his beer. He shifted his languid stare to the TV which was now showing the attack on the Capitol Tower from an exclusive new angle. "So does that mean that the Enemy is in cahoots with God? That God got mad at us for not believing, so he sent his henchmen to rough us up?"

HERESY!

The pig blinked.

Talia whispered harshly into Seven's ear, "Are you *trying* to get killed?"

"My theory," Seven continued, undeterred, "is that people like you are so worried about deviation within the country that you've forgotten that there's a dangerous world outside our borders. We're not being punished, we just weren't ready."

The pig's mouth fell open. "You're one of the goddamned Heretics!"

"He's really not," Talia pitched in. "He's just had a rough couple of days. He, um, lost a good friend in the attack."

"Stay out of this, *bitch*," the pig growled.

"Hey that's not nice," said Seven. "Simmer down."

"I don't believe this guy," the boar laughed. "The Heretic's trying to get *me* to shaddap." He slapped Seven's beer off the counter, and it smashed into several large pieces on the floor.

Talia glanced the bartender's way. "Can I close out?"

The pig threw a punch. Seven caught his attacker by the wrist and, redirecting his momentum, tossed him downward into the shards of broken glass. The pig squealed and the band stopped. A few skittish men darted out the exit, while some heavies lumbered toward Seven.

Talia pocketed her credit card and signed the receipt. "Seven?" she said. "I think it's time to go."

"Naturally, we intervened," said the sheriff. He popped a thick wad of chewing tobacco into his mouth.

"So this Talia has a brother in Loganville?" prodded Eve.

"Yessum. Man's name is Shaan—Shaan Williams, I think." He spun around and pulled open a dusty filing cabinet.

Coughing, Rodriguez whispered to Eve, "Kidding me? Don't they even have computers in this town?"

The old man slapped a file down on the table. Eve pulled it toward her and opened to the photograph. She scrutinized it for a few seconds, and then gasped. "I know this man," she said. "He was one of my Watched a few years ago. I thought he was dead!"

The sheriff laughed. "What? He's been living here for the past two years. I'm sure of it. You don't forget a man with a face like that and who spells his God-given name all wrong."

"He had a different last name back then. We have him on tape jumping his motorcycle off the Luna Coast."

The sheriff raised his eyebrows. "Did you find the body?"

"Just the bike at the bottom of the sea. But no one could have survived that fall."

The sheriff guffawed. "I guess sometimes them fish get away, don't they?"

Eve scowled. "Speaking of escapes, I don't suppose you've got Seven in your holding cell, do you?"

Frowning, the Loganville man bent over to spit some black juice into a stained bucket. "We chased him to the church," he grumbled.

A police siren rang out. Seven followed Talia into the shadows of an empty alleyway. It hadn't rained all day, but the narrow street was filled with puddles, dimly reflecting the yellow apartment windows above.

He shook off a shiver. Only a few hours ago Loganville felt relentlessly hot. But the air here was too dry to hold the warmth. The temperature dropped with the sun.

"Could you please stop being a stupid idiot?" demanded Talia. "Why would you start a fight? It's not even been twenty-four hours since our little adventure at the blockade. Don't the words 'lying low' mean anything to you?"

"Hey, going to a pub was your idea, not—ack!" Seven yanked his neck back, and began wiping frantically at the top of his head.

Talia took a step back. "What are you, some kind of crazy obsessive-compulsive invalid?"

HERESY!

Seven scowled. "You know, you've been asking me a lot of pretty insulting questions tonight."

"I'm sorry," she said insincerely, "did they sound like questions?"

"I jumped because something dripped on me," he explained, craning his neck to find the source. "Probably just an air conditioner."

"Too bad it wasn't hair conditioner," returned Talia, laughing at her own joke. "You could use some. Not to mention shampoo."

This time he ignored her. "Which way to Shaan's place again?"

Talia pointed down the alley. "Through here, across the church grounds, and then a few zigs and zags. But we should probably chill here for a little while longer."

She crouched behind a metal trash can. Seven started to speak but Talia shushed him. She mouthed something resembling "Did you hear that?"

Seven closed his eyes and listened. Somewhere a radio crackled. Then it spoke. "–proceed on foot." There was a methodical tapping from around the corner, and its volume was increasing. Someone was coming.

Suddenly, Talia gasped and reached for the back of her neck. As she did, her knee shot forward into the can, knocking it noisily onto the pavement. Several bottles of beer clattered out onto the street.

Collectively, the fugitives' jaws dropped. The slapping of soldier boots grew heavy.

"Run!" said Talia in a whisper that seemed only a few decibels short of a scream.

The stone cathedral seemed to bounce and expand as they approached. It looked far older than the high-technology monstrosities Seven had seen in the Capital. Those newer buildings were built like stadiums and even used jumbo screens to engage the parish. Of course, the comparison was no longer current, he realized. The Enemy had reduced all the Capital cathedrals to piles of rocks, accented here and there by shards of red and blue glass.

Talia darted around a conifer tree, avoiding a bright spot of light on the grassy grounds. Seven followed, looking back as he went. They hurdled into a dark patch beneath a stairwell in the back of the church. The low vibrations of an organ droned through an emergency exit at the top of the steps.

Seven looked thoughtfully up the stairs. Suddenly, he bounded upward and tore open the door. Talia cursed and scuttled after him.

There were more stairs inside, but these were steep and tightly coiled. The organ music reverberated off the heavy stone walls, drowning the fugitives in sound. Talia said something; Seven failed to respond.

"Well?" she yelled.

He pointed at his ear. "What?"

She clutched his shoulders and leaned in close. "I said these stairs probably lead up to the main hall!"

He nodded, and they climbed. And climbed. Finally, the stairs opened up into a long mezzanine running left and right to each end of the cathedral. Seven pressed up against the railing and ventured a look at the pews several hundred feet below. White candles all around bounced golden light up off cantilevers into a great painted dome.

"It's beautiful, in a 'fun with vertigo' kind of way," said Talia as she approached the ledge. "But where are all the big TV screens?"

Before Seven could respond, the organ stopped. The intruders froze.

There was a slight creaking and the soft shuffle of feet. Seven traced the patter to a bald priest walking up the aisle toward the entrance. He tugged open one of the tall, wooden doors, and three policemen stomped in.

"Is there a problem?" boomed the priest. His syrupy voice echoed around the cathedral.

"There was a fight at the tavern," explained a mustachioed old Guard in the center. "We're looking for the damned Heretics that started it."

"This is a House of God," answered the priest. "There are no Heretics here."

"We should still have a look around."

"You may not. The Great One will not have you dragging dirt into his church. You have no authority here."

"But–" the cop protested.

"Go," the churchman interrupted. "I still have much to prepare for tomorrow's sermon."

"Okay, sure," said Eve, gasping to find the words. "You lost him in the church. Fine. But they had to have been staying with Shaan, right? Please tell me you went there."

"We checked all right," said the sheriff, "but the guy said he didn't even know his sister was in town."

"And you just believed him?!"

"Whoa there, missy," he said like a cowboy calling to a beloved stallion. "My men searched the place good."

She was fuming. Didn't these hicks have any sense of protocol? "But did you post someone outside the house? Or the church?"

He flashed a look of annoyance. "For God's sake, lady, it was just a bar fight."

Eve nodded several more times than necessary, and then began to pace. Rodriguez sank into his seat one inch per second.

"Okay," she stated when she finally regained composure. "Would you mind if my partner, Rodriguez, and I paid a visit to Shaan's place?"

The sheriff's chair creaked as he leaned back. "I s'pose it's a free country."

CHAPTER NINE
Lost & Found

Eve and Rodriguez darted across the dead lawn in front of Shaan's town home. Eve pushed her partner aside at the entrance and pounded on the door. "This is the Guard! Open up!"

Bracing against the rail of the porch for support, Rodriguez gasped. "Is that necessary? I'm sure the doorbell is loud enough."

She turned with eyes like daggers. "Part of this job," said Eve, "is intimidation."

While it wasn't something she would admit, Eve did feel a little more charged up than usual. After all, all the evidence pointed to Jon spending last night in this house. Maybe he was still here.

"So what now?" asked Rodriguez. "Doesn't look like anyone's home."

She gasped. "You're going to make the assessment that this house is empty just because no one is answering the door? What makes you think they're not just hiding? We are chasing someone you know."

"No, sir. I made the assessment based on the fact that there aren't any cars in the driveway. The targets drove here in a purple minivan, right?"

Eve looked where Rodriguez was pointing and frowned. "A fair point. But we still better check the place out. If they're gone, we might at least find a clue about where they went."

She pulled a thin silver tube about the size of a straw from her pocket and slipped it into the key hole. Pushing a button on the handle produced a low buzz and then a click. She turned the knob and the door opened.

Eve gasped. The place was a total wreck. A floor lamp leaned diagonally against an upturned sofa, and a large crack stretched diagonally across the TV screen. Clearly, there had been some kind of fight.

Rodriguez looked at the screen mournfully. "You think someone got to him before us?" he asked.

Eve picked a worn paperback up from the floor and turned it over thoughtfully. "Well, it wasn't Guard. We're usually a bit… *neater* than this, even out here in the sticks. Also, as you noted before, their vehicle is gone. Seems likely they left the place on their own, unless someone decided to steal that van."

He laughed condescendingly. "Not sure who would want to do that."

Eve had a lump in her throat. On the way over she tried to prepare herself for the scenario that Jon wouldn't be here. But the disappointment hovered like a dark cloud anyway. The Elites' only lead had brought them here; now they were back to square one. Worse, she realized, Jon might be hurt. What had he gotten himself into?

The kitchen wasn't in much better shape than the living room, though it was unclear whether fighting or negligence was to blame. Rodriguez nearly slipped over some yellow mush on the floor, but caught himself just in time.

Eve pointed at an antique-looking computer consuming a wooden desk in the back of the room. "Can you hack into that?" she asked Rodriguez. "They might not have cleared their browser history–maybe they looked up directions or something."

"Yes, sir. No problem."

She thanked him and headed back to the front door.

"Where are you going?" Rodriguez called after her.

"To see if the neighbors can spare any flour," she said with a roll of her eyes.

Shielding her eyes from the beating sun, Eve scanned the

houses across the street. A lone white face peering out at her from one of the second-story windows made her jump. "Probably as good a place as any to start," she remarked to herself.

She raised a fist to beat the door, considered the doorbell for a second, and started pounding anyway. "Guard!" she shrieked.

A loud, fast clunk-clunk-clunk followed a shrill "Coming!" The door opened, revealing a rather short and chubby man in a grease-stained undershirt. He gave Eve's body a once over and grinned sleazily. "Why, hello, milady."

Eve sniffed and immediately wrinkled her nose. She flashed her badge. "I'm investigating a kidnapping at the house across the street."

He gasped. "What? I've never seen any young miscreants there."

"No," she snapped. "It was a man–there were no children involved. I'm checking around to see if anyone saw anything suspicious, either today or last night."

"Not I. Of course, I've mostly been engrossed in *World of High Adventure*."

"Excuse me?"

"You know, the MMORPG," he returned.

Eve blinked. He might as well have been speaking an alien language.

"A computer game of the highest caliber."

"Oh," she said, pretending to understand. "Does anyone else live here?"

"My wife," he said, dropping the royal embellishments from his voice. "She's always staring out the damn window so she may have seen something. Want me to call her?"

"Will she be back soon?"

"Huh? She's upstairs." He turned around and screamed up the steps: "*Cupcake*! Lady here wants to ask you a few questions!"

Almost instantly, Cupcake dropped down the stairs. "I saw 'em," she announced.

Eve recognized her pale face instantly–this was the girl she'd seen in the window before. The woman's clothes didn't hide her heft. She wore a baggy smiley face T-shirt that hung loosely over a pair of tight spandex biking shorts. She had a dingy old baseball cap on, with a shock of wheat-colored hair sticking out the back.

"You saw who?" Eve managed eventually. The Elite wondered if Cupcake had been eavesdropping on the entire conversation thus far. And was it really necessary to be so sneaky in the first place?

"Saw the whole thing–happened early this morning, maybe a few hours ago," Cupcake declared. "The door burst open and that shady fellow across the street comes out, carrying a huge duffel bag–no, a body bag. There was a girl, too, who kept yelling at the man and generally making a scene. But I guess she was helping him, 'cause she opened the door of that van and helped push the body bag inside."

Eve nodded. "Did you report any of this?"

Cupcake shook her head. "I'm not allowed to use the phone," she said. "Am I gonna be on the tee-vee?"

"No," stated the Elite.

Eve said goodbye and headed back. It appeared that Talia and Shaan had turned on Seven and packed him up to go. But where had they gone? She hoped Rodriguez had found the answer.

"I found some pretty messed up stuff," the rookie announced when Eve stepped back into the kitchen. "This Shaan guy is definitely with the Underground. Looks like he was sent instructions to take Seven back to their headquarters, wherever that is."

Eve raised her eyebrows. "Well, that meshes with what the neighbors said. Shaan and Talia were seen dragging an unconscious body into their van late last night. Do you have anything that might indicate where this Underground HQ might be?"

"I hacked into their network to find out, but got kicked out within seconds. Just had enough time to print out the message." He handed her the paper.

LOST & FOUND

Shaan:

Seven is wanted for questioning for his involvement in the capture and subsequent murder of Our Leader Daniel Alexander Young. Bring him to us.

HQ

"Damn it, Jon," said Eve, shaking her head. Taking a deep breath, she began to pace. In the living room, the toe of her shoe kicked something small and plastic, and it rattled into the foyer. She chased after it and gasped. "Oh, my God."

Rodriguez leaned over in his chair so he could see out of the kitchen. "What happened?"

With fingers like tweezers she plucked the object from the floor. "It's a memory stick," she explained as she plugged it into her tablet. Eve's eyes sparkled as its LCD backlight flashed to life.

Rodriguez's eyes lit up. "You mean *the* memory stick?"

This was the lucky break we needed, Eve thought as the surveillance app loaded. If this was indeed Seven's key, it meant she would have access again to Seven's GPS location and live audio feed.

She tapped a few keys and grinned. "The chip's still functioning," she reported breathlessly. "I know where he is."

CHAPTER TEN
The Prisoner

The white concrete walls pressed in upon Seven. He struggled to stand but ascent was impossible from the heavy steel chair in the center of the cell. He was tied down with nylon rope, and the chair was bolted to the cement floor. The prisoner allowed himself a moment to cry out for help, but quickly corrected the emotion with a deep breath and a shiver.

He searched his foggy mind for answers. When exactly had he been captured? He remembered giving the Guard the slip and running with Talia back to her brother's place. He'd gone almost immediately to sleep on the sofa. The next thing he recalled was a needle and syringe glinting in the morning light. He remembered a struggle and a quick fade to black.

Seven scanned his surroundings for weak points and possible areas of escape. The wall directly across from him was empty except for a poster featuring one of the Guard's most famous slogans. The last three words were struck out by lime spray paint, so that it read: *PATRIOTS ARE THE TRUE. HERETICS ARE THE DAMNED*. Stenciled beneath the words was a black visage with fiery red eyes.

He turned to a solid black door on the left. Hanging above it, a mechanical eye watched without blinking. Next, he traced two dim yellow rectangles on the floor up the wall on his right to a pair of single-pane windows. Dirt, grass, and weeds pressed up against the glass. The cell seemed to darken as he looked into the sunlight.

Seven smiled. The irony of an organization calling itself the Underground locking him in a basement had not been lost on him. Suddenly, Seven was ludicrous with laughter.

A sharply rational fear that he might be going insane shut him up. He couldn't stop his right leg from shaking.

A low rustle shifted his attention to the left. The door to the cell popped open, and a lanky young man pranced inside with the bounce of a court jester. The newcomer's pale fingers combed through short and slick blond hair and dropped cold onto the prisoner's shoulders. "Welcome, Seven," the man said with a roguish smile. "Do you know who I am?"

The prisoner blinked a few times. This was getting weird.

"I'll take your silence as a no. I guess it's true then, what my people tell me about you."

If his hands were free, Seven might have tried to cover his amusement.

"Something funny?" his captor asked curiously.

"You're old enough to have 'people?'"

The corners of the other man's mouth upturned so slowly that it unsettled Seven's own smile. "It's recent," the stranger explained. "You see, I've just become chairman of DAY Corporation. The name is Daniel Alexander Young, Jr., but please, call me Danny."

Seven remembered the name from the radio. Danny looked about his age, but was far more fashionable. He wore a tailored, chocolate suit with matching leather boots; he was a veritable urban cowboy.

"I heard your statement about severing DAY's ties with the Underground," Seven said. "I'm going to guess that wasn't completely accurate?"

Young smiled. "To be perfectly honest, I didn't even *write* that statement. But, you know, that's the game we have to play."

"And where do I fit into your game?"

"Straight to the point–very good!" Danny grinned. His teeth were even whiter than his skin. "We got your email.

That was one hell of an attachment, I must say. We're still working on the transcript."

It was hell getting that memory stick, thought Seven, recalling the horrible exchange with Eve, the narrow escape from the crumbling Capitol Tower, and the long run to the Underground hideout. Annoyed to hear it wasn't more of a priority, he seethed, "I was hoping you'd be able to use the information against the Guard."

Danny's expression turned severe. "You are some kind of enigma, aren't you? What, do…do you think you can just switch sides at will? Providing the cause with new ammunition doesn't change the fact that you *crippled* it first!"

The prisoner felt his blood boil as he realized his fears were coming true. The Underground had heard enough of Seven's recordings to piece together that it was he who had exposed the senior Daniel Alexander Young as the leader of the Underground. He had known this would happen—expected it—from the minute he clicked send, but he had held out hope that he would find a place to hide and escape any attempts at retribution.

"You want revenge," said Seven with only the faintest crack in his voice. "I get that, but I swear to you that I didn't know what was going on—what the Guard had done to me. I'm—I'm sorry about what happened."

Young's pole-like arms stabbed into the seat of the chair around Seven's legs. He screamed. "You're sorry? You're *sorry?*"

Their eyes linked.

Unexpectedly, Danny laughed and fell whimsically back onto his heels. Seven wasn't sure whether to feel angry or relieved.

The leader of the Underground kicked at a dust bunny and chuckled. "Fortunately for you, I see the bigger picture. Don't get me wrong—I certainly was mad about what happened, but time and meditation have convinced me to direct my anger more constructively. Let's be honest: killing you would accomplish nothing for the cause. I mean, you were just the Guard's weapon, really. A white knight wouldn't focus his energy breaking the black night's broad sword, would he?"

Seven wasn't quite sure what his captor meant by this, but nodded encouragingly since it seemed to support keeping him alive.

"Truth is, Seven, I need your help. The reason for all the dramatics–tying you to a chair and all that–is just that I wanted to make you squirm a teensy-weensy bit. Consider that my revenge...*for now*."

The prisoner froze.

"Joking!" Danny laughed. "Loosen up, will you?"

Seven breathed. "Kind of tough when I'm tied to a chair."

"Never mind that–hey, that was kind of a pun you just made, wasn't it? I like that! Seven's coming alive, everyone!" Danny's head moved up and down giddily as he laughed. "Seriously, though, I'll cut you free as soon as I decide you can be trusted. You *were* an Elite Guard, after all. Can't be too careful you know. Why don't we just chat a little bit more, and when I'm feeling a little more comfortable, we'll let you loose, okay?"

Seven kept quiet.

"Now," said Young, pacing toward the windows and back. "Tell me what it was like when you woke up with no memory a few weeks back."

"Um, well–"

"I mean, philosophically I just think it's so interesting! All of the propaganda fed to us by the Guard our whole lives–forgotten! Overnight! I mean, you became *tabula rasa*!"

"Yeah, it was–"

"–amazing I bet. You don't know what I'd do not to have a past. My life would be far easier, let me tell you."

Seven raised his eyebrows. "Easy is not the word I'd use."

Young ignored the remark and continued. "And how do you see our country now? Our way–the Underground way! You see this corrupt, broken government exploiting man's natural fear of God to keep everyone in check. You see everything my father taught, but without his teaching! Let me tell you that he would have loved to have met you. I know that might sound a bit ironic considering you indirectly killed the man–but it's the honest truth!"

Seven felt his blood pressure rising. "Look, all I've done since waking up this way is destroy lives. If you're trying to tell me all this is some kind of blessing–"

"Oh but don't you see? It absolutely is a blessing! You have the power to see things the way they are!"

"I'm not sure I–"

"The Cave!" interrupted Danny, barely able to contain his enthusiasm.

"Oh," Seven said. "Wait…what?"

"You're not familiar with the story? No, I suppose you couldn't be, even if you once did."

"What does this have to do with–"

"I apologize. Lend me a few minutes and I shall orate from the beginning. I'm not talking geology with you. The Cave is a famous philosophical allegory. Hopefully I'll be able to explain."

Seven got the feeling he didn't have a choice. Young's enthusiasm was exhausting.

Young began his retelling. "The Cave imagines a group of prisoners, chained inside a cave so that they can only see the wall. There's this…*bonfire* behind them–but they're unable to turn their heads to see it. And for their entire lives, their captors parade statues of various everyday objects–pots, fruit, animals–in front of the unseen fire, casting shadows on the wall. Because the prisoners are chained, they see only these shadows, and they believe them to be the true, natural form of the objects. Suddenly, their entire society revolves around this illusion. And in fact, they honor and elevate the prisoners who are most adept at reading the shadows and construing meaning from them."

Young's pointer finger sprung up into the air. "The exact same thing," he grinned, "happens in our nation. The people here see only the shades of reality cast by the Church and the Guard. To the average citizen, the priests teach the good, and the president is infallible. What's more, we place upon the pedestal those of us who most embrace the distortions. We call them Patriots."

Seven began to understand. "And the people who don't are called Heretics."

"Hey, look at that, you're getting it! This is great!"

Seven tried to force a smile but failed miserably.

Danny continued undeterred. "So anyway, the next chapter begins with an experiment: What happens when you release one of the prisoners from his chains? The freed man turns around and sees for the first time that all those shapes are just shadows. He sees the fire and the true form of the objects.

"This is where you come in, Seven. Let me ask you, how did you feel when you first took in our nation and realized you didn't recognize it?"

"How would you feel?"

"Just humor me."

Seven exhaled miserably. "Disoriented, I guess."

Danny grinned. "So was the prisoner. Here he was all used to living in a dark cave, and now there's this big bonfire stinging his eyes. I bet part of you wanted to go back to what you knew before, right?"

Seven considered. "I couldn't go back."

"Neither could the prisoner. Instead, he followed the path out of the cave. When he experienced the sun for the first time, it was even more severe to his eyes than the fire. But soon he became accustomed to the light."

Young paced toward the Guard poster opposite Seven, apparently to gather his thoughts. "Now that you know the truth about this nation, how does it make you feel when you meet people who blindly follow the Guard and the Church?"

Seven frowned at the floor. "I mean, I guess you just said it. I think they're blind."

"So did the man who escaped the Cave," he said. "Well get over it! Try to assimilate!"

THE PRISONER

A short laugh shot from the prisoner's lips. "It's not that easy."

"Of course not—it's too late, isn't it? When he tried to go back, he realized he could no longer play their game of shadows. For you it's the same. You don't understand how people can buy into the lies told by the Guard and the Church. And you must disdain so called Patriots, for they embrace the lies without question."

Seven gazed blankly at the white-tiled floor. "So what did the prisoner do?"

"The same thing as anyone who learns great truths. He tried to free the others so they could see the light, too."

"Did it work?"

"No. They insisted that the prisoner's eyes had been corrupted. When he wouldn't give up, the others decided there was only one solution."

Seven looked up at Young's index finger pointing high in the air.

"Kill the Heretic."

The prisoner frowned. "So you're saying it's hopeless."

"Not quite," Young returned. "You see, there's one important difference between the Cave and this world, Seven. You have allies."

Danny leaned against the fiery symbol of the Underground on the wall across from the prisoner and beamed. Seven exhaled, "What do you want?"

"It's just as I said before, Seven. You're a blank slate—well, blank enough anyway. That means your opinions are pure and not tainted by the Guard's propaganda. That's valuable to me."

"How?"

"I want you to be my adviser."

CHAPTER ELEVEN
The Promise

A black luxury sedan with armor that could withstand a machine gun snaked between two lanes of traffic. In the passenger seat, Eve stared at a red dot blinking on the screen of her tablet. "He's been in one spot for almost an hour since we started tracking him," she said.

Rodriguez kept his eyes on the road and returned, "This could be big. If he's really at Underground HQ, we're about to get a whole lot of extra credit from the president."

"Hey, let's not get ahead of ourselves, rookie."

"Can you tap into the live audio?"

"Don't have a strong enough wireless connection," said Eve, glancing at the red rocks whizzing by her window. "Probably just this damn desert."

"Well, we'll be out of it soon. Underground HQ isn't far from the city."

Eve thought of Jon and smiled. God was giving her another chance to convince him, she thought. She could practically taste their happily ever after.

Rodriguez tapped Eve's shoulder and pointed to the radio on the dash. "The president's on."

"My friends," drawled the voice on the radio, "we face an infestation. Victory is within our reach. The famed Guard—your boys and girls—are right now preparing to meet the Enemy invaders on Luna Coast. I've ordered our defenders to pull no punches. They will not rest until the termites–all of the termites–have been exterminated.

"This attack, while horrible, should give Patriots no reason to despair. It is rather God's hand pushing us to be better. The Great Power has merely identified chinks in our armor. It is our duty to seal them.

"My friends, the sad truth is that heresy runs like poison through the veins of our great nation. There are people among us–hiding in plain view–whose only ambition is to weaken us. These selfish men and women say they are working in our country's interest, but we must not believe it. We all know the truth–that they are working for the Devil and seek only to create chaos. We must weed them out, one by one.

"To that end, I am today announcing 'Patriot ID,' a national identification program to assist in the Guard's efforts to seek and destroy heresy. Under the program, which we will roll out soon after the Enemy is driven from our shores, your family doctor will administer a simple, painless procedure that will allow Guard to identify you and your loved ones more quickly than ever before. Patriot ID is more secure, efficient and effective than traditional documentation, and it will allow us to quickly separate the Heretics from the Patriots. Think of it as paperless billing from your friendly government.

"You see, my friends, in the never-ending race to protect our country, we have to stay one step ahead of a nimble adversary. That's just what Patriot ID is for."

Rodriguez chuckled. "I hope this doesn't mean we're out of a job."

Eve didn't respond. Her mind was replaying something the Headmaster said during her briefing: "It is of national importance that information about the technology in Mr. Wyle's head is not revealed to the public."

She felt sick. The president couldn't really be doing *that*, could he? Suddenly all she could think about was the promise she'd made last year to a good friend.

Eve remembered feeling very cold as she looked at the red and yellow flowers. Jon's hand dropped gently on her shoulder. "My love, you've had that door open for two minutes now."

Nodding, she snatched a bouquet of fiery wildflowers. "Sorry," she sniffled. "It's just really hard to pick flowers for a gardener."

They shuffled to the counter. "Hello," chimed the old lady at the register. Her gray eyes popped to the package in Eve's arms. "Those are beautiful."

Jon placed a glass vase on the counter. "This, too, please."

"Would you like a decorative tag?" asked the cashier, spreading five varieties out for them to see.

"Um," stammered Eve. She pointed at a cobalt one reading *Get Well Soon*, and felt the need to explain. "Not the most original, but he'll like the color."

No amount of gifts felt like enough. Bill had always been there for her, celebrating her successes and helping her through hard times—like when her mom…

Eve gulped.

She hadn't thought of her mother in years. It had been so long ago, that day when Eve came home from school and mom wasn't there. She remembered watching TV by herself, well past the cartoons and into prime time. At about 9:00 p.m., her father arrived with a grocery bag full of canned ravioli. He was crying. Mom had been shopping downtown when a protest broke out, Dad said. The Heretics brought out guns, and she was standing in the middle of it all, and…

Dad was a wreck for days. But old Bill listened to Eve, found pretty flowers for her, took her to the playground.

"Cry if you need to," he'd say. "You'll feel much better."

"After you," said Jon.

She was back in the hospital, standing in front of Room 303.

The old man lying on the bed seemed too frail to be her friend. "Hello, Uncle Bill," she greeted meekly.

Some color returned to the man's cheeks as he looked over. "Eve! Still on your Watched List, am I?" He beamed.

Chuckling, she took a seat by his side. "You're never going to let me live that one down, are you?"

"Never!" he declared. Suddenly he fell into a fit of coughs.

Eve tried to help but Bill waved her off. "Those are beautiful flowers," he said eventually. "Thank you for coming. And you too, Jon—you taking good care of my angel?"

Jon smiled. "Doing my best."

"Good," he said. "Sorry for excluding you—inside joke. Short story is she thought I was the Devil!"

Eve's boyfriend nodded knowingly. "Oh, she told me. She's still embarrassed."

"I'm not!" protested Eve, hitting him playfully.

A nurse, probably in her forties, stepped into the room. "Oh, visitors!"

Eve sprung up from her seat. "Sorry, do you need us to–?"

"Oh no, I have to give Bill his meds, but it's nothing that can't wait fifteen minutes. Take your time."

When the nurse had gone Eve turned back to Bill. "How are you feeling?"

"Not bad." He inhaled slowly through the clear tubes running through his nostrils. "I've accepted what's coming."

She frowned. "Bill…"

"It's okay. I've had a good life." He bobbed his head slightly. "Well, the last twenty years anyway, after your dad took me in. I'm especially proud of you—the first young lady ever to be inducted into the Elite Guard!"

"One of the first," she corrected with a blush. "Anyway, you inspired me. Ever since I met you, got to know you, I couldn't bear the thought of a good, innocent man being prejudged as a Heretic."

He gave her the warm smile that always filled her with cheer and optimism. Even now, with its owner on his death bed, the smile was infectious.

THE PROMISE

"You have a rare talent for reading people—like x-ray vision, but better," Bill replied. "That's grand, because not everything is black and white. It takes close and careful observation to see the grays, and an open mind to see the colors." He coughed again. "Will you promise an old man something?"

"Anything."

"There are people out there who will want you to rush to judgment, maybe because it's more convenient to theirs or someone else's agenda. But Eve, you mustn't let them. Promise me you'll always look for the colors."

CHAPTER TWELVE
Allies

"You've got the wrong guy," protested Seven. "I don't want to help the Underground or the Guard. I just want to be left alone!"

Young's face tilted incredulously. "This coming from the man who risked his life supplying evidence against the government?"

"I felt guilty for hurting the Underground. I did it to make amends, but that was it. I'm done taking sides."

Danny shook his head. "Repentance may have been part of it, but I think there was more," he said. "You made a judgment call. You decided that what the Guard was doing was wrong, and you wanted to do something about it."

Seven looked sullenly at the concrete wall behind his captor. "Maybe. I don't know."

Young squinted at him. "Do you disagree with our methods?"

"I just don't see the point," he sighed. "How is the Underground going to change anything? Do you even have the numbers to go up against the Guard?"

A smile crept slowly onto Young's mouth, and suddenly he was guffawing loudly. "I'm sorry," he said, "do you think our master plan is to start a civil war? A second Great War?" He shook his head. "No, Seven, we *don't* have the numbers for that, but my father never believed it would need to come to that."

Seven was speechless.

"I should probably explain how our government is structured, and give you a little history," said Young, licking his chops. "I always did love social studies. More than philosophy even."

Here we go again, thought Seven. He wondered why Danny hadn't become a professor.

"We have four branches of government: executive, legislative, judicial, and the Church," he explained. "They are supposed to have equal power, and in fact they had equal power, until one fateful day decades ago when the president and the Church decided to gang up and fight the *growing evil*." He made quote marks with his fingers around the last two words.

"Let me guess," Seven interjected. "Heretics?"

Danny grinned broadly. "You got it–a splinter church to be exact. The Headmaster at the time tried to convince then-President Frederick Wright that the new religion's growing prominence was a threat to the nation."

"Tried?"

Danny shrugged. "For a while it didn't work. President Wright held firm that Church and State should be separate, and wouldn't order the Guard to intervene. But things changed fast when the Heretics–allegedly, mind you–set off a bomb in the old Capitol building. The president was traveling, but his wife and the vice president were in the building. Neither survived.

"As you might expect that got Wright's attention. And so just like that the Headmaster had the president's full support. Together, they pressured congress into writing a law declaring the splinter church illegal. The so-called Heretics fought back, which in turn started what we now refer to as the Great War. It lasted four gruesome years, and the better trained Guard came out the victor.

When it was over people were weary of fighting and violence. The Church easily convinced them that it was heresy that began the war, and therefore it was heresy that needed to be prevented in order to keep the peace. So, President Wright pushed another bill through the Congress which he called the Heretic Act. The proposed law defined the differences between a Patriot and a Heretic, and laid out the punishments for being a Heretic. That law was rather loosely written, leaving the courts essentially powerless to side against the government whenever the Guard brought in a suspected Heretic. The result is that most people arrested for heresy in our country are quickly convicted."

Seven shook his head vigorously to stop Young. "Wait, why wouldn't more people resist a law like this?"

"Two reasons," Young said. "One, they were told that the law was critical to national security. When the president of the whole goddamned country says something is critical to national security people tend to be more receptive. Second, the Heretic Act was fully endorsed by the Headmaster, and everyone's priest espoused its virtues. Imagine you're at church, and your minister is telling you about a proposal that will lead to a purer society, usher in God's love, blah, blah, blah. Sounds pretty good, right?"

Seven felt a headache coming on. "But that's crazy!"

"It gets worse. Turned out the Heretic Act also gave the executive branch broad new surveillance powers. Again, very loosely written. As a result, the president suddenly was able to inflict pretty much any crazy paranoid measure he wanted onto the public. As long as he said the reason was to protect against heresy, he was in the clear. And he had the Church right behind him slapping everything with a big red 'Approved by God' stamp!"

Danny clapped, apparently for effect.

"Lucky for you, Seven, seems you woke up in a new era of *change*! It's easy to miss, but there is this growing…restlessness, I guess. For most people it's like this seed, or—no—it's like this *match* inside them. All we need to do is strike these God-fearing churchgoers in just the right way and—I promise you—they will ignite and fight on our side!

"The really good news for us is that some of these people have made their way into the Congress. Even with the Heretic Act, Congress still maintains the power to impeach the president and fix the laws. But the only way to do that is to get the other legislators to stand up against him and the Headmaster."

"Can't the president just block an impeachment?"

"No," said Danny. "Our country's founders gave the legislative branch the power to remove the president, and no one has the balls to throw out this country's first laws. The real problem is convincing a majority of the stubborn jerks in Congress to take action. Seriously, these fools will stalemate over naming a post office!

"Still, even with all that, my father believed it was doable if we brought forward some pretty compelling dirt. Unfortunately, it's near impossible to collect appropriately damning evidence without breaking the law."

Seven found himself perplexed as he thought about the chip in his head. "What about the evidence I sent you?"

Young shrugged. "While certainly concerning that the Guard would take such elaborate steps to infiltrate the Underground, it's difficult to make the case that they've overstepped their authority. For example, you–the old you–technically consented to having the chip installed."

"Yeah, but…"

"Don't get me wrong. What you got was great stuff. But to stage an uprising against the president…Unfortunately we're just going to need to find a few more skeletons in his closet."

Seven felt strangely invigorated by the fiery-eyed symbol of the Underground staring back at him from the wall. "I guess that's where we come in, right?"

Danny responded with a brilliant grin.

Young shoved a gun in Seven's back and pushed him stumbling up the wooden steps from the cellar. They made eye contact briefly. The prisoner's face showed no emotion. Danny's thin lips quivered up and down like a fish. Danny ducked around a lonely yellow bulb hanging from the ceiling, and pushed the door open. Sunlight rushed through, and for a split second Seven teetered off balance. A blunt stab in his lower back pushed him forward again.

"So this is my home," welcomed Danny. "One of them anyway."

Seven rubbed at some rope burn left on his wrist and looked around.

The living room was about what Seven expected, considering the Young family owned the top bank in the country. He couldn't decide of which feature he was most jealous—the tall floor-to-ceiling windows, the cushy leather sofas, or the cinema-sized TV screen. Then he saw the view. Through a shady thicket of giant oak trees Seven could see the ocean and a brilliant blue sky.

Danny smiled proudly. "You were expecting the desert?"

"Where are we?"

"On the coast, a few miles outside the Capital. My family came here often for summer retreats."

"Beats camping," interjected a breathy and familiar female voice.

Seven's head spun right and took in a tall, slender woman with short auburn hair, tortoise-shell glasses, and piercing green eyes. "Ana?" he made out.

He hadn't seen her since the attack. Ana looked like just another pretty face, but actually was an efficient and deadly spy for the Underground. Her only weakness, as far as Seven could tell, was poor taste in men. She was the type of girl who, faced with a crowd of suitors, always seemed to pick the biggest jerk in the pile. He knew that because he briefly had a crush on her. It hadn't worked out.

Ana pulled a skinny cigarette from her burgundy lips. "Hey, Seven, looks like you made it out of the city in one piece."

"More or less." He shrugged. "But what are you doing here?"

Young coughed, and then appeared to choke a little bit on it.

Ana shot him a look. "Danny and I are…old friends," she explained slowly. "I called him up after I got out of the city."

Seven looked around but couldn't locate Ana's most recent jerk-friend. "Is Eric here?"

She took a quick puff and considered the smoke curling

up to the ceiling. "After everything that happened…our arrest, the escape from the Tower…I guess he decided that he'd had enough."

Seven's eyebrows rose. He tried to think of something comforting to say, but couldn't come up with anything. He still felt guilty for getting her in trouble with—and nearly killed by—the Guard. The surveillance he had unwittingly done for the Guard exposed Ana as a Heretic.

Danny tapped Seven's back with his gun. "You can thank—or blame—Ana for your presence here today," he said. "She practically begged me to bring you into the loop after it became clear you'd escaped the Capital."

Seven shot his old teammate a puzzled look. "But…but it was my fault…"

"Danny told me about the tapes and your involvement with the Guard," she said. "But I know you didn't know what was happening. And anyway, you saved our lives."

"Yeah, after I got you arrested."

"We were a team, and you did so much to help us," she said. "No matter who you may have been before, I don't know how I could ever doubt your heart is now with the Underground."

Danny cleared his throat with such force that Ana looked concerned.

He waved her off. "I hate to break up the reunion," he said, "but we didn't exactly bring Seven here for pleasantries. Ana, could you please find Shaan and Talia and tell them we're having a meeting in my office."

Adopting the accent of a pirate, Ana returned, "Aye aye, Cap'n Young."

He laughed and told her to shut up. Then he jabbed Seven with the gun and pushed him out of the room into a bright hallway wallpapered with wildflowers.

"So your summer vacation home doubles for Underground HQ?" asked Seven.

"What?" Young shot back. His eyes narrowed and then lit up

quite suddenly. "Oh! No, no—you were brought to this particular location because I happened to be in the area. That's all. The truth about HQ is that it's everywhere and nowhere all at once."

"I...see," Seven said hesitantly. He was starting to wish Young was capable of giving answers that weren't long-winded.

Young took Seven's response as a request for more information. "You see, it would be child's play for the Guard to locate us if we kept everything in a single, centralized location. Instead we have an extensive network of small locations, each contributing to the whole. Are you familiar with cloud networks?"

"Not really."

"Shaan could explain it better..." said Danny, head swiveling wildly around. Shaan was nowhere in sight. "I know, think of it like a plant!"

First a cloud and now a plant; Seven was beginning to grow tired of all the metaphors.

"So imagine a large plant with, I don't know, how many leaves does a large plant have? Fifty or sixty? We have more bases than that, but for the sake of this analogy, let's go with that. So, what happens when one leaf turns brown? Does the entire plant die? No! Likewise, if one of our locations is detected, we can avoid having the entire Underground compromised by issuing a simple disconnection command, pruning the found station like the dead leaf."

"But you're the leader now, right? Isn't wherever you are the central base?"

Danny shook his head. "That's a common misconception, actually. Truth is no one is really the absolute leader. My dad founded the Underground, but he only directed activities in the Capital and surrounding region."

"Then who makes the decisions for the entire group?"

"Well, Dad was chairman on a board with several other directors. But his vote was equal to theirs. When he died, I took over as chairman."

"Interesting," said Seven. Finally, he worked up the courage to complain about the object that kept bumping against his back. "Hey, if I'm going to be your adviser and everything, is the gun really necessary?"

Young eyed his hand as if he'd just discovered a mysterious growth. "Oh," he said, dropping his arm. "No, I guess not."

Ana caught up with them. "They're on their way," she said. "Arguing about something trite, as per usual, but they're coming."

Danny pulled open the door to his office and wandered behind a big oak desk. The workstation was immaculate–so much so that Seven wondered how much use it got. Young grabbed the computer mouse and shook it furiously until the machine beeped. Satisfied, he fell into a red leather chair and motioned to a single chair near the door. "Have a seat," he told them.

Seven squinted awkwardly at Ana until finally she offered the chair to him. "Please, Seven, after everything you've been through today, you probably need it more than me."

A hushed warbling in the hallway of Young's vacation house turned to emphatic chatter. Shaan and his sister entered the room.

"Why does *he* get the chair?" Talia protested immediately, indicating Seven with a point of one of her long, slender fingers. "What happened to chivalry? And isn't he supposed to be our prisoner or something?"

Danny clasped his straw-like fingers and peered at them over his black flat-panel monitor. "Well, only in the philosophical sense." He guffawed for a long time by himself.

Shaan scrunched his lids tight, as if he expected his eyes to pop out otherwise. "All right, that's it!" he exploded. "What's this all about? Why is Seven here? When we knocked him out and drove all the way here, I *thought* we were bringing in some kind of traitor!"

"Seven's not working for the Guard, anymore," tried Ana.

"What do you mean, *anymore*?"

Young held up his hands as if trying to stop an oncoming bus. "Seven is one of our spies, and he's provided some very valuable evidence that we believe can help us take down the Guard. There was a bit of a…um…misunderstanding, which was why I needed you to use force to bring him here. But that's all cleared up now. Isn't that right, Seven?"

"Um," he hesitated. "I guess so."

Danny slicked back his blond hair. "Anyway, Shaan, it's good that you're here. We could use someone with your technical expertise. It's getting harder to come by good agents, what with the attack and everything…"

He peered down at the big man's sister. "And Talia, um… well, it's good to have you here as well."

She stuck her thumb up and offered a rather patronizing smile.

Young's eyes fell mournfully to the keyboard and for a while he said nothing. Finally, he spoke. "I'm not my father. I didn't…I didn't even really work with my father when he was alive. I always believed in the cause, but…I guess what I'm saying is I'm a bit new at this." He looked up at everyone. "I appreciate you all bearing with me as I try to figure all this out. I want to involve all of you in the decision-making process, at least until I have things under control again."

Ana smiled. "That's what we're here for. Just tell us our first move."

Danny turned to the monitor and fiddled again with the mouse. "Well, the situation's changed a great deal since the Enemy attacked. A new option has presented itself. You see, the Enemy sent a message to my father."

Talia gasped. "They what?"

"Listen." He clicked and the light fuzz of radio static filled the room.

"Hello, Mr. Young," boomed a heavily accented voice. "Our intelligence indicates that you lead a rebel movement in your nation known as the Underground. We would like to make our intentions known to you, because we believe our interests may align. In one hour, we will launch a 'shock-and-awe' attack on your Capital. We then intend to come to shore and take it."

Seven glanced briefly at Talia, whose mouth now hung wide open.

"You refer to us as the Enemy, but we are not the Underground's enemy. Our mission is not one of destruction, but rather salvation. We are here to free your nation from the tyrant William Drake and his wholly oppressive government. We are here to install you, the Underground, as leaders of this new, free republic."

The voice of the Enemy paused. "All we require is your allegiance."

Talia was so angry she was shaking. "Danny! You knew about the attack and didn't warn anyone?!"

Young stopped the recording. He looked surprised by the charge. "Well, no, I didn't know. With my dad captured, we didn't actually find the tape until after the bombing. By that time it was too late to do anything."

"Whatever," said Ana dismissively. "All we can do now is decide how to respond."

Seven wasn't sure what was more incredible–the message from the Enemy or the Underground's inability to make a decision about it. "Wait, let me get this straight," he spoke up. "Are we actually thinking about helping the Enemy take over?"

"Well," said Ana, "I mean they never said anything about conquering the country, right? They said they're here to help us overthrow the Guard."

Shaan considered. "Danny, what do they want us to do exactly?"

"As you know, the Underground has a sizable presence in every major city in the nation. We've got small armies that can fight the Guard if push comes to shove. And we've got people with access to critical infrastructure who can prepare cities for invasion."

"Prepare…?" Seven squinted at him. "Meaning what?"

"Well, for example, we've got insiders who can disable wireless communications, shut down the electric grid, or… um…do something clever with the sewage system. That kind of thing."

Shaan nodded. "All feasible options. But only if we manage to convince our people to sabotage their own country."

Danny laughed. "Well, you wouldn't pitch it like, you know, 'Hey guys, let's help the Enemy!' We could just tell them that we're enabling the war to continue a little bit longer, so that, when all's said and done, whoever wins will be so weak we can overthrow them in a matter of weeks, maybe days. And you know, to a certain extent it's true. Maybe the Guard will pull out a victory. If they do, we'll still have put ourselves in a stronger position."

Seven couldn't believe what he was hearing. "No," he said. "This doesn't…this doesn't feel right to me."

Danny held up his hands in surrender. "I'm not saying we should definitely do it. That's why you're here. Clearly, you think this is a bad idea. Why?"

"Look, the way I see it, we've got this bitter divide, right? Patriots and Heretics, Guard and Underground. I think it's what made us vulnerable to attack, and I think that maybe the Enemy knows it's the key to winning the war. How can we be so sure that, when it's all over and the Enemy has won, they're not just going to turn around and be just as controlling as the Guard?"

"I'm just playing devil's advocate here," said Danny, "but I'm not sure they could control anyone, even if they wanted to. I don't think the people would allow it. The Enemy would have to put one of us in charge to keep the peace, right?"

"But 'the people' aren't exactly on our side," said Seven. "They've been taught by the government to hate the Underground. If they see the Underground actually *helping* the Enemy take out soldiers—many of whom, by the way, are just following orders—it's just going to confirm every lie the Guard's told. Even if the Enemy makes good on its promise and puts us in charge, the people aren't going to like it. They're going to hate us even more than they do now."

"Seven's right," said Talia. "Every soldier has friends and family. Those people are going to care."

Ana shook her head. "But, I mean, we can't help the *Guard* win the war, right?"

"Don't think of it as helping the Guard," said Seven. "Think of it as defeating the Enemy. If the people see the Underground defending the homeland, it's possible they'll start trusting us. That trust will make them more open to what we have to say. And it's not just good public relations; it's the right thing to do."

Danny exhaled meaningfully. "Okay," he said. "I've got to think about this more, but you may have convinced me. Anyone else have anything to say?"

"Yeah," said Talia. "What's that high-pitched bleep-bleep-bleep noise?"

Everyone shut up. Something was indeed producing a high-frequency pulse.

"The alarm!" gasped Young, turning fast to the computer screen. "I think we may have visitors!"

CHAPTER THIRTEEN
Surprise

"Three," said Eve, and the Elites popped out of the car. Rodriguez ducked behind the purple minivan parked outside the ranch house and pointed a pistol at the front door. Eve approached the entrance and pounded with her fist.

After a minute of no response, Eve glanced at her tablet. The blinking red dot showing Seven's location was still frozen in place about a half-mile away. "This rancher is the only building in three miles," she said. "It's the only place Jon can be."

Nodding, Rodriguez procured a silver key and slipped it into the door knob. Eve glanced down at a pot of flowers on the porch and thought again of her old friend Bill and their last meeting.

"Are you ready?" said Rodriguez. The door was open.

Eve wasn't–she'd never been so confused in her life. But she couldn't tell her partner that. "Let's move," she said.

◎

"That looked like some kind of tracking app," said Shaan, eyeing Danny Young's monitor over his shoulder. "But who the hell is Jon?"

Seven felt his heart race as his worst fears were confirmed. Eve hadn't let him go even after their scrap in the Capitol Tower. She must have been tracking him ever since, he thought. "She found me," he murmured aloud.

Ana and Talia sent Seven a collective look of bewilderment. Danny spun around his chair to face him head on. "Wait, Seven, you know these people?"

He struggled to explain. "I don't know the guy, but the woman is Eve. She…she was the Elite tracking me on, uh…you know…my mission."

"Well," snapped Shaan with the face of someone stung by a bee, "it would appear she's still tracking you."

"That's impossible," said Seven. "The only way they could track me would be if they had…"

He reached into his pocket for the memory stick, but all he could feel was tattered tissues. "Oh shit."

"What?" snapped Shaan.

It didn't take much explanation to bring the short-fused engineer up to speed.

"You lost it?!"

"I must have dropped it when you rushed me back at your house!"

Shaan slammed his fist against the desk and bared his teeth. "She was in my house?!"

"Hey, everyone chill," advised Danny, rising to his feet. "We'll worry about all that in a minute. Right now we need to hide."

Eve nudged open the front door. Rodriguez darted inside and assessed the foyer with pistol outstretched. They edged forward toward an intersection with a long hallway stretching left to right. In the room straight ahead, Eve could see large windows and a windy forest.

Rodriguez gaped into the living room, too. "Nice TV!" he exclaimed.

She rolled her eyes. "Try to focus, please."

"Should we split up?" he asked. "You go left, I go right?"

She shook her head. "We don't know how many Heretics are here. Better if we stay together." She pointed to the right with her gun. "Go that way, I'll be close behind."

Rodriguez did as he was told. Eve's eyes lingered on the weapon in her hand and again felt racked with indecision. She

SURPRISE

had Seven, she knew it. But something kept gnawing at her. Was her whole mission here really just about Patriot ID? Was the Guard really going to help her fiancé, or did they just want to ensure there would be no backlash against installing chips into more people's heads?

"Promise me..." she heard Bill whisper in her ear.

"They're moving for the bedrooms," said Danny Young, squeezing past Ana's breasts to look at a TV screen displaying the house's security feed. They were lined shoulder to shoulder behind a faux bookcase in Young's office.

"Something tells me this room wasn't built for five," complained Ana, releasing herself from the wall.

"There's only two of them out there," whispered Talia. "Why don't we just jump them?"

"I think you're forgetting they're Elite Guard," replied Ana. "And more could be on their way. We have to be very careful about this."

"They're only tracking me," said Seven. "The rest of you should make an escape. I'll stay here and figure something out."

"No," said Young. "We're a team now. We're sticking together."

"But we can't just wait here!" protested Talia. "They're calling in backup. Maybe this parlor trick of Danny's can fool them temporarily, but it's not going to work forever. I've seen how the Guard operates. They'll burn this house down to the ground before they walk away from a possible Heretic nest. And anyway, if those Elites are tracking Seven, shouldn't it be pretty easy for them to figure out we're in here?"

"No, at least not right away," grumbled her brother. "This house is equipped with a device that interferes with wireless spectrum used by the Guard."

She nodded, but her expression was blank.

"It's a security measure," Shaan explained. "It's likely that this has neutralized whatever chip they put inside Seven's head."

She shook her head. "Then how did they find the house?"

He grimaced. "The range of interference is limited. If they started tracking Seven before he arrived, they'd know where he was when he dropped off the grid."

Talia looked more puzzled than ever before. "Then what's even the point of having an interference what-cha-ma-call-it?"

Danny shushed them. He was wide-eyed and pointing at the screen.

Seven couldn't believe what he was seeing. Eve had a gun aimed on her unwitting partner's neck.

Eve looked over her pistol at Rodriguez, who was currently conducting a futile search under the king-size bed in the master bedroom. She asked him to do it and he was stupid enough to follow. Now all she had to do was act.

"I'm not seeing anything," he said. "I mean, unless you care about a stray tissue."

She smiled. The rookie was actually kind of endearing once you got to know him. "They might be notes," she suggested. "See if there's any writing on them."

"Yes, sir."

Eve pulled the trigger. Her partner moaned slightly, then his arms and legs gave out and he fell into a useless pile on the floor. She flipped the gun around and tossed it lightly into the hallway. With a sigh, she sat on the bed and waited for the rebels.

CHAPTER FOURTEEN
Reunion

Even with three Heretics circling like hungry sharks, Eve couldn't help but smile. Finally, she had caught up with Jon and would have another chance to convince him to come back and leave the Seven persona behind.

It would, of course, be difficult to explain any of this to the Headmaster. Eve had always considered herself a good Patriot, and others seemed to think so, too. That's why she'd risen so high in the Guard's ranks, higher than any woman before her. It was true she didn't like what the president was planning–or at least seemed to be planning. But now, in retrospect, attacking her partner seemed a little…well…irrational. Well, she'd worry about all that later.

"Hey *bitch*, pay attention!"

Eve looked up at the tall brunette smoking a cigarette. She recognized her from the Guard's files as Ana Ivanova. The woman had popped up on the periphery of a number of cases, but had for years managed to keep her profile low enough to keep off the Watched list. Jon's mission changed all that. When he infiltrated the Underground, the once secret Heretic's voice began streaming live to Eve's tablet.

Behind Ana, a skinny man with slicked-back hair slumped lackadaisically against the door. He tapped a revolver against his thighs and yawned. Eve recognized him from the supermarket rags as playboy Danny Young. She wasn't entirely surprised to learn he was working with the Heretics. After all, his late father was behind the entire Underground operation. It would have been more shocking to learn he had no involvement.

"Where's Seven?" Eve asked.

"None of your business," Ana snapped. She wrenched Eve's arms behind her back and latched on a pair of handcuffs.

The Elite Guard glanced down with a sigh at Shaan, who until recently she thought was dead. Even though she'd seen his photo back in Loganville, part of her still hadn't believed he was alive. But here he was, on his knees trying to pull Rodriguez out from under the bed. Eve shifted a few inches down the mattress to give him more space.

"That's my partner, Rodriguez," said Eve. "He's just a dumb rookie, but you should probably find a way to keep him quiet."

He looked pretty stupid face down on the carpet, thought Eve. But then again, he always looked pretty stupid. Shaan touched the rookie's neck, presumably to check for a pulse.

"He's alive," he said at last.

"We were both armed with tranqs," explained Eve. "This isn't a *Jackson Danger* flick–we were never planning to kill anyone."

Shaan looked annoyed. "No, you were just going to arrest us so that we could be killed on live television," returned Shaan. His baritone voice was laced with disgust. "How merciful."

Eve shrugged. "Look, would someone just tell me where Seven is? I've got to speak with him."

"Go to Hell," shot Ana. The metal cuffs tightened suddenly and Eve yelped in protest.

"Now, girls, let's play nice," laughed Danny, who was apparently enjoying the situation. "Allow me to introduce myself. My name is–"

"Daniel Alexander Young, Jr.," Eve interrupted. "I already know all of you. The mean girl with glasses is Ana Ivanova, and the guy on the floor with a penchant for faking his own death is Shaan…Williams, is it now?"

Shaan gaped in horror, while Ana simply maintained her stink-eye.

REUNION

"That's an amusing parlor trick," said Young with a roguish smile. "We're told you are Agent Eve Parker of the Elite Guard."

He stretched out his hand, inviting a hand shake.

Eve scowled. "I appreciate the gesture, Mr. Young, but to be frank I'm a little tied up right now."

Danny erupted with laughter. "Oh, right, the handcuffs! Maybe later, then, assuming we don't kill you first. Kidding!"

Seven pushed up onto the hood of the purple minivan and spit at the driveway. One end of the saliva lingered in his mouth. He shook his head to free it and groaned in self-disgust.

The back door to the house opened, but Seven didn't turn to face the newcomer. "Go away," he grumbled.

"What are you doing out here?" demanded Talia. "They might need you inside."

"They might need you, too."

She approached slowly and turned her head sideways to match Seven's orientation. "No, I'm useless. The only thing I know how to do is run, and you've probably noticed I'm not even very good at that."

"Join the club." He leaned back on his palms and looked up at the trees. Talia found a small spot to sit next to him.

"You know, I got my name out here somewhere," said Seven.

Talia furrowed her brow quizzically. "What, the forest?"

He nodded. "My first memory is waking up among all these trees, looking up at the sun. I didn't know where I was or why I was there. Hell, I didn't even know who I was. But just when I was about to give up, I saw a sign."

Talia snorted. "What, you mean, like from God?"

"Nah, it was graffiti. The number seven carved on a tree. I remember it so vividly because up to then I could have been anywhere. I could have been hundreds of miles from civilization. The carving gave me hope because only a punk kid would do that kind of thing. And punk kids don't go hiking very far into a forest."

Talia laughed. "So, what, you saw this number on a tree and thought to yourself, 'Hey, that's pretty neat! That's what I'm going to call myself from now on.'"

He smiled. "Not exactly. I didn't actually think of it again until this old man asked me my name. I didn't know what to tell him, and I didn't want to sound like a crazy person, so I chose the first thing that popped into my head."

She blinked. "You didn't want to sound like a crazy person, so you named yourself Seven? Couldn't you have said, I don't know, 'Jake?' Or 'Scott?'"

He shrugged.

"I know, how about 'Steven?' That's close to Seven and actually sounds normal! We can start calling you that now, if you like."

Seven shook his head no. "I was going to pick a name like that later, but I guess Seven grew on me. It at least had some meaning. Anyway, it wasn't like I could just say to people, 'Oh hey, by the way, remember when I said my name was Seven? Yeah, I just had some amnesia for a while and forgot there was a "T" in my name.'"

They laughed together. A gust of wind blew through their hair and a few yellow-green leaves fell from above. Talia tried to snatch one but missed.

"My real name is Jonathan," he confessed. "Jonathan Wyle. But he was someone else, someone I never want to be again."

She put her hand gently on his. "Hey, I'm sorry, by the way," she said.

"For what?"

"Well, you know, the whole thing where my brother and I knocked you out and brought you here against your will. It was all kind of a last-minute decision, and mostly Shaan's."

He looked at her. "Well, I probably wouldn't have gone if you'd asked nicely. I guess you did what–"

"Wait a minute!" interrupted Talia, eyes lighting up. "I get it now! This Eve...this is the girl you told me 'it's complicated' with, isn't it? Back in the bar!"

Seven's mouth opened to speak but produced no sound.

"It *is*! It is the girl!" she exclaimed. "I guess being in love with an Elite *would* be compli–"

"I'm not in love with her!" he yelped. "Jon Wyle was in love with her! He was engaged to her. She doesn't understand we're not the same."

"Hey boy, calm down, calm down," she purred. "Anyway, I'm sure once she gets to know the new you, she won't want *anything* to do with you."

His jaw dropped. "You are such a…a…I can't think of a nice word."

She beamed. "Back at 'cha. Now, what say we go inside and see what the ex wants, hmm?"

"Tell me where he is!" demanded Eve. She was fuming.

Jon stepped into the room and Eve's heart leapt. A young woman Eve recognized from surveillance footage as Talia appeared behind him and laid a hand gently on his back.

Danny glanced at him out of the corner of his eye, but kept his gun pointed squarely at Eve's head. "Everything all right, dude?"

The man at the door nodded. "What does she want?" The voice was cold and detached.

"Seven," Eve acknowledged sadly. "I was sent here to stop you from spreading information about your mission."

"Too late," he said. "The Underground knows everything."

"It doesn't matter. That's why I was sent here, but I don't care about that anymore," she said, fighting back tears. "I'm really here because…because I don't think I can support the president and the Headmaster anymore."

The Heretics exchanged looks. Finally, Ana asked, "Why?"

"Have you heard about Patriot ID?"

"I meant, why should we believe you?" Ana growled.

"Let her talk," said Shaan, turning to Eve with interest. "Patriot ID was just on the news–an identification system without cards, right? Not exactly the scariest thing the Guard has ever come up with. What do you know about it?"

Eve smirked. "I have strong reason to believe Patriot ID is more than just identification. As Seven may have told you, we installed a chip in his head that records audio and sends it wirelessly to the Guard. I think they're going to do that to the entire country."

Seven looked sick. "Did you know–did I know–they might do this?"

She sighed. "We thought at most they'd try it on people on the Watched list. But now it seems President Drake wants to be able to watch everybody."

"That's ridiculous," said Seven. "He's just going to throw the entire country in with the Watched?"

"Yes and no. The Watched–the people we had a reason to suspect–are being rounded up and arrested."

"Wait, wait, wait," said Talia, flagging down the conversation with her hands. "Didn't you people *block Seven's memory*, too? Are they going to do that to everyone?"

Eve shook her head. "I don't know…probably not. Not sure what the point would be."

Shaan raised his eyebrows. "Knowing the Guard, they'd probably at least leave the capability in the chip–just in case someone's mind needed a factory reset."

Seven broke in impatiently. "Why are you telling us this? What's your game?"

"No game. I know what you all think of the Guard, but we're not all mindless drones. Personally, I don't believe it's right to watch someone unless and until there's good reason. A long time ago, I made the mistake of prejudging a good man to be a Heretic. Patriot ID does the same thing, but for the entire country. There's no way I can support that."

Ana rubbed her temples. "Do you have any proof that the Guard is mass producing these chips? Anything we can use to expose Drake?"

"Nothing solid. But I can help you find it."

CHAPTER FIFTEEN
Plans

The floor-to-ceiling windows in the living room of Danny Young's vacation home became black mirrors. Seven edged closer to the glass and cupped his hands around his eyes to see dark branches bounce to the rhythm of the wind. Suddenly the forest ignited in a flash of orange. For that split second, he could see the blue ocean dotted with gunmetal boats. Then darkness returned and he could see only his reflection.

A moment later he heard thunder but knew it didn't come from nature.

Talia strolled into the room grumbling about how dull she found her brother. She was holding two glasses of mysterious blue liquid. "You should never have let Shaan take a look at your dumb memory stick. What a bore."

For the first time since they met, Talia had let down her hair. It fell black, straight, and damp onto a white baby tee.

"You look refreshed," he commented.

Talia beamed. "You've got to try the shower here. It's brilliant."

"When you threw me in the trunk, did you remember to throw a towel and a change of clothes on top?"

She cackled. "Steal some shirts from Danny. Rich guy like him probably won't even notice."

"Hard day?" asked Seven, indicating the liquor glasses.

Talia glanced down at her hands. "Oh! Sorry, one's for you if you want it."

"What is it?"

"Something I learned at college. Try it. I'd say it's just what the doctor ordered given your ex is in the house."

Seven accepted the drink. "You've got me there."

She pointed to the sofa. "Guitar?" she asked.

The light cherry wood instrument was taking up two-and-a-half out of three seat cushions. "Sorry," he gasped, hustling to remove the obstruction. "Do you want to sit?"

"Don't put it away!" she cried. "Do you play?"

He stopped short. "I don't know. I, uh, I can't remember."

"I used to play a little," she said. "Let's see what you've got."

He looked at the guitar like it was some kind of alien squash. "I…uh…okay," he stuttered.

Seven took a swig of his aqua-colored drink and found that it tasted almost exactly like a sweet and sour candy. He wondered how much alcohol was in it. He couldn't taste anything, but that didn't mean it wasn't there. With some hesitation he set the glass down on the coffee table and picked up the guitar. Talia fell into the spot next to him on the sofa and eyed the instrument curiously.

Seven pulled up to the edge of the cushion and curved his left hand carefully around the neck. Three fingers fell naturally into place and he stroked it gently.

The girl gasped. "A-minor, the saddest of all chords. Like, you really do have issues, don't you?"

Seven grinned stupidly and plucked a tune that sounded a little bit country. "Better?"

She laughed. "No!"

Eve's ears perked up as a familiar tune leaked through an air vent into the basement, filling the prison with life. She stared at the source and wondered.

A low groan interrupted her thoughts. Eve looked down at the crumpled body of her partner.

"What happened?" managed Rodriguez.

She didn't respond. He'd been asleep for hours, and yet Eve still hadn't quite worked out what to tell him.

Rodriguez tried to pick himself up from the floor to stand, but only got as far as sitting up. "Where are we?"

She sighed. "The basement. They got the jump on us and threw us down here."

He nodded. "Any way out of here?"

Eve opened her mouth to speak, but was interrupted abruptly as the door swung wide. Ana stepped into the room with her arms crossed.

"Eve," she said calmly. "We need to talk to you upstairs."

Rodriguez looked at his partner in confusion.

Eve gritted her teeth. She couldn't let him know what she was planning. Think, Eve, think!

"Well? Is that okay?" Ana sneered.

"Whatever you want to say to me, you can say in front of my partner!" she called back.

Ana shook her head. "To be honest, we don't really care *where* we speak, but it's gonna have to be with you *alone*. So I guess that leaves you with two options: either we have a nice, peaceful chat upstairs…" She drew her pistol and pointed it at Rodriguez. "…or we stay here after I shoot your partner in the head."

Eve looked at the gun, and then her partner. "Probably best if I do what she wants," she told him.

Seven found himself utterly amazed at his ability on the guitar. Playing beautiful music wasn't really the kind of thing one thought to try right away when they woke up with amnesia. But then again, he had spent some time around musicians after waking up as Seven, so why hadn't he tried this before?

Boredom and curiosity led him to the wooden instrument. The former Elite had come upon it while wandering about the mansion, torturing himself about what he would say to Eve the next time he saw her. The guitar was leaning against the inside of a coat closet. Seven thought it looked a bit lonesome, so he took it out and carried the new friend into the living room.

He couldn't say whether he intended to play it. But pretty girls had a way of getting men to agree to things they weren't confident about in the least. This time luck had been on his side. But there was an unfortunate side effect, he realized. The warm tones reminded Seven of his first real friend since the rebirth.

"Ever hear of a band called Beacon?" he asked Talia suddenly. She was lost in the music and missed the question, so he repeated it.

Talia considered. "Sounds slightly familiar."

"They were a local rock group from the Capital. I actually stayed with their singer for a short while when I was trying to figure out who I was."

"Are you trying to tell me that you're gay?"

Seven went on without acknowledging the comment. "His name was Adrian."

"Isn't that a girl's name?"

"He was a good guy and an even better guitarist."

"And where is this Adrian now?"

He stopped strumming. "The Guard killed him."

Talia blinked. She looked taken aback but not entirely surprised. "Why?"

"He was on the Watched list because of something his dad did a while back. The Guard had him under close supervision, like they were daring him to say something traitorous. He kept himself under control his whole life. Then he met me."

Seven shook his head woefully. "He had all this anger about the government bottled up inside of him. And then I show up asking him, like an idiot, why things are this way and that. I got him talking about things you can't talk about when you're on the Watched list, and guess what? Turns out I'm a walking voice recorder. The Guard listened to the files and shot him."

Seven let the guitar fall forward into his lap and his face contorted into bleak sorrow. "They just shot him."

Talia rested a hand on his shoulder. "I don't have any stories like that," she said eventually. "It's not like I'm a fan of the Guard or anything–you've probably figured that out by now–but I don't really–you know–have anything driving me to action or whatever. I don't really know what I'm even doing here."

"So how did you end up on the Watched list?"

She scrunched her nose. "I don't want to tell you. It's embarrassing."

"Come on," prodded Seven. "Are you really going to turn down a wandering minstrel?"

She laughed. "That's true. Fine, it was something I asked in college…"

"You mean a professor reported you?"

"No, not exactly. The question was sort of directed to President Drake, and well, I guess the Guard didn't get the joke."

Seven opened his mouth to speak, but a murmur from the hall diverted his attention. Eve floated past the living room left-to-right and her eyes cut into him like razors. Ana followed close behind with a pistol aimed at his fiancée's back.

"Does she have to stand there like that?" Eve asked Danny. They were in his office. Young leaned back in his computer chair while Ana stood to his side, once again aiming a gun at Eve's skull. "I let you all capture me. Why would I run?"

"Trusting your enemy doesn't get you ahead in this line of work," Ana replied. "And don't give yourself so much credit. We would have pinned you even if you had fought back."

Eve raised her eyebrows. "You know what? I think I've changed my mind. She's feisty. I like that."

He grinned broadly. "You should see her in–"

Young caught himself before going any further. He stood and started pacing around the office. "We've been looking into the information you provided about where the Guard is manufacturing the surveillance implants. So far, it looks pretty solid. We've had teams down in Engine Valley check out most of the government factories there, but there's one place we haven't been able to get into because it's too high security."

"Let me guess," Eve yawned. "Facility B?"

"Facility B," he confirmed. "And we have reports—although hearsay mainly—that they have some kind of microchip in production. Given all the talk about Patriot ID, it seems logical that Facility B is producing the chips. It seems to me—to us—that this might be worth checking out, but we need a way in."

Eve nodded. "I should be able to get clearance, but it's not going to be as easy as me just asking for a tour of the facility. I'd need to give my bosses a pretty good reason."

Danny bit his lip. "I was afraid of that. Any ideas at this point?"

A warm tingly sensation enveloped Eve's heart as she realized suddenly that she had the perfect answer. "My mission was to bring Seven in so that we could restore his memory," she said, making every attempt to control her enthusiasm. "It's a procedure that can only be performed by top surveillance technicians. Well, Facility B has got them in droves."

Young considered. "I think I understand. You'll pretend to bring in Seven, and then the two of you will collect information on Patriot ID…"

"…and send it back to you."

"Sounds brilliant to me," he said. "What do you think, Ana?"

"It's not bad," she replied, shaking her head, "but I don't trust her. I know we can trust Seven, but I'd still feel more comfortable if we had a more veteran Underground operative with them."

Eve exhaled in frustration and shook her head. "We have to do it alone. Any other factory and I might be able to fake a clearance for someone else, but I don't think I could even get Rodriguez into Facility B without fighting my bosses."

Young began to speak, but the Elite Guard's mind drifted to the living room where she'd seen Seven serenading Talia with ballads he used to play for Eve. He'd always been so shy about bringing the guitar out in public—who was this girl? Did he really think Talia was prettier than her?

"Eve?" prodded Young.

She looked up. "Sorry, what?"

"You mentioned your partner. Can he be of any use?"

"No," she said. "He's a rookie and lacks training. The only thing he knows at this point is how to be a Patriot. Keep him out of this."

Young paced to the wall and back. "Then we'll leave him here, down in the basement. After you help us in Facility B, someone at the Guard will realize Rodriguez is missing and track him here. We'll just fill his food dish a little higher than usual."

"You're not worried Rodriguez will identify you when the Guard finally rescues him?"

"This building isn't registered in any government database, and your partner hasn't seen my face. Despite what the tabloids may indicate, I'm very good at covering my trail when I want to keep hidden."

"So why didn't you evacuate the Capital right away?" asked Seven. "I think you know now why I was still hanging around."

She looked down at her feet and kicked them forward like a little girl. "I was in my dorm room when the bombs hit the Tower. I'd just had kind of a rough night, and now suddenly everyone was freaking out and running around. All I wanted was to be alone. I mean, like, the idea of leaving my bed to run with all those idiots? I couldn't do it."

"So you stayed."

"I slept on it," she replied. "Of course, a few hours of sleep and a little TV helped me realize who had been the true idiot. Suddenly it occurred to me that I was upset but not ready to die. So I grabbed some things and left. The building was completely abandoned, so I stole a gun from the security desk and headed for the car rental place. You know the rest."

Seven nodded. "So…you're still in college?"

"Was supposed to graduate in eight months," she said with a grin. "Guess that's not happening."

"Huh," he replied thoughtfully. "So you're what, twenty? Twenty-one?"

Talia eyed him curiously before responding that she was twenty-one. "Why?" she asked. "Are you worried I might be too young for you?"

He shivered as a single finger ran gently up his thigh. There was another shuffling of feet in the hallway, but Seven felt no need to verify that it was Eve.

Pushed by Ana, Eve went careening back into the basement prison. The door slammed behind her. Rodriguez was sitting up against the wall that read *PATRIOTS ARE THE TRUE HERETICS,* stirring water in a plastic cup with his pinky. He looked up at her and smiled. "Welcome back, boss."

Eve's eyes narrowed. The rookie's inclination was for the happy-go-lucky, but this particular grin carried a menace she hadn't seen before. "Everything all right?" she asked.

"Fine and dandy," he said. "But then, I'm not the one they dragged upstairs. Care to tell me what happened?"

She shrugged. "What do you think? They tried to get information out of me and I kept my mouth shut."

He looked up and down her skin. "No bruises," he observed. "They must not have tried very hard."

Eve nearly accused him of insubordination but held her tongue. "They're rebels, not…I don't know…savages or something."

She slipped into one of the olive-green sleeping bags the Underground had provided. It provided little padding atop the hard concrete slab, but at least it was snug. "Look, let's just get some rest for now," she said. "I'll have a plan all thought out and ready to go tomorrow."

But it was hard to fall asleep. Partially because she didn't like lying to her partner, but mostly because of how Seven had behaved since she arrived. She hadn't exactly expected him to run to her with open arms, but he'd just been so cold to her, she thought. He may have lost his memory, but love–real love–well, it had to be about more than a happy history, right? And what was that Talia girl's angle anyway?

It was probably all in her head, she decided. She would talk to Jon about it tomorrow.

Eve's neck suddenly felt hot, and she was overcome by the strange sense that eyes were trained upon her, watching every toss and turn with great interest. She peeked out from the covers. Rodriguez stared back at her.

CHAPTER SIXTEEN
Doors

In his first few seconds of morning delirium, Seven thought a woodpecker might be at his door. He blinked a few times at the maple-paneled ceiling and remembered he was lying in one of several guest rooms in Danny Young's family vacation home.

"Jon–Seven!" The shouting voice on the other side of the door was Eve's. "Can I come in?"

Seven, sleeping on the right side of the queen-sized bed, looked worriedly to the empty space on the left. Then another fear seized him and he shot upright. Eve should be in the basement.

"How did you get out?" he yelled at the door. "What have you done to everyone?"

There was a long pause. "I–I haven't done anything to anyone…"

"It's okay, Seven," said another voice–it was Ana. "She's on our side for the time being, but her one condition was that she'd get a chance to talk to you. If you don't want to talk to her, then I'd say we've kept our word and given her the chance."

"What?" yelped Eve. "That's not what I…Seven, please!"

Seven fell out of bed in only his boxer shorts and considered the golden door knob. With a sigh, he pulled it open.

Eve's cheeks were red but her complexion seemed to improve the second she saw him. "Hi," she said meekly.

Ana glanced at Seven's bare chest and burst, "Well, good morning!"

Seven turned to her. "I think I missed something. We're *working* with her now?"

"I know, I don't trust her, either," whispered Ana as if she thought Eve wouldn't hear. "But she gave us solid information about Patriot ID, and Danny says we need her to get inside the Engine Valley factory where they're making the chips. We're going to leave after breakfast."

"Who's leaving?"

"Everyone."

"Except Rodriguez," Eve interjected. "We're ditching that loser here."

Ana leaned in closer to Seven's ear. "Do you want me to stay," she whispered, "in case she tries something?"

He waved her off. "No, I'll be fine. Thanks."

Ana held five fingers up in Eve's face. "This is how many minutes you have, bitch." And she strolled out of the room.

Seven closed the door after her and turned coldly to his fiancée. "So what do you want?"

Eve's face fell. "Jon–Seven–I'm here to help. I told you, everything's changed…the president has gone too far, and–"

"No, I don't believe you."

She took a deep breath. "Well, why do *you* think I'm here?"

"I think that you still think you can reverse everything that's happened and change me back into the man you knew. If you can capture a few Underground agents in the meantime, I guess that's two birds with one stone, right?"

"It's not about you," she said. "And if I had wanted to round you all up, I don't think I would have shot my partner and let myself be captured."

He shook his head in aggravation. "How do I know you're not wearing a microphone under your shirt? Maybe reinforcements from the Guard are on their way as we speak. Look, I don't care what our relationship was or wasn't before. I don't trust you, Eve, and there's nothing you can say that's going to convince me otherwise."

The air seemed to go out of the room. Trying to find something, anything besides his ex to look at, Seven turned left to consider a painting hanging over an antique butler's desk. It depicted an autumn scene of orange, yellow, and red leaves. He didn't like it.

Eve slumped. "I guess your point of view is fair," she mumbled. "I should have listened to you before this all started."

He looked at her blankly. "What do you mean?"

"You didn't want to take the mission. I was the one who encouraged you."

Seven paced toward the window and pretended to look at the conifers.

"I thought it would be good for your career," continued Eve, "and I didn't want to stand in the way of that. You were worried about exactly this happening–that you'd forget me. I promised you that it wouldn't change anything…that we'd be able to turn you back. You didn't think that was enough, so you…well…you…"

He turned and found Eve staring pitifully at the sparkling ring on her finger. The diamond had caught the sunlight from the window. Seven felt a sudden and strange desire to hold her, do anything he could to stop her from crying. But he chased the feeling with cold rationality. "I don't know what you want me to say," he gasped. "Maybe Jon loved you, but I…"

Their eyes met.

"But I…" Seven tried again.

"You've only lost your memory!" protested Eve. "What does your heart say?"

He turned away and cursed himself for letting this conversation go on for so long, for even allowing it to happen in the first place.

"Oh, my God," Eve gasped suddenly.

Seven followed her frightened gaze to a pink lacy thing that lay discarded on the carpet. He tried to speak but couldn't figure out what to say. His mind flashed to Talia's warm skin and the way she had nibbled his ear. "I…"

"Oh, God!" cried Eve. "I have to go. I'm sorry…maybe we can…maybe we'll talk more later…"

He was surprised to hear himself tell her to wait. But Eve didn't listen, and she left him holding the door. For a long time, Seven stared down the hallway, bewildered. Then he turned around and considered the scandalous object on the floor.

Ana glanced up from her mug as Eve stormed into the kitchen. The Underground operative was by the coffee machine, leaning over a slate counter that separated the cooking area from the breakfast nook. She took a tentative, noisy sip before addressing the newcomer. "You didn't try to escape. Good girl."

"I have no reason to do that," replied Eve. In truth she had thought about leaving just so she could get away from Seven. But there were too many of them and they were too far from town for escape to be realistic. Eve had no desire to hide out in the forest. Anyway, she had unfinished business.

"Well, don't think that I trust you now. I was just thirsty and needing my caffeine fix."

Eve sighed. "Does that mean I've got to go back to my room?"

Ana nodded. After taking another gulp of coffee, she slapped the mug on the counter. "Let's go."

They walked side by side to the heavy metal door that led into the basement prison. Ana patted down each of her pants pockets and then finally withdrew a large key chain. She had to use three to pass all the locks and get the door open. The rebel directed the Elite inside with a point of the finger and a raise of the eyebrows, and then followed her down the steps.

Immediately, Eve sensed something was wrong–Rodriguez was missing.

"Hey!" exclaimed Ana. "Where the hell is your–"

She gagged suddenly, and Eve whirled around to see what had happened. Rodriguez had Ana's neck in the crook of his elbow, squeezing so hard that the rebel's face was turning tomato red.

"What are you doing?!" Eve yelled at him.

Rodriguez looked confused. "What does it look like I'm doing? We're getting out of here. Help me."

She blinked a few times. "No, dammit. We're staying."

Ana kicked a few times to no avail, and then her eyes rolled back and she passed out. Rodriguez let go and the rebel dropped like a marionette whose strings had been cut.

"Then you're a goddamned Heretic," he sneered. "Fine, stay here. But don't try to stop me."

Eve watched dumbstruck as her rookie partner bounded up the steps.

Talia bit her lip slightly when she saw Seven standing outside her door. She was wearing a long, white T-shirt that draped gently against her small frame. If she was wearing shorts, they weren't visible.

Seven tossed her the pink bra. "You left this," he said without expression.

"Thanks, I couldn't see it last night. It was, like, really dark." With two fingers she worked a tangle out of her jet black hair. "Where did you find it?"

"I didn't," he said. "Eve just stopped by for a visit. She found it on the floor by the bed."

Talia gaped before bursting into hysterics. "Oh, my God that's fantastic! Oh, and she totally deserves it, too!"

Seven tried to smile, but couldn't figure out how to make the expression look genuine. Something about the incident had left a sour taste in his mouth. He knew that he would have had to tell Eve about Talia eventually, and yes, he wanted her to know he was an independent person...but it was weird—something just didn't feel right.

The swirl of gloom around Seven's head apparently escaped Talia's notice. "This is great news," she chattered on. "Now she'll leave you alone!"

"I don't know how I feel about it," he confessed.

All the warmth drained from Talia's eyes, and they looked almost black. "But..."

"I mean," he corrected, "last night was great. But it must be hard for her to–"

"Hard for *her*? It's been hard for *you*! You've been in the dumps since the moment we met, and I'm fucking sick of it. It's about time you had a little fun. You had fun, right?"

He nodded, but the expression on his face betrayed him.

Talia's jaw dropped. "Oh, my God, you still have feelings for her! Don't you?"

"No," said Seven. "I don't know," he added after a few seconds of consideration. "Look, I like you a lot, and honestly, I want to make this work, but–"

"Make what work?" She shook her head in disbelief. "Seven," she scolded. "It was just sex!"

He blinked. "What?"

Talia shrugged. "S-E-X. Who cares? Maybe we'll do it again sometime. Now if you'll excuse me, I've got to tidy up and get ready for the day. See you at breakfast." And she slammed the door in his face.

Seven sighed in resignation as he took the long walk back to his room. Turning the corner, he noticed the cellar door was ajar. He stopped short as a tan face with short-cropped hair peered out from behind it.

Rodriguez took one look at Seven and got moving. He swung the door just wide enough to block the amnesiac's path, and darted off down the hall. Acting on instinct, Seven charged the obstacle like a bull, and the door splintered off its hinges. He saw Rodriguez several paces down the corridor, tearing left around a corner toward the mansion's front entrance.

"They're loose!" Seven yelled at the top of his lungs. He heard some stirring behind closed doors but no one came out to help. Seven rounded the corner in time to see Rodriguez pull the front door closed behind him. Seven tore it open and plunged forward.

Now Rodriguez was running for the road. It was a long trek to the nearest town, so Seven presumed the Elite was seeking the vehicle in which he and Eve had arrived. Seven continued chase, but Rodriguez, stretching his legs like an Olympic runner, kept widening the gap.

No matter, thought Seven. Even the fastest man in the world couldn't get into a parked car, start the engine and pull out in the time it would take Seven to catch up. He knew he could stop him.

Seven leaped over a pothole and slid over some small rocks on the landing. He barely maintained balance and continued on. Suddenly the black sedan was in sight, and Rodriguez was nearly upon it. Seven gritted his teeth and pumped his legs hard. About ten paces from the vehicle, Seven lunged and tackled Rodriguez to the asphalt.

The escapee writhed violently but Seven held him tight against the black pavement. Finally Seven lifted an arm and delivered a right hook that hit solidly against Rodriguez's jaw. The Guard stopped moving.

Seven relaxed his grip and looked around. Still no one else from the house had come. He wasn't looking forward to dragging Rodriguez all the way back. The guy wasn't huge, but he would be all dead weight. He sighed and glanced backward again. Hadn't anyone heard him? What, were they all sleeping?

When he turned back, Rodriguez's eyes were open. Before Seven could react, a huge gob of spit shot from the runaway's mouth into Seven's eye. Rodriguez got a hand free. He flipped Seven onto his back and squirmed free.

Seven got to his feet just as the other man pulled open the car door. Rodriguez leaned into the vehicle but didn't sit down. When he came back out, he had a gun in his hand.

Seven felt a sharp pain in his left shoulder and the forest flashed white. As he stumbled forward, he felt a rush of panic like that he'd felt when he first woke up in this world.

Rodriguez drew closer, lining up a shot that Seven knew would be impossible to miss. "You ruined two good agents, you know," the Elite said.

"What?" choked Seven, heaving to catch his breath. He knew his best chance would be to keep the man talking.

"We knew we'd lost you, but we had hoped Agent Parker would stay true to God and country. But it's clear to us now that your refusal to return has…damaged her…irreparably."

Seven couldn't believe what he was hearing. "You mean you were watching her!"

Rodriguez pressed his weapon into Seven's forehead. "My orders were to find and terminate you. If Eve refused to go along with it, I was to terminate her as well."

"You should have made me first on your death list," interrupted a familiar female voice.

Rodriguez's head spun wildly toward the trees just as a deafening crack cut through the gentle breeze. The fugitive's gun hand burst red and the weapon clattered to the ground. With a low bellowing yell, Rodriguez ducked for cover behind the door of the black car. Another bullet smashed the vehicle's driver-side mirror.

Seven heard the engine rev. The car started with a screech and then roared away. The back window exploded in a burst of glass but Rodriguez kept driving and the vehicle soon disappeared down the road.

Seven squinted into the thick forest where the shots had come. It was getting harder to stay awake, and the trees blurred with every blink. He saw a rifle sticking out of a patch of brambles, and then a blond woman emerging from the greenery. She was running toward him and screaming a name that wasn't his.

"Jon!" yelled Eve, dropping the hunting rifle. She ran as fast as she could but, as if in a nightmare, felt she was moving through molasses.

Seven was lying on the cracked pavement, looking up at the sun. Dark crimson ooze dripped from his shoulder, but if he was in pain, his face didn't show it. For an instant, his eyes seemed to register her presence. But then they shut and his head fell to the side.

Eve fell on her knees next to him and verified he was breathing. Next, she tore Seven's shirt off and checked his shoulder. It was a mess, but she knew he would survive if she could manage to stop the bleeding–she just needed a tourniquet. Briefly, Eve considered using Seven's black T-shirt, but she decided against it because it was already so soaked with blood and sweat. Finally, she grabbed her own blue tunic by the bottom and pulled it up over her head.

"Damn it, Jon," she said, tying the shirt around his wounded arm. "What the hell were you thinking?"

It was only then, when she was satisfied with her treatment for Seven's wound, that she considered her former partner, Agent Rik Rodriguez. He was obviously no rookie. She had figured the Elites didn't trust her when they set her up with a partner, but she couldn't believe they'd actually asked someone to take notes on her. The one mystery she couldn't figure out was how Rodriguez had passed himself off so convincingly as a rookie. Eve thought she had met most of the Elite Guard–well, the good ones, anyway. The Guard would not have sent just anyone after her.

A gentle breeze brushed through the trees. Eve held her arms over her chest and shivered.

It occurred to her that she'd have a fine mess on her hands explaining all this to her superiors. She had just tried to kill her partner, Rodriguez, in order to save her Heretic fiancé. The government and the Church could form only one rational explanation, which was the same explanation that had apparently led them to watch her in the first place. Eve loved Jon more than she loved her country.

Eve jumped at the blast of another gun. She looked up the

road and saw Shaan racing toward her with pistol outstretched. The rebel had fired a warning.

"Step away from him and put your hands where I can see them!"

Eve raised her hands but not very high. It looked more like a shrug.

Shaan looked at her accusingly. "You shot him."

"No!" Eve protested. She struggled to explain. "Rodriguez shot Jon–Seven."

"Then where's Rodriguez?" he demanded.

"I tried to stop him, but he got away. If I hadn't been here, he may have killed Seven."

Shaan's eyes narrowed. "Why isn't either of you wearing shirts?"

Eve glanced down to verify she was still wearing the sports bra. "There's nothing funny going on. I used my shirt to stop his bleeding. It's standard issue from the Guard and made of a cloth that's particularly absorbent, so–"

"Fine," he interrupted. Shaan tapped a button on his ear piece and spoke. "Danny, it's me. Our prisoner Rodriguez is gone and Seven is out cold."

There was a question on the other end.

"No, she's here with Seven–claims she saved his life. Just send Ana out here right away with a stretcher."

"Actually," said Eve, clearing her throat, "Ana might be passed out in the basement."

Shaan's eyes widened.

"What?" she asked innocently. "I didn't do it."

CHAPTER SEVENTEEN
Bridge

Eve frowned at her shackled wrists. "And why are handcuffs still necessary, exactly? You're going to have to take them off me for the mission anyway."

Ana, sitting next to her in the first back row of the purple minivan, replied, "You ever consider we might trust you more if you didn't do things like steal a hunting rifle and run away?"

Eve was flabbergasted. "I stole that gun to save Seven's life!"

Shaan's eyes appeared in the rear-view mirror. "And we appreciate it. But please understand we have to take every precaution. In some ways, Agent Parker, you are even more dangerous in a moving vehicle."

The Elite cackled. "What am I going to do? Jump over the seat, grab the wheel and steer us into oncoming traffic? I'm not the one here with a history of dangerous driving."

Eve intended the jibe for Shaan, but he failed to respond. His sister, however, suddenly perked up. She was perched over Eve's shoulder one row behind. "That's actually a good point, Shaan. Which is why I should be driving. It's my van, anyway."

"It's not your van," responded Shaan. "You stole it."

"Oh, *whatever*," snapped Talia.

Eve fought back the temptation to push the girl by the forehead back into her seat. She glanced at Ana for possible support, but the Underground agent was busy blowing hot air into her glasses.

"Hey, don't I get a little credit for the van?" Seven said weakly.

Eve, Talia, and Ana turned excitedly. Up until now he'd been slumped unconscious in the seat next to Talia.

"How are you feeling?" Eve asked.

Seven rubbed the bandages on his shoulder. "Could be better, but I guess I'm alive, so that's good."

"You're lucky it was your left arm. You'll still be able to shoot."

Talia laughed. "Seriously? Who says that?"

He brushed the comment aside. "Where we going?"

"Engine Valley," replied Ana. "We're going to expose Patriot ID for what it really is."

"Great. Well, I'm sure someone will brief me later." He turned to Eve. "Thanks, by the way."

His smile was warm and contagious. But then Talia laid a hand on his neck. Going red, Eve turned quickly back to the front of the car. She bit her lip to keep the emotions at bay.

Danny Young, riding up front, pushed his seat back and lifted his legs onto the dash. The seat bumped into Ana's knees but she didn't protest. "Sorry to keep you in the dark, Seven. I was going to brief you last night but you'd already gone to bed."

Talia coughed awkwardly.

Danny continued. "So then I was going to talk to you this morning, but you got shot."

"So can you tell me now?"

"Well, it really would be better to brief you one on one," Young replied. "I think it's best that we wait until we get to the Valley. In the meantime, let's all just enjoy this luxurious ride in the stolen minivan. You know, it's been a while since I've been on a proper road trip. Kind of makes me miss my college days, when…"

Eve tuned him out and focused instead on a steel suspension bridge rising over the horizon. It seemed to hang from the clouds by a trio of dirt-caked towers. The bridge stretched long into the distance toward a smoky black blur of factories. She remembered the Engine Valley was ugly, but she'd forgotten just how ugly. For a second, she wished that the Enemy had directed its attack here rather than the Capital, but she immediately felt guilty for thinking it. "God help me," she murmured.

The car's tires produced a deep, echoing grind as the vehicle transitioned from the highway to the bridge. Eve looked down at the brown river for inspiration. "By the way, Shaan," she said, interrupting Young's story. "Don't you dare drive us into the water. Not all of us are so good at cheating death."

In the rear-view mirror Shaan's cheek bones rose just high enough that he might have been smiling. Eve immediately felt like a bitch for bringing it up again.

Finally, Shaan responded. "It makes you angry that I escaped you."

Hot despair overtook her as the memories flooded back. She could see that static, black-and-white CCTV image of Shaan's back as he drove the motorcycle straight off the edge of the Luna Coast cliff. The bike lifted briefly into the air…and she had not been able to watch the rest. When she finally looked there was only sky and endless ocean.

"It wasn't so much the escaping as how you went about it," Eve said. "I thought you had…well I thought you had killed yourself…and that maybe I…"

"You blamed yourself for my death?" prodded Shaan. There was a hint of pride in his voice.

Eve searched for the right words but came up empty.

He nodded. "That's good. That's what I wanted."

Ana, who had been looking lost the entire exchange, tapped Shaan suddenly on the shoulder. "Wait, you drove a motorcycle?"

"Yes," he exhaled with apparent perturb.

"That's sexy," she said, smiling like a girl in a candy store. "I've always wanted to ride."

Shaan didn't respond.

"Do you still have it?" she continued.

"Do I still have what?"

"The motorcycle."

"No."

Ana gave a frustrated sigh and slumped back into her seat.

Eve reached for her phone and came up empty. She'd forgotten they had taken it from her.

"Agent Parker," said Shaan, "you said Rodriguez was an Elite Guard like you, correct?"

She looked up in surprise. "Right. I mean, I think so."

"You have suspicions?"

"Well, they told me he was a rookie. But he was obviously more than that. But I never met or heard of him before."

"Interesting," he said enigmatically.

"Why?"

"Without going into details, the Underground has ways to identify undercover agents. You came up in our database; Rodriguez did not. At first I assumed it was because Rodriguez was new to the Guard and our records were out of date. But now I'm not sure."

Eve frowned. "Well, without going into too many details either, the Guard has ways to erase people from government records. We did it to Jon. I mean, Seven."

"Hmm," pondered Shaan. "But why would they erase Rodriguez? If anything, they should have modified his entry in the database so that you yourself would have no suspicions he was anything but a rookie."

Eve shook her head and sighed. "I don't know."

The group was quiet for many minutes. Finally, Danny disrupted the silence.

"Why do they call the front passenger seat 'shotgun,' anyway?" he asked. "Is it because my body would shoot out the windshield like a bullet if we stopped suddenly and I wasn't wearing my seatbelt?"

Eve ignored the question. "So tell me again, Mr. Young, we're meeting who in Engine Valley?"

"No," corrected Danny, "his name is Haru. He leads a team of Underground operatives down in the Valley. He knows the area, and he's providing some clothes and equipment we can use for the mission."

"He's cute," noted Ana, "but also…kind of an asshole."

The radio volume went way up. Danny's hand was on the tuner as the booming baritone voice of a local news anchor replaced the chatter.

"…the Luna Coast about an hour ago. The Guard has so far kept the invaders from entering the city proper, but the Enemy is putting up an impressive fight on the beach. Casualties are heavy on both sides. Let's go to Roger Phelps, our war correspondent, who's currently high above the scene in the WCCN chopper. What's it look like out there, Roger?"

A rush of crackle and the thunk-thunk-thunk of a helicopter filled the speakers.

"It's…it's absolutely horrifying," Roger Phelps yelled over the din. "There are bodies everywhere. The Enemy came in by boat so most of the corpses near the water are theirs, but they've been steadily working up the coast. Some of them have handheld missile launchers and have simply been blowing through the Guard's defenses."

"How are the Guard holding them back?"

"Well, I talked to one of the commanders for the Guard, and he told me we have snipers set up in the cliffs. They've been doing a good job targeting the invaders carrying heavy weaponry and limiting that kind of damage."

"Is the Guard planning to bring in any more air support?"

"Well, it's too dangerous to our troops to have our planes targeting the invaders on the beach, but the Guard's jets are further out at sea dogfighting the Enemy's airplanes. It's difficult to see the planes, but we can certainly hear and feel every explosion out there."

"At this stage, on the coast, does it look like one side or the other has the advantage?"

"It's still hard to say. The Enemy has made pretty stunning progress up the beach, but we're told the Guard has reinforcements on the way, so the situation could change in a heartbeat."

"Fascinating. Well, Roger, we'll check back with you later for updates. Thank you for the report, and stay safe out there."

The background noise cut out as the radio returned to the news studio. "We'll have more after the break," the newscaster announced.

Eve was surprised to hear that things were getting worse. Maybe she had been naive, but she thought that by now it all would have been over and done with. The Enemy certainly had used the element of surprise to their advantage, but certainly the Guard should have been ready. How could the Guard's defenses possibly fail in the Capital of all places?

What had she and Jon been working for all these years if not to secure the nation from attacks? What had they accomplished by rounding up Heretics? People were dying, and it was obvious to Eve that the country's Heretics had nothing to do with it.

"I just hope the Enemy lets us live long enough to fix things," said Ana. "I mean, this whole mission–if the Enemy wins the war, it won't mean anything, will it?"

"That's not something we can control," Danny said with a level of tranquility that astonished Eve. "But we sure as hell aren't going to wait around twiddling our thumbs while our president tries to use a war to tighten his grip around the people of this country. Our work will be important in preventing tyranny, no matter which side comes out the victor."

The purple minivan fell into silence as the rebels absorbed their leader's statement. Suddenly, Seven let out a short, falsetto whoop of approval.

"Yeah!" added Talia. "Fuck the man!"

One by one everyone lost it.

CHAPTER EIGHTEEN
Engine Valley

The six of them stepped off the parking lot blacktop onto a barren concrete avenue. The only color came from a line of orange flags strung along the roof of a gas station to a fading plastic palm tree.

Eve coughed on the fumes that Engine Valley residents regarded as air. It was hard to imagine why anyone would want to live here, but this city employed more working class men and women than any other in the country. From an aesthetic standpoint, it felt wrong to refer to the Valley as the heart of the economy. A more accurate description, perhaps, was that it was the blood and sweat.

"Where the heck is everyone?" Talia asked.

Shaan shook his head. "Perhaps Haru can say."

Young and Ana kept close to Eve. They had freed the double agent of her handcuffs, but Ana was making it clear with her body language that she still considered Eve a prisoner. Shaan pushed on ahead, increasing his distance from the women with every step. Seven and Talia lingered behind the pack.

Ana held her nose. "For some reason I expected the Guard's most well-protected science facility to be located somewhere a bit–I don't know–greener, I guess. And more…campus-y."

"Well, it's not exactly a wind farm," replied Eve.

Ana retrieved a smoke from her crimson clutch and lit it. "At least tell me they've got some good strong men here. They'd have to in a place so…industrial, right?"

Eve shrugged with a glance back at Seven. "I guess. They're not really my type."

"Really?" Ana smiled mischievously. "I like factory men—they're aggressive. Not even a sparkly ring stops them." She pointed to Eve's hand. "It's pretty, by the way."

The fiancée of Jonathan Wyle gazed sadly at her finger.

Ana exhaled a cloud of black air. "So I guess your little chat this morning didn't go well…"

That's it, thought Eve furiously. "Okay, what is your problem with me anyway? I can understand why Talia's ticked, but you've just been bitchy to me for no reason."

"Whoa-kay!" exclaimed Danny, walking alongside them. "I think I'm going to go try and catch up with Shaan."

Eve didn't notice him go. "Well, Ana? What is it? What did I do to you?"

Ana gritted her teeth. And then out of nowhere came tears. "You people killed Eric!"

Eric? The name was familiar, but where had she heard it?

Suddenly, she remembered. When Seven was doing Underground missions with Ana back in the city, there was an Eric on the team. He and Ana had been romantic. The Guard had been holding them in the Capitol Tower when the bombs struck. Seven rescued them from the building, but Eve wasn't sure what had happened to them after that. Frankly, she had been a little surprised to see Ana at Danny's house.

"I'm sorry, Ana, I didn't know," she said. "What happened?"

Ana shrugged her shoulders pathetically. "We were trying to evacuate. We got to the blockade and the Guard stopped us. They wouldn't let us through. Eric went ballistic and they…they just shot him."

Eve gasped. "How did you get through?"

Ana sniffed. "They let me turn back to the Capital. When I was far enough out of sight I hitched a ride in this guy's trunk. It was humiliating, but what else was I supposed to do? I just wish I could have seen Eric one more time."

Eve shook her head sympathetically. "I want you to know I don't approve of the blockade. I think that was an absolutely ridiculous policy."

"Look, I know you didn't pull the trigger. But you're the reason we got added to the Watched list. And…and you make such a goddamned big deal over losing Seven, but the reality is you didn't lose him. Not really. At least he's still alive."

Eve nodded. "I'm sorry. I'll try to make up for it the best I can."

They didn't say anything more to each other. Eve glanced at her wristwatch, but quickly remembered that Shaan had taken it along with her cell phone. She was pretty sure her timepiece wasn't a tracking device, but then again it *had* been made by the Guard. She had to admit this motley bunch was thorough.

Now Eve looked at the sun for clues about the time, but the great ball of fire was hidden beneath plumes of smoke. She was about to ask Ana when a digital *3:13 PM* flashed at her in red from a building on the corner of the next street. A few seconds later, the black board provided the temperature.

Squinting at the name under the sign, Eve realized they were heading for a DAY Bank. On his mission back in the Capital, Jon had spent days in the basement of one of these, she recalled. Apparently this financial franchise, owned by Daniel Alexander Young, was a popular nesting spot for the Underground. This, of course, had all been in her report to the Guard.

"You know, you Underground types might want to reconsider your policy about hiding in places named for your leader," she suggested.

Ana smiled. "Oh, we're not so predictable. That's not where we're going."

Seven felt obligated to walk with Talia for the same reason he'd felt obligated to sit next to her in the van—he felt guilty. She seemed to be mad at him, even though it seemed to Seven that he should be mad at her. After all, it was *she* who had dismissed last night as nothing at all, wasn't it? Seven didn't think he was being overly clingy. It wasn't like he needed this to turn into a relationship or anything like that, especially if that wasn't what Talia wanted. He just wanted things to be cool between them.

If only it weren't so damn impossible to start a conversation.

"Kind of windy today," he tried, immediately regretting it as an opener.

She shrugged.

"Is everything all right?"

"Yup," she replied without even a glance.

"Is this about Eve?"

"Nope."

She was only giving one-word answers and they weren't even insulting. Talia wasn't being herself; things obviously weren't cool.

"I really don't have feelings for her anymore," he said.

She looked at him skeptically.

"It's difficult. I'm sorry."

She provided an expressionless nod. It wasn't encouraging.

Seven sighed. "Look, let me know if you want to talk about it later. What happened between us last night…Well, I don't regret it, and I'd do it again."

That last line made her laugh. Seven wasn't sure he was out of the woods, but the smile was nice.

"How's your shoulder?" she asked.

"It's a little stiff."

Actually, it hurt like hell, especially when he moved his arm more than forty-five degrees. The stiffness came mainly from the pile of bandages which further restricted his movement. There was so much tape hidden beneath his T-shirt it looked like he had developed a strange growth.

Talia stroked the bump gently with the tips of her fingers. "Does this hurt?" she asked.

"No," he said. "To be honest, I can't feel your hand at all."

"You've got to be more careful," she scolded him. "What were you thinking, running off after an Elite Guard without even taking a weapon? Why are you so stupid all of the time? I can't believe I slept with such a moron. I hope you didn't interpret it as some kind of encouragement to be dumb."

Seven smiled. He wasn't sure how he'd done it, but he had the old Talia back.

Eve reached for her bare arms as the wind picked up. Across the street up ahead, Shaan paused by a shop with the words *Harry's Donuts* written across the window in pink florescent tube lighting.

"Shaan always did have a soft spot for sweets," remarked Eve.

Talia, catching up to the other women, regarded Eve like she was expired milk.

Eve returned the stare. "What?"

"You talk about him like the two of you used to be B-F-Fs!"

"Excuse me?"

Talia groaned. "It means best friends forever."

Eve shrugged. "I know him pretty well. I watched him for years."

"And you don't think that sounds creepy?"

"I guess I never thought of it like that," she reflected. "I was just serving God and country."

"Oh, okay, well as long as you were serving God and country," she retorted sarcastically. "By the way, my brother is not getting donuts; that's the base."

As it turned out, Eve wasn't completely wrong about Shaan's intentions. While *Harry's* was indeed a cover for a secret Underground hideout, to maintain appearances the shop really did sell fried pastries. Shaan was quick to take advantage of the situation. When the girls finally caught up with him inside, they found him munching on a powdered jelly.

A languid teenager manning the store counter perked up upon their entrance. He adjusted a humiliating string-and-paper cap and sputtered out a greeting: "H-hello, may I…may I help you, ladies?"

She thought that Seven, standing alongside him, looked a bit put off by the statement.

Shaan swallowed a thick gob of jelly and answered, "They're with me. We're here to see Haru."

The kid turned red. "Oh, I didn't realize…if I had known I wouldn't have made you pay for–"

"It's not a problem," said Shaan. "Good donuts are worth paying for."

"Hey, write that one down, cutie," said Ana. "You could get rich with a slogan like that."

The teen appeared dizzied, as if he'd found black-and-white pinwheels swirling in Ana's tortoiseshell frames.

"Right," said the boy. "Well, Haru's expecting you. Come around back. Take the stairs down to the basement."

Shaan thanked him, and the team shimmied past a refrigerator of iced tea and lemonade.

The stairwell was quiet except for the occasional drip. Also, it was hot. "What is with you people and cellars?" Eve remarked. "Is it really that important for you all to live up to the name Underground?"

Seven and Danny laughed while the others groaned.

They came upon a thick steel door at the bottom of the steps. Danny pulled at the handle but it didn't budge. "Haru?" he said, tapping the door.

No answer.

"Let me try," said Eve.

But the door spoke before she got the chance. "What's the password?" it said.

Danny laughed. "Fuck you, motherfucker."

The door swung open, revealing a friendly looking man with spiky black-and-gray hair. "Fuck *you*, motherfuckah!" he bellowed back. They performed an elaborate handshake.

It was strange, thought Eve. Haru looked middle-aged but acted like he was fresh out of high school. She decided there was some history here that she was missing.

Ana rolled her eyes. "Boys."

"Been a while, Ana," said the basement dweller. "And this is our Elite-in-Crisis?"

"Eve," she introduced herself.

"I'm Haru." He held out his hand.

She looked at it. "I'm not confident I can pull off that same dance of the fists."

"Dance of the fists?" cackled Haru. "That's funny. I like that."

"Haru," said Danny with a wave to everyone else. "This is the gang. Gang, this is Haru."

Seven and Shaan mumbled introductions. Talia kept quiet.

Ana cleared her throat impatiently. "Well? Shall we?"

Haru waved them in. It wasn't much of a hideout. There were a couple of computers, a boxy television, and two seedy-looking sofas.

"This looks like a college dorm," commented Eve. "Do you sleep down here, too?"

"No, no," Haru replied. "We only use this for biznatch."

"Excuse me?"

"That's what I call business. There's about five of us who work out of this location, but we all have apartments in the city. By the way, you're all welcome to sleep here tonight."

Charming, thought Eve as she fell into one of the couches. Shaan took the other one and Ana sat next to him.

Haru looked upon his reclining audience. "So, what's the word?"

"Where is everybody?" Talia asked impatiently. "This city's even quieter than the desert."

The Engine Valley rebel looked up at a brown stain on the ceiling and sighed. "People are scared the Enemy's next attack is going to be here. The Guard hasn't actually ordered an evacuation but a lot of people have left, and still more are hiding out in their homes. The other issue is that this city is fucking boring and no one who has any sense of fun lives here. So let's talk about something else. I hear you guys want to break into Facility B."

"That's the idea," said Danny. "We have a plan to get Eve and Seven inside without arousing too much suspicion."

"Well," said Haru, "I guess that little ace up the sleeve might upgrade this mission to improbable. Let's hear it."

CHAPTER NINETEEN
At Second Sight

With a deep breath, Eve pulled open the door to the bookstore and made a straight shot for the escalator. It was one of those mega stores that were becoming increasingly out of fashion–two floors, the aroma of coffee, and rows and rows of books, movies, and music. She knew exactly where to find her Watched. He was working the music section on the second floor, manning the information desk.

This would be the first time they had made contact since the mission began. Everything had so far gone according to plan but her Watched needed someone to push him in the right direction. Eve's superiors had assured her it would be a piece of cake, that he would be drawn to her instantly, but she wasn't so sure. There was no way she could recreate the circumstances of the first time they met. What if he didn't look at her the way he used to?

Eve's heart leapt when she saw Jon, and she felt suddenly naked without her engagement ring. He was sitting behind a wooden stand marked *Information*, reading a heavy-looking book. Sitting next to him was a stylishly dressed man with long black hair and a tight-fitting black T-shirt. She recognized him as Adrian, the musician on the Watched list with whom Jon had become fast friends.

"Excuse me," she said.

Eve thought it was cute how their heads bobbed up at the same time. For a while the two men just stared at her, but finally Jon spoke up. "Can I help you?"

She had known he wouldn't recognize her but somehow it hurt all the same. "Yes, I was looking for a particular album—"

"—I'll be happy to look it up for you," he said with surprising quickness. "What was the title?"

She couldn't help but smile. Maybe this wouldn't be so difficult after all.

"The title is 'Dark As Day,' and it's by Strider."

Jon tapped at the keyboard. He appeared completely bummed with the result. "We don't seem to have it," he reported sadly. "Rock album, huh? Who do you like?"

Was he actually flirting with her or was that just what she wanted? She listed a few bands, but thought he seemed more interested in her lips than what she was saying.

"I was actually planning to see a concert for this local band tomorrow night," Jon said eagerly. "If you're not doing anything, I'd like to…"

Adrian covered his mouth in a failed attempt to push back the laughter.

"I mean," stammered Jon, "would you like to…um, meet at the show and, um…I don't know…rock out, or–?"

Eve decided it was time to come to the rescue. "That sounds like fun! I'm kind of in a hurry right now, though, so, uh, call me later, okay?"

His eyes lit up as she wrote down her phone number and the name she had made up for the mission.

Jon looked down at the slip of paper. "I'm Seven," he said.

⊙

She found Seven leaning over a light wood fence on the boardwalk, gazing out at the moonlit ocean waves. He was wearing a cute blue button-down and black jeans that were tight in all the right places. She wondered if the clothes were on loan from Adrian.

"Hello there," she greeted.

He turned excitedly to her. "Hey. How's it going?"

"It's going good. How are you?"

"Can't complain," he said. "So…dinner…"

"There's a pretty good pizza place a few blocks down this way," said Eve, pointing the way. She already knew that he would like the restaurant. It was where they had eaten on their first date.

They walked close together and made pointless small talk. Jon seemed nervous, even more than he had the first time they had done this. He asked her about her job and she made up a lie about waiting tables and studying to be a lawyer.

"Want to ride?" he asked suddenly.

Her eyes widened.

"On the roller coaster," he explained quickly, clearly embarrassed. "Over there."

She looked ahead and saw the crimson red tracks snaking around the stars. Now she felt humiliated, too, for misinterpreting his words. It had just been so long since the last time they…well, now wasn't the time to be thinking about that.

"Yeah, let's go!" she said.

"All right, and then we can get something to eat afterward. I figure it wouldn't be a good idea to do it the other way around," said Seven, laughing slightly.

She chuckled and in a low voice said, "Nooo, no it wouldn't."

It felt good to laugh with him. She felt as light as a child. "Hey, I'll race you!" she exclaimed.

"You're on."

They lined up behind one of the boardwalk's wooden planks. Eve counted down. "Ready…Set…*Go!*"

Eve and Seven took off down the boardwalk. Clearly, he didn't remember how fast she was. He didn't catch up until just before the imaginary finish line. Eve flung out an arm to stop him from passing and crossed first.

"Hey, wait a minute!" he protested.

"Yeah! Take that!"

They strolled laughing into line for the roller coaster. The guy running the ride must have thought they were crazy, but she didn't care. When she was with Jon, nothing else mattered.

The Red Lion was a dank and dingy club that smelled thickly of cigarette smoke. But being here with the love of her life made it somehow easier to stomach. He was coming back to her now with drinks in his hands, looking at her like she was the only girl in the room. Just the way he used to.

Even though she had encouraged Jon to take the mission, at the last minute she got so worried that things would never be the same between them. She felt so relieved knowing that even without memory he still desired her.

She took the pint from his hand. "The band should be coming on soon," she said.

He took a sip of his dark beer and some of the foam transferred to his lip. "You just can't wait, can you?"

That was true, thought Eve, but probably not for the reason he was thinking. She just wanted to get to the part where he'd be holding her close.

"What can I say?" she laughed, sticking out her tongue. "I love this stuff."

He kissed her as the lights dimmed. The little girl inside jumped for joy.

The crowd began to cheer. They got louder still as Adrian and his band, Beacon, strolled out onto the stage. Without saying a single word of greeting they began to play. The sonic boom took her breath away.

Eve leaned back into Seven's arms. She could feel him wanting her as she brought his hands around her hips. She half-turned and gave him a devilish look meant to show him the feeling was mutual. Eve began a slow grind to the thump of the bass. Sometime into the third or fourth song of the set, Eve took Seven's hands and brought them gently up to her breasts. At first he was hesitant, but with a little encouragement began to understand what she wanted.

"Thank you very much," Adrian was telling the crowd. "Okay, this next song is about living in fucked up times. They took my parents. Don't let them take you."

AT SECOND SIGHT

The audience roared, but Eve felt sudden fear as she realized the time had come for the next phase of Seven's mission. She wasn't sure she was ready. Adrian was a Heretic, yes, but he was also Seven's friend. It broke her heart knowing how much pain this might cause her fiancé. She prayed he would forgive her.

The world shifted into slow motion as Adrian began to play. A red light appeared in the center of his forehead.

CHAPTER TWENTY
Division

Danny Young lifted his semi-automatic pistol and squinted down the barrel. He smacked his lips a few times, took a deep breath in and blew out one quick stream of air. Finally, the leader of the Underground pulled the trigger. The recoil shook his hand and he nearly dropped the gun.

Seven stepped up to the counter to see what damage Danny had done to the paper man hanging several meters back. He failed to detect any.

Haru whistled.

"Well, that's a turn off," Ana said dryly.

"Shut up," Danny replied. "Shooting is what I pay you people to do. Speaking of which, Seven's up."

The excitement in Young's voice made Seven cringe. He didn't like how eager everyone was to see him fire a gun. It was Ana's fault. She kept bragging to everybody about how sharp a shooter he was, hyping him up like he was some kind of legend. Honestly, he didn't know what to expect. Knowing that Jonathan Wyle was an excellent fighter didn't give him any confidence. Someone might as well tell him that his older brother was a great shot. So what? Sure, Seven had survived a few scraps, but maybe he'd just been lucky.

"They had to send two Elites after the guy," bragged Danny. "Two!"

Seven's shoulder cried out in pain as he picked up the gun. It hurt enough that he had to drop the left arm entirely and shoot with just his right. He knew he wouldn't have as steady a shot, but he didn't have much choice.

The truth was that he had been dreading this. When last night Haru suggested that the four of them visit a firing range in the morning, Seven immediately resisted, pointing out–cleverly, he thought–that they didn't want to arouse suspicion. But Haru reassured Danny that he had a "hookup," and that his Engine Valley based team of operatives had been shooting there for years.

Now the owner of the range strolled over to watch. He had a stinky cigar in his mouth and a bag of potato chips tucked beneath a flabby forearm. Haru had introduced him earlier as Pug. He wasn't in the Underground, but Haru called him an honorary member since he always let the rebels use his firing range, no questions asked.

Seven took a deep breath. Then, in one quick and easy motion, he lined up a shot and fired.

Potato chips and profanity sprayed from Pug's mouth. Ana laughed giddily. Everyone else was speechless.

Even Seven felt a little awestruck by the perfectly round hole he'd cut into the center of the paper man's forehead.

Eve bit into the donut and regretted it instantly. This was already her third–at least. It seemed entirely possible that her hand had picked up and fed her another without Eve ever realizing it. It was difficult to resist the treat in a place that smelled so good all the time. She wondered why Haru wasn't fatter.

She was sitting on the sofa, half-watching the TV with Talia. All she could see of the girl was a blue handkerchief poking above the coffee table. Its owner was sitting cross-legged on the floor with all of her attention on the screen.

They were watching a documentary titled "The Amazing Story of Susan Levi." The film consisted largely of interviews with Levi, her friends and family. It was supplemented by photographs and video footage of Levi looking triumphant about this thing or that. The film had begun with Levi's mother discussing her daughter's birth and first years on Earth. Apparently, when little Susan was eight years old, she told her mother she wanted to be president. The film had just gotten to the point in Levi's life when she began to seriously consider a run for the Loganville city council.

"But how would Susan Levi reconcile a career in politics with a blooming romance?" the narrator asked. "More after these messages."

Eve was beginning to regret declining Haru's offer to join them at the local shooting range.

Shaan had been sitting with them earlier, but left after becoming frustrated with the TV show and subsequently losing an argument to switch the channel. Talia resisted vehemently, until finally Shaan bolted up from the couch and went away to fiddle with a computer. The weird thing was that Talia didn't seem to like the show that much, either. Every few seconds she made a snarky comment about what Susan Levi said or what she was wearing.

Eve had a simple solution–she stopped paying attention and thought about how she was going to get Jon back.

"Danny, seriously, I am fucking impressed by your man here," exclaimed Haru. "Not in a gay way. Well, maybe a little in a gay way. No, I'm just fucking with you. But I mean, damn, Seven, you want to join my squad here in the Valley?"

"He's mine," said Danny, taking an ambitious bite of a roast beef sandwich.

The three men were sitting in a booth at a deli a few blocks from the firing range. Seven wasn't quite sure why they picked this particular establishment; the only thing slimier than the floor was the turkey in his sub. He took another, tentative nibble before giving up on eating completely. "So, Haru," he said, "are you on the Underground's council or whatever?"

Haru nodded. "For the Engine Valley region. Originally I worked under Danny's father in the Capital when Danny was still a teenage street urchin. Now he's an urchin with power."

Danny smirked. "Don't make me fire you."

Haru cackled. "I'm just jealous because Danny gets all the fine ladies while I'm stuck here in the fucking Valley."

Seven's eyebrows shot up. "Not so many fine ladies in the Valley?"

He shook his head. "People don't come to the Valley to play. They spend all day breaking their backs in the factories and spend all night forgetting about it, first in the bars and later at the strip clubs. They're mostly men, and the few women we do have look like they need a bath more than a man. And yeah, that includes the strippers."

Danny pounded the table, laughing.

"You got some nice ones in your crew, though. I like that Eve babe. She seems feisty. Did you know her when you were in the Guard, Seven?"

He hesitated. "I don't remember."

"Oh that's right. Danny was saying you've got amnesia. Sorry, I forgot. Well, for what it's worth, I hope you banged her."

Young dropped his sandwich. "Now come on, Haru, she's promised to help us take down the president. Let's treat her with a little dignity, shall we?"

Returning to the table, Ana sat down next to Seven. She looked miserable. "Just a heads up," she warned, "if you need to use the restroom, wait until we get home."

Seven changed the subject. "So Haru, based on your condemnations of the proletariat, I take it your day job isn't in a factory?"

Haru smiled. "You saw—I run a donuts shop. Keeps me relatively busy when I'm not conspiring against the government. Ironically, my best customers are with the Guard."

"Oh," interjected Ana, "tell him why it's called *Harry's*."

Haru groaned. "Because the people here are too dumb to say

my name right. When I first moved to the Valley, I introduced myself to five goddamned people. Apparently, all of 'em heard 'Harry.' When I opened the shop, I figured I might as well make it easy for the—"

"—Hello," came a meek voice behind Seven's back.

The others looked curiously over his shoulder. Seven swiveled in his chair and, despite being in a sitting position, found himself at eye level with a young woman, probably in her twenties or, at most, early thirties.

"May God be with you," she said, frowning slightly.

Seven realized he must be making a face, and tried to force a smile. He wasn't quite sure what to say. May God be with you, *too*?

Ana spoke up. "Can we help you, miss?"

"Did you hear what I was saying over there?" she asked, indicating the far corner of the room where no one was sitting.

"Uh," said Ana, "no, we were having a conversation here."

"Oh," said the small woman, frowning again.

"What did you say?" Danny asked brightly.

Haru scowled at him for the question.

"It's important to go to church," she said. "Were you in church today?"

Haru glanced whimsically at his phone. "Oh darn! Is it Sunday already?"

The girl opened her mouth to speak but didn't say anything. She just gaped at them.

Seven felt uncomfortable so he turned back to the table. The group exchanged looks.

"The thing you have to understand about the Engine Valley," Haru told them, "is that this place is more full of 'sin' than most towns. Unfortunately, a town full of sinners tends to attract missionaries."

"You should have gone to church today!" the girl yelled louder than Seven could have ever anticipated. She stormed off before they could respond.

"So if this place is so bad," asked Seven, smarting a little from the outburst, "do you really think the Enemy is going to bother with it?"

"This place may be a shit hole," said Haru, taking a huge bite of his sandwich and then talking with food in his mouth, "but it also represents a huge chunk of the economy. If you wanted to bankrupt this country, blowing up the Engine Valley is a good place to start."

Seven thought about the Enemy's offer to put the Underground in charge if the rebel organization assisted in the invasion. "Did Danny show you the message from the Enemy?"

He nodded. "I'm not going to lie and say I wasn't intrigued by the idea at first. I mean, shit, we're already a bunch of traitors. But Danny talked me out of it. He reminded me that our goal is to make this country a better place, not blow it all to Hell."

"Don't give me all the credit," said Young, turning to Seven.

The acknowledgment surprised Seven. "Oh," he stammered. "Well, all I said…I mean, we're not going to win people to our side helping someone whose idea of bringing freedom is dropping bombs all over our Capital. And anyway, I kind of think the Enemy might be a symptom of a larger problem in this place."

Haru looked intrigued. "How do you mean?"

"It's so divided here. Guard versus Underground, Patriots versus Heretics. Of course we're under attack. We were all so concerned about our internal issues that we forgot to worry about threats from the outside. Now the Enemy is here and they're taking advantage of the disharmony. Maybe they sent that message because they want to exploit our problems and tear us apart from the inside."

Young agreed with a solemn nod. "Divided, we fall."

"So what," asked Ana, "are we supposed to make nice with the Guard?"

"I'm not saying that Danny and the president should hold hands," said Seven. "But fighting each other isn't going to get the Enemy off our shores. The only way we're going to end this war is if we stand together as one nation."

"But what about our mission here?" said Ana. "If Eve can get us information about Patriot ID, and it stinks as bad as it smells, we need to get it out to the public immediately. We can't just hold that information back until the War is over. That could take years."

"If we do it right, I think we can avoid anarchy and maintain a united front against the Enemy," said Young. "I mean, no one is actually going to support Patriot ID when they find out what it is. It's the president who wants it, and everyone else has just been following orders.

He put down his sandwich dramatically. "When we tell everyone about it, we just have to emphasize that the answer is not a violent revolution, because that–as Seven says–would cripple us at a time when we need to be strong. Instead, our message must be to let our democracy take care of the problem. My family has connections in the Congress, and I have it on good confidence that they will support impeachment if we provide them with enough dirt."

"What about the Church?" asked Seven.

"If the Headmaster has any brains, he won't let the president drag the Church down with him. The politics will be so rotten that he'll have to separate himself and support impeachment."

Haru scratched his head. "Supposing all that goes down like you say," he said, "how do we ensure the next president isn't even more of a prick than Drake?"

"Well...as you know, my father ran one of the largest corporations in the country, not to mention one of the largest foundations for charity."

"So what?"

"So, when an election is announced, the son of philanthropist Daniel Alexander Young–a martyr executed by the bad old president for his opposition–intends to announce his candidacy for president."

The announcement hung in the air for what felt like an eternity.

"I've been thinking about it a lot," Young continued. "I've got a face that ordinary people recognize and a name that unites the Underground. I know my father would have been the more logical candidate, but there's nothing we can do about that, is there? I think he would have wanted me to do this in his place."

Haru smiled encouragingly. "I think you're right."

"This isn't to say I completely know how to do it," Young hedged. "I'm going to need all of your help and advice."

Haru smacked Danny lightly on the back. "You're going to do fine, dude."

"Good luck, Mr. President," Ana said in a breathy voice.

"I think it makes a lot of sense," said Seven, "but we're going to have to work on your image."

Danny checked to make sure he didn't have any blond hairs sticking up. "What do you mean?"

"On the radio the other day, they basically called you a rich playboy who parties hard every night and every day. I'm just not sure you'll have the family values vote."

Danny laughed and waved it off. "Oh, *that* image. That's just a cover. I do all that just to throw people off the scent of my role in the Underground."

Haru cackled. "Yes, and he also does it for the women."

Young grinned. "Okay, so it's *mostly* a cover. But I must concede the point to our friend Seven. I'll probably have to start spending nights in."

Ana tapped him lightly on the shoulder. "If you want, I could pretend to be your first lady."

Haru couldn't contain himself. "Oh, you wouldn't be his *first* lady!"

"Hey, shut up," Danny whined. "You are so not helping my image right now."

○

"What a whore!" The exclamation from Talia snapped Eve out of her musings. On the TV screen an absolutely radiant Susan Levi was exchanging rings with her groom.

"Hey, come on," said Eve. "I hardly think it's slutty to get married."

"Right," said Talia, laying on the sarcasm. She didn't bother to turn from the TV. "Like you're qualified to say what's a healthy relationship."

Eve couldn't believe the amount of estrogen she was having to put up with lately. "Excuse me?" she said finally.

Talia sprung to her feet and pointed accusingly at Eve.

"Seven told me all about you, how you won't stop hounding him. You need to get over it. Seven's moved on."

Eve's cheeks turned red. "It's…it's none of your business."

"It's totally my business. Like, I know you found that bra in his room. Maybe you weren't totally clear on this, but that was mine. I left it. Me." As if feeling the point was not already clear enough, Talia grabbed her own black spaghetti string top by the neck line and tugged it down to reveal the pink undergarment.

"What, is that the only bra you own?"

Talia stuck out her tongue. She let go of the shirt and it sprang back into place.

Eve could feel her blood boiling. Talia was practically a teenager and she dressed like a boy. What could he possibly see in her?

"J-Jon," stammered Eve, "doesn't know what he's doing."

"For your information, I'm a who, not a what." She shook her head. "And, like, reality check? Jon's dead. The sooner you accept that, the easier it's going to be for the both of you. The two of you are about to work together on what everyone says is a pretty damn important mission. The kind of mission that could bring big changes to people's lives. But mark my words, if you take all this baggage with you, you're going to fail."

Eve wasn't about to take this from a goddamned little girl. She stood up and told Talia to go straight to Hell.

"Is that the best you got?" asked Talia, beating her chest. "Want to take this outside?"

Eve was flabbergasted. "What? I'm not going to fight you."

Talia grinned victoriously and sat back down in front of the TV. "That's what I thought."

Grumbling, Eve reached for another donut. She wasn't going to let the brat get to her. Things were too far along, much too far along. Jon was hers, and when everything was said and done, she knew she would have him back.

CHAPTER TWENTY-ONE
Facility B

Eve's heart beat faster as she led Seven, handcuffed, up the black steel steps to Facility B. The moment had played through her mind a thousand times, but now, finally, it was happening.

Facility B was a huge complex that most closely resembled a metropolitan hospital. It was only about five stories, but had several mile-long extensions that stretched out from the center like the arms of an octopus. The first time Eve visited this place, she'd gotten hopelessly lost and spent an hour trying to get back to the front entrance.

A Guard, standing erect outside the door, saluted Eve as they approached. He was a standard-issue soldier—shaved head, broad shoulders, and midnight blue uniform. He licked his lips upon eying her pink button-down top. She wouldn't normally have worn it on a mission but she considered this home turf.

"At ease," Eve said as calmly as she could manage. "I'm Agent Eve Parker."

The soldier hid his tongue. "Yes…they're expecting you."

He turned and opened the door.

Orchestral strings whispered through the lobby. The melody was tense, but the volume was turned down low enough for the piece to work as ambiance. A female Guard sitting behind a granite counter saluted Eve. "Welcome to Facility B, Agent Parker. I'll let them know that you're here."

After a few minutes, the large elevator doors behind the counter slid open. A middle-aged man in a white lab coat stepped out with a soldier on either side.

"Hello, Agent Parker," the doctor said. "My name is Dr. Fitch."

Eve grimaced slightly as she got a whiff of Fitch's coffee breath, but quickly transitioned the expression to a smile. "Nice to meet you."

The soldiers grabbed Seven by either arm and led him into the elevator.

"Hey, watch the shoulder," protested Seven. But he didn't resist.

Eve bit her lip as the silver doors slid shut.

"They're taking him to the holding cells," explained Fitch, laying a hand comfortingly on Eve's shoulder. The doctor's smile emphasized his two front teeth, and Eve thought he looked a bit like a mouse. "My team is prepping upstairs for the operation, and we should be able to get under way in about forty-five minutes. Would you like to wait down here until then?"

That should be enough time for me to investigate Patriot ID, thought Eve. "Actually, I was hoping you could give me a tour. My superiors asked me to check on the Patriot ID project while I was in the area."

Fitch frowned and furrowed his graying brow. "I wasn't told about that."

Eve was afraid she might face questions, but knew what to say. "It was a last-minute assignment," she lied. "Since I oversaw the pilot run of the surveillance chip, they want me to get up to speed on the countrywide expansion."

With a shrug the doctor pulled a phone from his hip and began to dial a number. "Sounds reasonable enough," he told Eve. "I'm not sure security will like it, but I'll see what I can do."

Fitch stepped away and began to speak in a hushed mumble that Eve couldn't make out. Finally, he pulled the phone from his ear and clipped it to his belt. "Come with me," he said.

Eve looked uncertainly at the small black box in her hand.

"Open it," said Dr. Fitch.

She pulled up the hinged top and a tiny object inside sparkled back at her. "It's tinier than Jon's," she said.

Fitch smiled. "Yes, in fact it's about eighty-seven percent smaller. The microchip in Agent Wyle's head was just a prototype. Since then we've been able to shrink much of the circuitry. At this size the chip requires much less work to attach."

The doctor held up an orange gun that looked like a hand drill. "With Jon we had to do surgery. But since the new chip is no bigger than a deer tick, we can actually staple the chip directly onto the user's skull. You can't see it beneath someone's hair. The procedure takes a few seconds, and the program is immediately operational."

Eve tilted the chip in the light and held it level with the middle button of her shirt, which was actually the lens of a small video camera. Now she just had to keep him talking about the project.

"So this little thing has all the same functions as the chip in Jon's head?" she asked.

Fitch grinned. "It records audio and uses satellite GPS to track location. The data is sent wirelessly to a computer database in this facility. We have an advanced filtering program here that automatically flags suspicious behavior."

"And then what?"

The scientist shrugged. "That's for the government to decide. We just build it."

Eve could barely contain her objections. Yes, the Guard had long used machines to compile its Watched list, but never had those tools been used to label people as Heretics. With President Drake's recent order to round up everyone on the Watched list, the government was trying to short circuit the Elites' careful process for separating real threats from false positives. If implemented, she realized, Patriot ID would hugely increase the number of arrests unchecked by human analysts.

Expending every ounce of willpower, Eve let the matter drop and changed the subject. "What about the memory blocking function we used for Jon?"

"Well," said Fitch, "we didn't remove it, but of course it's been turned off. We aren't looking to create a country full of amnesiacs, obviously."

"But it can be turned on once it's in someone's head?"

"Well, yes, technically. But I can't imagine why we would do that."

Smiling, she closed the box and returned it to Fitch. "Are these under production here?"

"Yes," he replied. "If you'd like, the factory's about a ten minute walk from the lab. We won't have to go outside."

Eve looked at the thin gold watch on her wrist. They still had almost a half hour until the operation was to begin. "Why not?"

Eve leaned over the railing and took in the big steel boxes and conveyor belts. She focused on one machine in particular that was cutting up sheet metal into hundreds of tiny squares. She guessed they would become the casing for the chips.

"So many!" she yelled over the noise of whirring and hammering.

"We've got a big population!" Fitch shouted back.

Suddenly, Eve was struck by the enormity of what she was doing. The information she was gathering could be catastrophic–the kind of thing the president would never be able to talk his way out of. If the Guard found out Eve was to blame, she'd certainly lose her job. In fact, Eve realized, she'd be lucky if she kept her life.

It's not too late to turn back, she thought. The evidence had been recorded but it didn't have to be saved. She could still destroy it.

Eve didn't feel like a Heretic, but this Patriot ID program sounded…well…evil. Watching a dissident was one thing, but watching everyone? Casting a net that large went against everything she believed in. If she stood by and let that happen, wouldn't she be breaking her promise to Uncle Bill?

The doctor tapped her on the shoulder. "It's almost time for the operation. You ready to head back?"

"Yes," she said. As she followed him to the exit, the sparkling diamond on her finger caught her eye.

Jon will know what to do, she decided. She reached into her shirt and disabled the camera.

CHAPTER TWENTY-TWO
Seven v. Jon

The nurses tied Seven down to the hospital bed with thick canvas straps. Then they left him alone to wait for the doctor. The bonding restricted most movements, but he could turn his head sideways for a disconcerting gander of scalpels, syringes, and other surgical equipment lying on a metal side table. Beyond that, he could see a large rectangular window spanning the entire wall. A single white door with a vision chart stood just around the corner on the wall closest to Seven's feet.

He'd maintained his cool until about a minute ago. Now he was worried. According to the Underground's plan, Eve should have come to rescue him by now. Where was she?

The doctor stepped inside, flinging the door back behind him so hard that the eye chart shook. He strode alongside Seven and tied a surgeon's mask over his mouth. Peering down at a clipboard, he introduced himself as Dr. Fitch.

Seven didn't respond; he was focused on the blond woman standing on the other side of the glass.

The betrayal was in Eve's eyes. He wondered how he could have been so foolish as to trust her, how they all had been so stupid. He was supposed to be Danny Young's adviser, but he had failed–barely even tried–to convince the Underground that Eve couldn't be trusted.

"Well then," said Fitch, "looks like we're finally going to get that chip out of your head."

He convulsed involuntarily. The chip had been a curse but he didn't dare remove it. The contraption was what made him Seven.

Fitch wiped Seven's brow with a napkin. "Now, now, no need to get all worked up. This is going to be quick and easy, and if you cooperate, you won't feel a thing. That gorgeous woman out there—well, she says she loves you. And when you wake up, the two of you will be together again, like none of this ever happened."

Seven struggled against the straps. He thought he felt them loosen, but not enough.

The doctor fit a clear plastic mask over Seven's face. It was connected by a thin plastic tube to a metal tank on the lower shelf of the bedside table. Fitch leaned over and twisted the knob on the tank, and instantly Seven felt a rush of warm air against his lips.

Gas. He tried not to breathe.

"Relax," commanded Dr. Fitch.

Still Seven would not take a breath. He pushed harder against his restraints.

Fitch shook his head. "I told you this would be painless," said the doctor, balling up a blue-gloved fist, "as long as you *cooperated*." On the last word he struck the patient hard in the diaphragm. Seven felt the air shoot out of his lungs. Wheezing painfully, he gulped down the gas. It tasted sweet, like cotton candy.

But he felt much too drowsy to eat.

So Joanna and Shaan are going out, he reflected. How did they miss that?

Agent Eve Parker seemed to be taking it especially hard. It was cute how pathetic she looked, standing there at the bottom of the lighthouse.

"Hey," he tried, "I mean, it seemed reasonable at the time they might be trading weaponry, or illegally obtained data…"

She shook her head. "They were trading spit!"

The Luna Coast looked beautiful at sunset. As they walked to their cars a gust of wind blew gently through Eve's golden hair. He found himself admiring her slender hourglass figure, and the confidence with which she walked. Suddenly he felt overcome by a strange sense of longing, and he realized he wasn't ready to say goodbye. He tried to think of something to say so she wouldn't go, but everything he could think of sounded like something a stalker would say. And he wasn't a stalker. He just wanted to see her again, maybe.

He could feel his heart beating harder. They were getting close to her car. Soon she'd be gone. If he was going to say something, he realized, he had better say it now. But what?

Eve spoke first. "Well, it was nice working with you, Jon."

He realized she was saying goodbye. Jon told himself to stop stalling, but all he could manage to say was "Yeah…"

Her eyes were on him, and he wondered if she could read his mind. Had he blown his cover so easily?

"Well, uh, it's still pretty early," he managed finally. "Do you maybe—I mean, do you have any dinner plans…currently?"

Her eyes widened. After what felt like hours, her lips curved into a smile. "No, not currently."

They were in a restaurant. The red pepper burned his throat, and Eve was laughing at him. On the beach, she drew near and said, "I guess we ended up getting a little action tonight anyway."

Suddenly, they were running down a small hill off of the paved park trail. The next thing he knew, they were in the grass and she was straddling his waist. He kissed her hard.

Then she was off, running through a swirl of orange, yellow, and red leaves. Eve's soft black jacket vanished behind a tall oak in the distance. He went after her, and soon had Eve trapped against the bark.

"Hey!" she protested, running a finger down his chest. "You were supposed to count."

He let go and dropped to one knee.

There was a blinding light and he was alone. On the tree where he had held Eve, there was now only a simple engraving of the numeral 7.

He heard an engine in the distance, and the forest began to glow white. A silver train hurtled toward him. He shut his eyes but the impact never came. When they opened he was sitting inside one of the cars. The locomotive shot out of the forest and carried Seven into a vast city by the sea. The track lifted and a silver skyscraper floated by his window. Suddenly the tower exploded and fire rained down upon the train.

The other passengers glared at him. Someone shouted, "Heretic!"

He heard the heavy stomp of a soldier's boots coming fast down the aisle. The guy sitting next to him, a young man with frizzy black hair and a guitar case, stood up and shouted something at the oncoming Guard. A shot rang out and the musician fell to the floor.

The Guard was soon upon him. Seven turned to meet the soldier's gaze and saw Jonathan Wyle staring back. Wyle pressed Seven's face against the train window and stabbed the barrel of the pistol into his head.

The other passengers chanted: "Drop him, drop him, drop him…"

Seven's foot shot up into Jon's left kneecap. The Elite Guard loosened his grip on Seven, who took the opportunity to swat the gun away and rise to his feet.

Jon Wyle roared furiously and lunged at Seven, but Seven leaned to the side and redirected his attacker's momentum toward the window. The glass shattered and the Elite's head went through. Wyle's face was a bloody mess when he pulled it back inside.

The train seemed to pick up speed. Seven ran down the aisle and slipped through the emergency portal into the next car. He heard a shot and a ricochet as the doors slid shut behind him.

A hundred turned heads met him in the next car. He pushed through the crowd, occasionally grabbing hold of the backs of seats for balance. Seven saw, too late, the outstretched leg of a teenager. He tripped and fell crashing to the floor. With his ear to the carpet he could hear the loudening reverberations of his pursuer's feet.

Seven picked himself up and ran through car after car until finally he reached the front of the train. There were no more doors to run through. He glanced outside at the burning city and then spun back around. He could see Jonathan Wyle stampeding toward him like a wild animal.

Wyle burst into the car and pointed his gun at Seven. "End of the line," he said. "You can't run from me any longer."

"You're right," said Seven, suddenly overtaken by a strange sense of calm. "But maybe I don't have to run. I think, maybe, that you can't kill me."

Jon's eyes narrowed. "Isn't that an awfully high risk to take?"

"You're my past, but so is all of this," said Seven, waving out the window at the burning city. "You can restore my old memories, but you can't take away my new ones."

"Wrong!" screamed Agent Jonathan Wyle. He cocked the pistol and pulled the trigger.

Seven saw the bullet go through his chest but it left no mark. He charged down the aisle and lunged at the other man.

CHAPTER TWENTY-THREE
The Return

Eve awoke with a crick in her neck. She was slumped on a scratchy blue couch and didn't remember falling asleep. Taking only a few moments to compose herself, Eve launched herself onto her feet and strode purposely toward the room where they were holding Jon.

Dr. Fitch had prohibited Eve from seeing him immediately after the surgery. He said Jon would be too disoriented to see her right away. The nurses moved her fiancé to a room with a comfortable bed and told Eve to wait an hour.

She'd been asleep at least that long, her watch showed. Enough time, she decided. She had to see him, had to see if the man she loved was back. She was worried sick that the operation failed or had unforeseen side effects.

A Guard met her at the door to Jon's room. "Name and business," he asked.

"Agent Eve Parker. The man in there was–" She stopped short to correct herself. "The man in there is my fiancé."

The soldier immediately stepped aside.

The man she loved was sitting up in bed, staring out into the night sky.

"Not much of a view, is it?" she asked him.

He turned to her and smiled warmly. "Eve," he said knowingly. "You always did hate the Engine Valley, didn't you?"

She felt a pit in her stomach. "Jon?" she made out finally.

"Close the door and c'mere," he replied.

She sat on the bed next to him. At once he had his arms around her. "I'm sorry," he said.

Eve's heart felt warm under Jon's gentle squeeze. "Why?"

"For becoming Seven. I've treated you so badly...hurt you."

A tear fell from Eve's eye. "It's fine," she said. "You didn't know what you were doing. I always knew you didn't mean it. When I first met you as Seven, I could tell that you still loved me. And so even after everything went mad, I knew that if I could just help you remember, you would be mine again."

"And now I am," he said. He pulled her close and kissed the bead of salt water on her cheek. Eve kicked off her shoes. She pushed Jon down onto the bed and stretched out next to him. He pulled her mouth against his. When he eventually tried to come up for air, she pulled him back. When finally Eve, too, was breathless she pushed Jon onto his back and tucked her head into his neck.

Into his ear, she whispered, "I'm in trouble, Jon."

"What?"

"Don't talk–the Guard might have this room bugged and I don't want them to hear this. Do you remember our mission with the Underground?"

He nodded slightly.

"I don't know why I went through with it, but I collected the evidence they wanted."

Jon exhaled deeply.

"I'm not a Heretic, but I don't understand why they need a machine to watch everyone. I've spent nearly my whole life watching people and deciding if they're Heretics. What they're talking about is a program that makes everyone a Heretic until proven innocent."

She sighed. "But at the same time, I don't know if I can turn on the Guard. Maybe there's a larger story here that I don't know about. Maybe Drake is completely justified in launching this program.

"I don't have to do it. The evidence was recorded to a flash memory card. I can still destroy it. But for some reason, I just can't decide if that's the right thing to do."

Jon's lips brushed gently against her ear. "Then give me the burden of deciding," he whispered. "Give the flash card to me and I'll destroy it."

The more she thought about it, the more she liked the idea. She knew she'd regret either choice. But if she let Jon decide…

She reached into her jeans pocket. Keeping the card hidden in the palm of her hand, she straddled Jon and kissed him. She gently placed the object in his hand and closed his fingers over the top. Then she began to unbutton his shirt.

"You know there's a camera in here," he managed to say eventually.

She brushed her hair out of her face and laughed. "Maybe they'll send us a copy."

"As much as I'd like to proceed," said Jon, "I'm also starving."

She gasped. "Haven't they given you anything to eat?"

He furrowed his brow. "I think they gave me some kind of consommé?"

"You poor thing!" She got off him at once. "In that case, I'll get you a proper supper. We can catch up afterward…I know a hotel not too far from here where we can go when they release you. It's still the Engine Valley, but it will have to do."

"That sounds nice," he replied.

Eve leaned over to kiss him one more time. Then she adjusted her hair and left the room. She was grinning ear to ear as she walked past the Guard and down the hallway.

In the cafeteria, Eve piled a plate high with grilled chicken, mashed potatoes and some kind of pea/carrot mixture. She poured Jon a cup of cola. She didn't get anything for herself except for a bottle of water. She was too excited to eat. All she wanted to do was sit by Jon's side and look at him.

When she returned, Eve found the door to Jon's room unattended and slightly ajar. Then she saw the Guard lying still on the floor. She dropped the dinner tray and the peas and carrots went flying in different directions. Some of the brown soda splattered onto the fallen soldier's face.

Eve checked the Guard's pulse and found none. Only then did she notice that his revolver was missing.

Pulling together what courage she had left, Eve stood up and pushed open the door. "Jon?" she whimpered.

The bed was empty except for a single scrap of paper. She picked it up and read a message scrawled in her fiancé's handwriting:

Thanks for the evidence!

It was signed *Seven*.

The alarm sounded and Seven cursed. He'd hoped to have made it a little closer to the exit before the hunt began, but instead had gotten hopelessly lost. Facility B was much too large, with far too many branching hallways. As far as he could tell, he was on the fifth floor, but it was unclear how to get down, and he still felt a little woozy from the gas.

He remembered being in Facility B once before, a long time ago when he was Agent Jonathan Wyle. But maybe he had been in a different wing. He thought he was heading in the direction of the fire stairs, but all he had come across so far was a water fountain.

It was strange remembering this place, or remembering anything at all for that matter. But Seven didn't have time to give it much thought. Thinking was a distraction.

"Hey, you!" someone shouted. Seven spun around and saw a pair of Guard jogging down the hallway. When they saw Seven's gun, they picked up theirs.

Seven ducked behind the water fountain. An errant shot struck the faucet and water began spraying out of the top of the machine. Seven leaned out, and with his good arm fired back at them. The shots hit their targets straight on, and the soldiers slumped to the floor.

The fugitive did a quick survey of the area. A red exit sign glowed like a beacon down the hall to the right. He ran toward it, eventually coming upon a big door with a metal push bar. Ignoring an all-caps warning, he charged through, setting off another alarm.

"Damn it!" Now they would know exactly where he was. "Stupid, stupid, stupid!"

Now he had two choices: take the stairs, or look for another exit. If he took the stairs, they'd certainly be waiting for him at the bottom. But there were plenty of Guard up here, too, and if he stayed in place he'd be no closer to the exit.

Seven had thought he was pretty clever after collecting the evidence on Patriot ID and giving Eve the slip. Well, the rush from that experience certainly had been short-lived. All of that effort would be meaningless if the Guard caught him now.

He decided on the stairs and took them two steps at a time. He cleared the fourth and third floors easily, but stopped short upon seeing a heavily armed Guard step onto the second floor landing. Seven bounded back up the stairs and took the third floor exit. He came out in another corner intersection that looked nearly identical to the floor he'd come from.

A trio of Guard came running down the hallway in front of him. This group didn't hesitate to fire their weapons. Seven squeezed off a few shots to disorient them and then turned right. He drew close to the wall and, for the heck of it, slapped the elevator's down button. He hadn't planned to wait, but after only a few strides past the machine he heard the doors slide open.

Seven couldn't believe his fortune. But as he turned, he saw that the elevator was not empty, but in fact held four more soldiers. These men were more heavily armed than the previous ones he had seen. They were obviously reinforcements brought in only when matters got serious. They carried not only rifles, but an entire utility belt full of grenades and other contraptions.

With barely a pause, Seven took aim at a can of tear gas attached to one of the soldiers' belts. Instantaneously, the elevator exploded in smoke, leaving the men inside choking and hacking away.

Seven shook his head. He'd been lucky so far, but there was no way he could keep this up forever. He had to find a way out of this building, and fast.

The orange moon caught his eye. Stopping short, he approached the big plate-glass window. It looked out at one of the outer edges of the complex. Down and below was a grassy courtyard with a couple trees and benches–this was probably a place where workers went out to have a quick smoke, or maybe even to eat lunch when it was warm.

He wondered if he was close enough to the ground to survive a fall without breaking anything. It might hurt a little, but maybe if he landed it just right…

"Stop! We have you surrounded!" a Guard yelled.

He checked both ways and confirmed there were soldiers on either side of the hall.

"Drop the weapon and put your hands in the air!"

He didn't have a choice.

"Drop your weapon, I said."

Seven blasted the window and dove through. A bullet cut through the back leg of his hospital pajamas, just missing his flesh.

The ground came faster than he expected, but he broke the fall with a forward roll. Soon he was up on his feet again and running for a reinforced concrete wall. He scanned the barrier left and right but couldn't find an obvious weakness. He thought about scaling it, but it appeared to be iced with broken glass and barbed wire.

Seven couldn't believe he had been so shortsighted. Why hadn't he thought of this before?

A heavy thunk interrupted Seven's despair. Instinctively, he curled up into a ball. A moment later, there was an ear-splitting explosion directly in front of him.

When the smoke cleared, he discovered an elephant-sized hole in the wall, opening onto the street. Parked on the other side of the road was a purple minivan. Shaan stood out in front, holding some kind of detonator.

"Seven!" he shouted. "Let's get out of here!"

"Agent Parker?"

She was sitting on the bed where Seven had lain less than a half hour ago. Eve looked up, and for the first time saw the Guard standing in front of her. "What is it?" she said.

"Wyle has escaped, sir."

She shook her head. "Wyle is dead."

The Guard looked confused. "With all due respect, sir, we're sure he's on the move. Shall we send cars after him?"

She thought about it. "No," she said finally. "Let him go."

"Yes, ma'am. Anything else?"

"No, you can go."

The soldier saluted and walked away. Eve fell back into the bed and closed her eyes. She was angry with herself for thinking she could ever bring Jon back. She held her left hand up over her head and watched the diamond on her finger sparkle. The clomping footsteps of the Guard returned.

"I said that you could go," she said without looking up.

"Agent Parker?"

It was a new voice. She looked up and saw that it was a priest.

"Oh, hello, Father," she said. "Can I help you?"

"I'm afraid I need to ask you to come with me," the clergyman said. "The Headmaster has some questions about your recent tour of the facility."

"How did you find me?" asked Seven as the van sped away from Facility B. He was stretched across the first row of seats in the back. Shaan and Talia monitored him closely from a row back.

Danny Young, riding shotgun again, twisted around in his seat. "One thing I learned from my dad is never to trust strangers," he said. "Eve was the key to the mission, so I decided we should take a few extra precautions. Shaan was happy to oblige."

"The flash card we gave to Eve was also beaming us her location," explained Shaan. "When it became clear that she was planning to break from the plan, I immediately alerted Danny and we started packing our things. Only a few minutes after we pulled up to launch a rescue, the card's GPS signal started moving erratically. We decided that one or both of you was on the run. Then it was just a matter of finding you outside."

"Why didn't you try to rescue me right away?"

"Since Eve knew about our base, we first had to erase all traces of the Underground's presence in Engine Valley," said Ana, who was driving. "Haru's on his way to a safe house now."

"For the record," Talia chimed in. "I wanted to come right away."

Shaan chuckled. "And she nearly gave me a black eye trying to convince me."

Talia blushed. She seemed to Seven almost embarrassed that the topic had been breached. Maybe she really was starting to care for him, he thought. Seven liked her, too, but now there was a new feeling inside holding him back—a sort of emptiness that he couldn't explain.

"Did they hurt you?" Talia asked.

Seven hesitated.

She turned him around and looked him in the eyes. "What did they do to you?"

He sighed. "They removed the chip."

The statement sucked all the air out of the car.

"But it's okay, I guess," Seven continued. "I've got my old memories back, but I still…I still feel like Seven."

Shaan rubbed his chin thoughtfully. "You maintained control," he said. "Interesting."

Danny Young shook his head. "Well, there goes your usefulness. I guess you're fired."

Seven smiled. "Hey, I could use the vacation."

"Seriously, though," said Young, "it's good to have you back. Did Eve get the evidence, at least?"

"So she claimed," said Seven, handing Young the flash card. He wondered what was in it for Eve if she really had betrayed the Guard. They would certainly find out she had leaked information, and now the Underground couldn't provide her any protection. What had she been thinking?

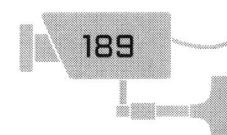

He thought about how her cheeks turned apple red when she saw him after the operation. And then there was the way she kissed him—it felt familiar and yet like nothing he'd ever experienced.

Seven came out of the daze and asked where they were headed next.

"My family has another little cabin outside of Loganville," said Danny. "We'll hide out there for now and go through the evidence. Then we'll send it to my connections in Congress and the press."

"What about the Enemy?" asked Seven. "There might not be a nation to save from Patriot ID."

"Don't worry about it," said Danny with a grin. "I took your advice."

"You mean...?"

"Yes. As we speak, the Underground is sending its men and women down to the Luna Coast to help drive the Enemy off the coast."

"What?" asked Ana. "Why?"

"It's the right thing to do. If I'm serious about leading this country, there's no way I can stand by and let the Enemy wipe us out. The Underground has the resources to help, and so that's exactly what we're going to do."

"But like, this all assumes we make it to Loganville alive," interjected Talia. "I still think we should have taken a different car. Like, maybe one that Eve doesn't know about."

Remembering the conflict he'd heard in Eve's voice, Seven shook his head. "I don't think she'll come after us. Eve went through with her part of the mission, and I think she genuinely wanted us to report the truth on Patriot ID."

Talia nodded thoughtfully. "But I guess she just couldn't get over you—the old you anyway."

Whatever she decided, thought Seven, he couldn't imagine

this was going to end well for her. The Guard was bound to find out what part she played in all this. When that happens, he didn't know what she would do. He wondered why that made him feel so worried.

CHAPTER TWENTY-FOUR
Until Death...

A Guard led Eve handcuffed into the dark chamber and pushed her into the cold metal chair in the center of the room. Her arms twisted awkwardly as she landed, but she kept the pain to herself. The Guard took a swift turn that looked almost ceremonious, and headed for the exit. The heavy metal portal slid shut behind him, leaving Eve in darkness so black she couldn't see her hands. The click of the lock was the last sound she heard for many minutes.

A spotlight snapped on overhead. Eve could see herself, and an empty floor about a foot in each direction, but the rest of the room remained hidden from her.

"Eve Parker," said a familiar deep and syrupy voice. "We are very, very disappointed. You have disgraced God and country."

It was the Headmaster. She concentrated on her diamond ring, but for the first time found it powerless to calm her.

"Father, I..."

"Silence!" the Headmaster's voice boomed. "We need not waste time discussing your failure. You know what you have done. We know what you have done. And most of all, He knows what you have done. You are a Heretic and your destination is the Infernal Flames. There is nothing you or we can do to change your fate. Your soul is lost and cannot be Saved."

Eve wondered if he was referring to her feeding the Underground incriminating details about Patriot ID, or letting Seven get away. She didn't regret either one. The tour of Facility B had confirmed her worst fears about the Patriot ID program. She knew then that it had to be exposed and shut down. She did feel bad about nearly destroying the evidence, but she wasn't going to tell the Headmaster that.

"You will be moved temporarily to a prison cell here in the Desert Base," the Headmaster said. "For thirty days you will consider all the evils you have committed against God and his people. Then you will be dropped."

"An execution?" Eve gasped. "I believe the law says I'm entitled to a trial."

"Heretics are entitled to nothing but death," was the high priest's icy response.

Finally finding the power to raise her voice, she exclaimed, "You can't do that! I want to speak to the president!"

The Headmaster made no answer, but Eve could sense that he was grinning through the darkness.

Eve didn't resist as a Guard led her down the hallway to her prison cell. It was quiet, and the heavy steel doors prevented her from seeing whether any of the cells had inhabitants. The Guard, a brown-haired woman with astonishingly large biceps, stopped at a cell marked 05 and sunk a card into the door.

"In there," said the Guard, shoving Eve forward.

When they were inside, the Guard directed Eve to stand against the wall. Eve did as she was told. The Guard pulled back Eve's shackled wrists and unlocked the handcuffs.

"Your ring…it's beautiful," said the Guard. "Unfortunately, you can't have it in here."

Eve's eyes widened. "What? Why not?"

"That's the policy. We'll keep it in a safe place, and your family can come pick it up when they see fit."

"Please," Eve begged. "One woman to another, you've got to understand. I need it! You can't take it away from me!"

The Guard shook her head. "Don't make me use force."

Eve fought back the tears. "But it's mine!"

And with that she leaped at the Guard and wrestled her to the ground. Eve grabbed the soldier's throat and squeezed until the woman's face turned red.

As she held the Guard tightly between her fingers, it occurred to Eve that she didn't have much of a plan—subdue the Guard and make a run for it. Chances were good someone would see her and the whole Desert Base would come down on her.

The Guard got a hand free and used it to knock Eve's arm out from under her. Off balance, Eve was easily pushed off onto the concrete slab. The Guard pinned her down with one hand and pulled out a club with the other.

"You can't have it!" screamed Eve. "It's my ring!"

The blow came like a flash of light. Eve's vision cleared just long enough to see the Guard's fist hurtling toward her.

Red and golden leaves sashayed through the air as Jon and Eve walked through the tall gates and into the tree-filled commons.

"I'm sorry about encouraging you to take the mission," she told him. "I love you, and the last thing I want is for us to be apart."

He looked her in the eyes and smiled slightly. "No, you were right. I do have to think about my career, and this is an opportunity that I'd be foolish not to take up."

She scrunched her eyebrows questioningly. "You mean…?"

"Yeah. I told them I'd take the mission."

For a second she couldn't breathe.

"You approve, right?"

Her lips twisted cautiously into a smile. "Of course. This is great news. What you're doing…well it will be historic."

Jon's eyes narrowed. "What's wrong?"

"Well," she said, grabbing his hand, "I'll miss you."

They paused and Jon kissed her on the lips. "Yeah, I'm going to miss you, too."

They walked on through the foliage, stopping occasionally to take wild and usually futile grasps at the falling leaves. Jon stopped suddenly and pointed off the trail down a yellow slope, where months ago they had tussled in the grass. "Do you remember?" he asked.

Eve grinned. "Up for round two?"

Jon stroked a pretend beard, as if to weigh the pros and cons of the suggestion. Then, without warning, he smacked her on the back and ran down the hill. "Tag!" he bellowed.

Her blue eyes displayed something between shock and amusement. She chased after him but he was already far away. "Jon, stop!" she called after him. "C'mon, we're too old for all this running around. Let's play something else. Please?"

He came out of the forest holding his hands in the form of a T. "Time out," he explained. "Fine, we don't have to play Tag. But what mature game do you have in my mind?"

She bit her bottom lip as she thought. "How about Hide and Go Seek?" she offered, adding quickly, "I get to hide first!"

Jon laughed. "That's not fair; you were just 'It.'"

"But now we're playing a new game," she said. "You said we could!"

Jon held up his hands in surrender. "Fine."

Eve smiled triumphantly. "Close your eyes and count to thirty!"

And she was off. Eve looked from tree to tree to find the best place for hiding. Finally, she settled on a mammoth oak tree that must have been hundreds of years old. Seconds after settling herself, a pair of muscular arms came around her and pinned her against the bark.

"Hey!" she protested. "You were supposed to count."

Jon smiled at her mysteriously.

"What do you want?" she asked, drawing a line with her finger from his belly up to his chest.

Finally, he let go and dropped to one knee.

"Jon, what are you—?"

"So, this is going to sound cliché," he said, "but Eve, you make me happier than anyone I've ever met. And the hardest–the hardest thing about this mission is going to be not having you by my side. So I want–I want to make sure that, when it's all over, we'll never be apart again."

He reached into his pocket and removed a small, cherry-wood box. He pulled the top open carefully and held the sparkling rock to her eyes. "Eve…will you marry me?"

She smiled so hard her face went red. "Yes," she whispered.

Eve awoke with a throbbing headache. She was lying atop gray sheets on a thin mattress. Her throat felt scratchy and she tasted blood.

The bed squeaked as she sat up. Gray walls oppressed her from four sides. She felt like she could reach out and touch each of them. There was a lone toilet in the back corner. It didn't have a seat and there was no tissue paper. She had the cell to herself, but she could faintly hear the sound of someone sobbing.

"Hello?" she called out, but her voice was hoarse.

The whining continued unabated.

It wasn't fair, she thought. After all the years of service she had given the Guard, they'd sent her to a prison like a common Heretic. She may have helped the Underground, but she had only done what she thought was right.

Something didn't feel right when Eve rubbed her goose-bumped arms for warmth. She looked at her ring finger and noticed it was naked. She thought she would cry but the tears never came. Eve got down on her knees and prayed.

—PART TWO—
United

CHAPTER TWENTY-FIVE
Last Days

She felt most paralyzed in the morning. Every day she woke up with what she called "the knowing and the not knowing." She knew that she was soon going to die, but she didn't know if she'd go to Heaven with the Patriots or to Hell with the Heretics.

Never before had Eve met a problem she couldn't overcome. Sometimes all she had to do was wait around. Things always seemed to resolve themselves. But it had already been an entire month, and still she was here in prison, waiting to be dropped.

In her first few days she had carried some hope of escaping the concrete cage. By the end of the second week Eve had given up on being rescued by the Underground. She may have helped them expose Patriot ID, but they had no reason to risk their lives for her. As far as they were concerned, Eve had served her purpose. They wouldn't need her again. If there was any doubt, pulling that stunt on Seven had certainly sealed her fate. Heck, the Underground probably *wanted* her dead.

The only thing that made the mornings at all bearable was reading the news. Every morning at 8:25 a.m. a slot on the heavy steel door would flip open and deposit a tabloid. Reading the news this month had been like watching a dystopian sci-fi movie, the kind that usually resulted in the real government arresting and subsequently dropping the filmmakers.

It began with reports that men and women without uniforms were fighting alongside the Guard on the Luna Coast. They were referred to as civilian soldiers. That was the line from President Drake, too. But then someone found a dead body of one of the civilians, and noticed something surprising. Tattooed on his arm was a black silhouette of a head with fire in his eyes–the sign of the Underground.

Drake denied that the rebels were assisting the Guard. But then a story broke that a Guard was seen in a fight with one of the "civilian soldiers," calling him a Heretic and a traitor. Someone snapped a photograph of the Guard holding a gun to the civilian's head against the background of the Enemy's boats at sea. The newspaper ran it on the front page, under the headline,

WHO IS THE ENEMY?

Drake was forced to go on TV to apologize for the Guard's actions and praise the assistance of civilian soldiers, who he acknowledged were making a key difference in the war. Eve saw no more reports of fighting between the Guard and their civilian allies after that.

Finally, the news broke that the Guard had driven the Enemy off the Luna Coast and out of the country. This Eve learned without reading a paper, when a great cheer went up among the prison guards outside. They danced about the hallways spraying champagne in every direction. One soldier directed a bottle through the small window in Eve's door, and the popping cork almost nailed her in the head.

The Underground did not waste a day before making its next move. Eve was in the recreation room when Daniel Alexander Young, Jr. appeared on TV. He revealed that he was the leader of the Underground and confirmed that the civilian soldiers who fought the Enemy belonged to the rebel group.

"However, these men and women are not Heretics," he said. "The Underground loves its country too much to stand idly by and watch the Enemy take control. We could not allow that to happen."

Then he revealed Patriot ID and called out "the true Heretics."

Dick Randall, majority leader of the Congress, called immediately for a formal investigation to find out if President Drake had violated the law. Not surprisingly, Drake balked. He denied that Patriot ID was a secret surveillance program and ordered Young's arrest. As far as Eve could tell from the papers, the Guard never caught Young, but that was the least of Drake's problems. Protesters, chanting for justice and holding banners with the Underground's sign, sprang up in cities and towns across the nation. In a reversal of the evacuation, they descended en masse upon the Capital.

The outrage was what surprised her the most. The church-going, God-fearing public had always seemed to accept surveillance before. How long had they been harboring this anger? Sure there were dissenters, most of whom were linked up with the Underground. But never did she dream there could be so many others.

The newspaper didn't come for several days after the first reports of the protests, and the television disappeared from the rec room. Eve had paced around her cell, wondering what was happening.

A new edition of the newspaper finally appeared on the floor of her cell yesterday morning. The headline read,

HEADMASTER CONDEMNS PATRIOT ID, DEMANDS DRAKE RESIGN

Below that,

President Drake To Testify Before Congress Today

Last night the prison guards refused to tell Eve anything about the congressional hearing. But she knew today's paper would have the answer. She slid off the bed and dropped lightly onto her bare feet. The stone slab sent a shiver through her body, but she pushed through the discomfort. She snapped the tabloid from the floor and brought it back to her bed.

As with nearly every recent newspaper story, the headline made her gasp:

PRESIDENT DRAKE STEPS DOWN AFTER HEARING BLOWUP!

PRESIDENT WILLIAM DRAKE resigned from office last night amid a wave of controversy over the government's strategy for identifying Heretics. Drake made the surprise announcement hours after admitting the secret and possibly illegal nature of the Guard's Patriot ID program.

While Drake initially pitched it as a more convenient driver's license, the president confirmed at a congressional hearing yesterday afternoon that the microchips could record citizens' conversations and track their geographic coordinates. The surveillance would not have been limited to Heretics or the Watched, he said.

"It was a mistake to hide certain details about Patriot ID from the public," Drake said at a 9 p.m. press conference. "It would be another mistake for me to stay in office. I have undermined the people's confidence in their president.

There is nothing left for me to do but step down."

The disgraced president did not say who would replace him, but multiple government officials said Majority Leader Randall of the Congress plans to take the job, at least on a temporary basis. Randall led the interrogation of Drake at the hearing.

"President Drake's announcement that he will resign is an unprecedented decision," Randall said. "It's a good decision, and that's why it's unprecedented. Drake is making the right choice after committing high treason against his people."

Randall declined to say whether he would take the job of interim president, but the senior congressman promised an announcement shortly. Government officials said that could happen as soon as today.

"God acts in unexpected ways," the Headmaster said of the president's resignation.

"While shocking, we must remember that God has a Plan. He will certainly deliver us from this dark time into a bright and infinite future."

In sworn testimony at the hearing, Drake for the first time validated evidence introduced by DAY Corporation Chairman Daniel Alexander Young, Jr.

Young, who recently revealed that he leads the Underground, testified at the hearing that the Guard intended to relay audio recordings of citizens to a central database, where a computer would scan for "concerning" keywords and phrases. If the computer counted a minimum number of these keywords, the citizen's name and location would be forwarded to the Guard for immediate review, Young said.

Young provided several examples of how this could lead to "false positives," situations in which he said the Guard's computer could flag a person who voiced certain keywords but actually had no plans to do anything heretical.

"Actors could be flagged for playing Heretics in a play," Young said. "Your offensive uncle could be flagged for making a 'Heretic walks into a bar' joke. Patriot ID throws out the old standards of evidence and reasonable suspicion. You could be followed, wiretapped, even thrown into jail, all because a machine has calculated you might be up to something."

Drake said the intention behind Patriot ID was to prevent future attacks, both from inside and outside the nation.

"Patriot ID will find Heretics, period," the president said. "The only people who need be scared are the Heretics."

But then Drake indicated that Patriot ID was part of larger and possibly illegal government surveillance program.

"This is no worse than anything [else] we've been doing," he said. "This is just the next logical step."

Randall seized upon the statement. "Why don't you take a step back, then, and tell our nation's people what else their government has been up to?"

A sudden click turned Eve's attention to the door. The heavy steel portal pulled out and rolled to one side, revealing a pair of identical looking Guard.

"Parker," one of them said. "You've got a visitor."

They brought her into a chamber about the size of an outhouse. She found a single chair facing a reinforced glass window. Eve's heart skipped a beat when a red-robed priest stepped through the door on the other side and sat down in front of her.

"Daddy?" she whimpered.

He considered Eve with an expression so full of pity that she wondered if her father thought she was suffering from some terrible disease.

She hadn't seen him since before the Enemy attacked. She called him once, to make sure he was still alive, but that had been the end of it. She had been too ashamed to tell him about her arrest, even though she knew he would find out eventually.

"Why didn't you come sooner?" she asked anyway.

He let out a deep sigh and shook his head. "I raised you better than this you know."

Eve swallowed hard.

The priest's eyes widened. "This is Bill's influence, isn't it? I should never have let him get so close to you. I suppose we can only be grateful that he's not alive to do any more harm."

Eve was furious. "How can you say that? He was your friend!"

The old man sighed again and she saw unfamiliar dark bags beneath his eyes. "I'm sorry, Eve," he said. "Attendance at the church is down. My flock shows up asking questions I can't answer."

"What's the Headmaster saying?"

Her father shook his head slowly. "The Headmaster is distancing himself from the president. What else can he do?"

He stared blankly at the wall behind her. "Did you see the news last night?"

"They forgot to give me a TV," she said dryly, "but I saw the papers. What happens now?"

"An election," he said. "Randall said he'll protest any member of the administration who tries to take Drake's place. He wants everyone out."

"Everyone?" Eve couldn't help but laugh. "How convenient for Randall."

He held out his hands in question. "Well, he is next in the chain of succession. Given he's led this entire investigation, his appointment makes sense."

He glanced at his watch. "There's supposed to be an announcement at noon. Randall could take the oath of office as soon as tonight."

"That's quick," she said, "but then I guess everything has been."

Her father shrugged. "I don't think they want to take any chances with the Enemy breathing down our necks. They may have retreated, but we didn't win the war. They could strike again."

He looked at her sadly. "I suppose you won't have to worry about that anymore."

Eve chose pizza for her last meal. The warden seemed to think she was kidding.

"We can get you anything you want," the fat man said. "It's the only perk our law gives you."

Eve shook her head. "No, all I want is a few slices with meatball and onions, and please, some red pepper on the side."

"You're certain?"

She raised her eyebrows with perturb.

The warden let out one final frustrated sigh and held up his arms in defeat.

An hour later, a Guard brought Eve to a plushy dining room. An entire fourteen-inch pie was waiting. The smell was intoxicating.

"Do you mind if I put the TV on?" the Guard asked. "Majority Leader Randall is supposed to speak soon."

"Please," said Eve, reorienting herself toward the flat panel on the wall. She had to admit she was curious what he would say.

The Guard walked to the screen and slapped it on. Instantly, applause filled the room. "Thank you," said Randall. "Thank you."

He looked old but stood with the conviction of a hardened policeman. "We were all encouraged last night to learn that the tyrant William Drake has resigned from the presidency," said Randall. "His reign of terror, I am proud to say, is over!"

There was an ocean roar of cheers.

"Now we are faced with the question of succession," he said. "Our nation was founded on the principle of democracy, and in that spirit I believe it is only right that we have a fair vote. This is not a process that will happen overnight, but given the ongoing war with the Enemy, we in the government would like to run as expeditious a transition as possible. I am announcing today that we will have a general election in exactly sixty days. That should provide sufficient time for interested candidates to mount a campaign and make their case for reforming our nation.

"In the meantime, we must have an interim president to ensure our interests are promoted at home and abroad, and to protect us from the ever-present threat of war. According to our country's rules of succession, the role of presidency falls to the majority leader of the Congress."

Randall winked at the camera.

The crowd laughed and a million flashbulbs burst.

"I am honored to accept this job, and am proud to announce that I have already taken the oath of office. I am your interim president."

More wild applause.

"I promise to begin turning things around in this country, but remind you that the real work will begin after the election. Thank you, and God bless our fair nation."

He began to walk off stage but one of his aides stopped him and whispered something in his ear. Randall turned back to the podium. "Are there any questions from the reporters?" he asked as an afterthought.

The press contingent buzzed to life. Eventually one of the older looking reporters won out by shouting his question the loudest and refusing to back down. Eve could only make out the end of the question: "…the Enemy really gone for good?"

"As you know, about a week ago the Guard successfully drove the Enemy away from the Luna Coast. There are sea battles ongoing many miles off the coast, but we have the Enemy on the run. Soon, we will dispatch a surge of troops to Enemy territory. We will show them that our country does not roll over so easily, and that there are consequences to attacking us in our homes. Meanwhile, we have repealed the evacuation order for the Capital, and are urging all citizens who left their homes to return as soon as they feel ready."

"What about the Watched?" another reporter yelled.

"My predecessor made a terrible mistake in trying to block the evacuation of citizens on the Watched list," said Randall. "The government formally apologizes for the stress and hardship of the last two months, and I urge them to come out from hiding and rejoin us. We shortly will be combing through the Watched list and reevaluating who should and who should not be on the list."

"Does the Headmaster approve of your interim Presidency and the election in sixty days?" asked another reporter.

Randall grimaced. "I would not dare speak for the high priest, but I will tell you that the Headmaster has raised no objections."

"Has anyone come forward yet to run in the election, and will you be endorsing anyone?"

The interim president regained his composure. "Daniel Alexander Young, Jr., the man who made all of this possible, told me this morning that he plans to run for the presidency. I believe that his patriotism combined with his family's long legacy providing jobs and important services for our people makes him an excellent candidate. I believe he would be a dramatic symbol of change for our fair nation."

Eve looked down at her slice and discovered she'd layered it with way too much red pepper. It reminded her of Jon and she started to cry.

Eve's legs went stiff at the entrance to the death chamber. The two soldiers escorting her had to drag her arm-in-arm the rest of the way to the center of the room.

She wobbled inside a black circle marked with an X in duct tape. A priest was mumbling some kind of prayer and making strange gestures at her.

A soldier holding a thick rope noose advanced. He tossed it over her neck and then dropped a black fabric bag over her head.

In the bleak darkness all Eve could see was Jon's face. For the past month she had avoided thinking about him, convinced herself that he was dead and never coming back. But he wasn't dead, not really. And he wouldn't be waiting for her in Heaven or Hell or wherever she was going.

"Please, God," she heard herself saying. "Oh, God, please…"

She had watched Heretics dropped before. She knew what would happen next; the trapdoor would open and she would fall away forever.

The room went silent and Eve wondered if it had happened.

Then she heard frantic whispering. Every now and then she could make out a word, but it was difficult to make sense of anything.

"Now…my orders…Randall…I know…yes."

She heard footsteps.

"What's going on?" she asked the void.

The shroud lifted and she was blinded by the chamber's fluorescent lights. Eventually her eyes adjusted and the chubby face of the warden came into focus.

"Agent Eve Parker," he said. "I'm pleased to inform you that you've just been pardoned by Interim President Randall."

CHAPTER TWENTY-SIX
Regrets

From his eighth floor Capitol Tower office, Agent Jonathan Wyle reviewed the activities of Joanna Phelps. Using the Blue Wall program, he had logged into her computer and could see that his Watched was composing a blog post for the paper. In an hour all she had written was one cryptic sentence. She had revised it several times, adding a word here, subtracting one there. Currently, it read:

He has an army.

Wyle tapped his pen thoughtfully against the desk. It was four-thirty in the afternoon, and Joanna's newspaper required her to file an editorial for the blog every day at five. Joanna never missed a deadline.

Jon clicked open the main menu of Blue Wall and selected a button called *History* that opened a click-by-click summary of Joanna's activities. Ten minutes ago the sentence had read,

The Headmaster has Saints.

Twenty minutes before that it had been differently phrased as,

The church has soldiers.

He wasn't sure what to make of it. The Church didn't

have soldiers. Unless, he considered, she was referring to the Guard. There was a popular urban myth that the Guard worked for the Church.

Wyle tapped a key and up popped a live video feed from Joanna's webcam. She appeared to be in a state of deep thought, sitting perfectly still with one hand covering her mouth. After a minute she took a deep breath and ran a hand through her brown bangs.

Jon's mind wandered to Eve. His lips were still sore from their rendezvous last night in the park. He remembered the feel of her blue jeans and the soft cotton pressure of her chest against his.

Suddenly, Blue Wall's keylogger came to life. Joanna was typing.

He has an army. He teaches unwavering faith in his leadership. And President Drake is his puppet.

"Shit," muttered Jon.

Joanna had kept her views relatively private before, but now she was on the cusp of airing them publicly. Wyle didn't trust Joanna's editor to stop her. She was an experienced writer who usually demonstrated good judgment, and lately her editor had gotten lazy about checking her copy.

Joanna continued to type, and the article was only getting more controversial. Cursing again, Jon picked up his desk phone and dialed his boss.

The phone rang twice, followed by the sound of someone clearing mucus from his throat.

"Captain?" said Jon.

"Oh, hello, Agent Wyle," the old man said at last. "What's the good word?"

"We've got a problem. Watched #55078 is about to publish heresy in the *National News* blog."

The captain clicked his tongue. "Oh, that's a shame. Quite a shame indeed. You're certain the target plans to go through with it?"

"She looks pretty dead set, sir."

"How long do we have?"

"Her deadline is in less than an hour. What do you want to do, sir?"

"I suppose we have only one option," the captain returned. "Freeze her system and I'll order the arrest. Good work as usual, Agent Wyle."

Jon placed the handset gently on the desk and let out a deep sigh. He reopened the Blue Wall menu and selected an option marked *Disable Destination Computer*.

The webcam showed Joanna shaking her mouse vigorously. "C'mon, you goddamned machine!" she yelled at the PC. Futilely, she tried hitting various combinations of buttons on her keyboard. After a minute of further profanity, a tall man in a midnight blue uniform appeared in the background. He tapped on the green-carpeted wall at the entrance of Joanna's cubicle.

"Sorry, it's just my crap computer. It froze," said Joanna, turning to the visitor. When she saw it was a Guard she turned frantically back to the monitor and tried to shut it off. Her face went white when she couldn't.

Jon felt obligated to watch the executions of people on his Watched list. He didn't have to, and he knew some other Elites who didn't watch. But for Jon Wyle it didn't seem right not to see things through to the end. It lent a sense of completion to the whole affair.

Eve had been weird about this particular execution. Jon suspected it was because of the whole Joanna-Shaan dynamic. Eve had seen a lot of that romance. The fact that this execution meant the end of it seemed to bother her.

Jon smiled. She's so cute, he thought.

A highly made up woman in a pantsuit strolled onto the TV screen. Jon leaned back into his leather sofa and turned off the mute.

"Welcome to the lower basement of the Capitol Tower!" the TV lady exclaimed. "Next to be dropped this morning is Joanna Phelps. Phelps was a journalist with the *National News*, and she had some funny views about the Church. Turns out she was plotting to use the paper as a vehicle to spread heresy!"

The camera zoomed in on Joanna. She was standing on a black metal stand with a noose around her neck. There was a yellow circle around her feet.

Jon knew the routine. In a minute, the circle would open up and this particular Heretic could be scratched off his Watched list forever.

A rock 'n roll number started up. It took a few seconds for Jon to realize it was coming from his cellphone on the desk. He picked up the device and saw that it was Eve calling. Indecisively, he looked at the TV and then back at the phone. Finally he pressed the receive button on the handset. "Hey, baby, can I call you back in a minute?"

"Are you watching?" she asked.

He loved how breathy her voice sounded.

"Yeah."

"I turned it off," she said. "I don't think I can watch this time."

On the television a priest with a Bible read Joanna her last rites. She started bawling.

"Uh huh," said Jon. "Hey, they're about to start. I'll call you back."

He put the phone down, hunched forward and licked his chops.

The priest stepped away from Joanna. A soldier walked up and threw a black bag over her head. The camera zoomed out to the pretty TV announcer. She began to count from ten, and the numbers flashed on the screen as she said them. "Three, two, one…"

Jonathan Wyle smiled as the floor fell away and Joanna dropped.

Seven's eyes snapped open. He was sweating and breathing hard.

It was still dark and had begun to rain. The radio alarm clock on the bedside table glared 3:48 a.m. in crimson digits. Sighing, he realized it was too early to get up; he'd have to risk another nightmare.

For a few seconds he considered the shape under the covers next to him. He touched the girl's light brown skin, felt its warmth.

Talia groaned and rolled away.

He fell on his back and listened to the rush of rain hitting against the window. The room seemed to darken and then grow bright.

Jon stared vacantly out the window at the apartment building across the street. The rain was coming down in sheets, beating against the glass like it wanted to be let in. The Elite looked at his watch and took a first sip of the red wine he'd poured for two almost an hour ago.

A light but steady tap–different from the rain–stirred Jon from his trance on the sofa. He put the wine down on the coffee table and took to the foyer like a man on a mission.

Eve stood pathetically in the doorway with matted hair. Her gray coat was so drenched it looked black. She dabbed at her eyes. "I forgot my umbrella," she moaned.

He took her coat and left it dripping in the closet. Eyes to the floor, Eve trudged toward the couch and collapsed.

"Have some wine and dry off," Jon called from the kitchen. "We can head over to the restaurant in fifteen minutes."

Eve eyed the wine glasses on the coffee table. "I'm sorry I'm so late," she whimpered.

Jon brought in a plate of bread and dipping oil. He looked up and Eve was crying.

"Are you okay?"

"It's Shaan…he's dead," she managed.

"What?!" he exclaimed, sitting beside her.

She nodded sadly. "H-he took his motorcycle to the Luna Coast. And he just jumped it, right into the ocean! You know how high those cliffs are. I had no idea he was going to…I was monitoring him from my apartment, and I couldn't get to him in time. I…I couldn't…"

He put an arm around her. "Maybe we should stay in tonight. I'll order some food."

She nodded and ran a pale hand through her hair. She stared wide-eyed at the blank TV screen while he dialed. Occasionally she shook her head in disbelief.

Jon dropped the cell phone on the table and pulled her closer.

"I let myself get too close," she explained. "I saw so much of his life; it was almost like we were friends…or something. I mean, I guess 'friends' isn't a good word for it–we never really talked or anything. But I felt like I knew him."

Jon nodded. He'd heard of this happening to Elite Guard before. It was why he always tried to separate himself as much as possible from the people he watched.

"And yet I *didn't* know him," she continued. "I never determined one way or the other whether he was really a Heretic. And I definitely didn't know he was depressed enough to…to…"

"Right," he said, putting his arm around her. For a while they said nothing, and together looked out at the falling rain.

Jon exhaled. "You think it's because of what happened with Joanna?"

Eve leaned into her hands. "Well, he certainly didn't take that well," she answered. "But…you shouldn't blame yourself. You were just doing your job. She was a Heretic."

Jon said nothing. He was perplexed as to why Eve would think he would blame himself. He shrugged it off as stress on her part. Or maybe, he thought with a frown, she was on her period again. When had they last had sex?

"I don't know…I guess it's just that I'd been watching him so long, and he was really a likable guy. I mean, you know, for a suspected Heretic. After a while I kind of…I guess I kind of forgot why I was watching him in the first place."

Jon nodded. "Well, you know, not all Heretics act like Heretics."

"That's it exactly. And I think the other thing…"

"What?"

She shook her head. "No, it's dumb."

He squeezed her. "Tell me."

Eve bit her lip. "Well, Shaan and Joanna…they were in love, you know? It's just such a tragedy. I mean, what does that say? Why can't God let two people that make each other so happy be together? If those two weren't destined to be together, is anyone?"

He felt frozen under her gaze. Finally, he broke free and pulled her close. "I love you," he said, kissing her hard on the mouth. He began to peel off her wet shirt, revealing soft pink skin and an ivory bra.

CHAPTER TWENTY-SEVEN
Politics

The couple considered the open elevator door, but neither made a move.

"Maybe you should go up first," offered Talia.

"What, and you'll wait down here?" asked Seven. "For how long? Won't they wonder why we didn't run into each other if we arrive only minutes apart?"

"We'll brush it off as coincidence."

Seven rubbed his temples in exasperation. "Then we might as well just go up together, right? And call that a coincidence?"

"Maybe…"

"They probably won't even ask."

"Hmm…"

The polished silver doors began to slide shut. For the third time, Seven stopped it with his arm. The elevator opened on reflex and beeped in horror. "Please stand clear of the doors!" exclaimed an automated voice.

"You're right, this is stupid," said Talia. "Let's just go."

As they entered the chamber, Seven wondered why relationships had to be so complicated. That is, if this fling with Talia could be called a relationship. He supposed that, whatever this was, it was at least less painful on a minute-to-minute basis as whatever the hell had happened with Eve. He still wasn't sure how he felt about that, and the recent rush of happy memories had made that whole situation even more confusing. At least, before the operation, he could brush Eve off as a stranger, or at least a one-time date that didn't quite work out. But now when he thought of her he felt the crushing force of love gone cold. It wasn't that he wanted Eve back, but it was harder now to pretend nothing had happened. Even if he could distract himself during the day, he couldn't prevent his subconscious from conjuring images of the girl in his dreams.

"Welcome to the DAY Center!" burst the elevator. "Please say—"

"How sweet," remarked Talia. "Guess it's forgiven us for that unpleasantness earlier."

"Sorry, I didn't get that," said the elevator. "Let's try again. Please say a floor number between one and one-fifteen."

"One hundred and fifteen," Seven replied.

"One-fifteen," the elevator confirmed. "Is that right?"

"Uh huh."

"Sorry, I didn't get that. Let's try again. Do you want to go to floor one-fifteen?"

Seven winced. "Yes."

"Thank you," it said. "Are any other floors requested?"

"No."

"Thank you. Off we go!"

Seven wondered if it had been Danny's idea to have a talking elevator in the building. It was definitely his style to choose futuristic over practical. In fact, the whole architecture of the DAY Center was styled in that weirdly cold, city-of-the-future fashion. The Center was also one of the tallest skyscrapers in town. Danny, of course, chose the top two floors for his official presidential campaign center. An army of political whiz kids were on the 114th grinding out political messaging and other details. The 115th was reserved for Young and a small team of "senior advisers."

Through the glass side of the elevator, Seven and Talia watched the cityscape descend. Other than the demolished Capitol Tower and churches, the city was mostly intact. The sky was silver but visibility was good, and over the theater district Seven could see the dark blue ocean. There were no boats today.

POLITICS

There hadn't been for quite some time. While some people were trickling back into the city, the vast majority of evacuees had not. The protesters had swarmed the Capital only a week ago, but only a handful stayed. Seven figured there were at least two reasons for that: the first, more obvious reason was that it had only been a few weeks since the Enemy retreated, and it was difficult to say if it was really over. The other reason stemmed from former President Drake's evacuation policy. By preventing the evacuation of the Watched, he had effectively turned the Capital into a quarantine zone. He might as well have told the country that a horrible and highly contagious virus was sweeping through the city. In the end, people were left thinking it was dangerous to live in the Capital.

Seven couldn't help but notice Talia was standing almost three feet away from him. He felt the need to ask her if she was feeling okay.

"Fine," stated Talia. "You?"

"I didn't sleep well last night."

"Nightmare?"

He shrugged. "Something like that."

The elevator dinged. "Welcome to floor one-fifteen! Have a good day!"

They found Danny, Ana, and Shaan in the lobby, huddled around a sixty-inch flat-panel TV on the wall by the couches.

"What's with the sad faces?" asked Talia. "Someone die?"

"Where the hell have you been?" demanded Ana with a glance at her watch. "Haven't you seen the news?"

Seven and Talia glanced helplessly at each other.

"That bitch Susan Levi," continued Ana, "just won an endorsement for president from the Headmaster!"

"What?" gasped Seven.

Levi was on the TV screen with a big smile and two thumbs up. "I'm just so proud to accept this pledge from his holiness, the Headmaster," Levi said. "While disappointing that Interim President Randall chose to support my opponent, I must say it's a big boost knowing I've got the angels on *my* side. As president, I will return the favor, honoring our loving God by restoring normalcy and good morals to His wonderful nation."

"Angels?!" protested Talia. "Normalcy?! What is this girl smoking?"

"I believe Levi means square one," groaned Shaan. "If she becomes president, it's likely we're back where we started."

Seven exhaled. "And here I thought we had won."

"We never declared victory," said Young. "Getting rid of President Drake was a good first step, but we knew the man was just a puppet for the Headmaster. They might not say it out loud, but the Church has always had the real power in this country. The Headmaster probably supports Levi because he thinks he can control her. Judging by what I've seen of her, he probably can."

The doom and gloom soon devolved into jokes and unflattering anecdotes about Susan Levi. Young took Seven aside. "I need to talk to you privately," he said.

Seven followed the leader of the Underground down a wide hallway past a series of offices. Since their team hadn't expanded since the mission at Facility B, most of the rooms were dark and unused. At the very end of the hallway was a thick mahogany door leading to Danny's executive suite.

The heir to the DAY empire plunged into a high-backed red leather chair behind a heavy maple desk. Seven sat in a flimsy metal folding chair on the other side. For many seconds he marveled at the view through the floor-to-ceiling glass window behind Danny's back.

"Hey, over here," called Danny. He was holding up a small blue poster that read:

POLITICS

A NEW D.A.Y.

VOTE
DANIEL ALEXANDER YOUNG

"The boys downstairs just mocked this up for the campaign. What do you think?"

"Clever," Seven replied.

"You get the pun then?"

"I do."

He looked concerned. "Is it too obvious?"

Seven smiled as politely as he could. "No, it's great. Really."

Danny breathed a sigh of relief and let the sign fall on his desk. "So, how's the new apartment?" he asked, unclasping his fingers. "All moved in?"

"There wasn't exactly much to move in," said Seven. "It's great, except that I don't feel worthy of it. Sure you wouldn't rather make some money renting it out to a rich bastard who can actually pay?"

Young had put Seven up in a beach-side living complex called the Ravenwood Estates, one of several apartment buildings around the city owned by the Young family. Danny had generously offered rent-free pads to all the members of the team. Only Ana declined, because she already had a flat in the city. Seven expected a nice flat, but nothing could prepare him for the hardwood floors, fireplace, and whirlpool bath. He had a regular swinger's pad.

"Brilliant ocean view, right?"

Seven grinned. "You might say I've got a front-row seat if the Enemy ever attacks again."

"Maybe that's why I put you there," joked Young. "You're our lookout."

"Yeah, right. I'll be the one yelling, 'Look out!'"

Danny let loose one of his now trademark howling laughs. "In all seriousness, though," he said, "you should check out the Luna Coast when you get a moment. About a mile down the beach from you, there's some stairs up the cliff. Or at least, there were. Not sure what kind of damage there was during the battle." He considered the matter further. "On second thought, I probably wouldn't recommend Luna for a few months, give or take."

"That's okay, I'm not in any rush to see it," confessed Seven. The name Luna Coast had sent a shiver down his spine. He remembered it was the place where Jonathan Wyle had first struck up the nerve to ask Eve on a date. No need to stir up those memories again.

"And the car?" Danny asked. "Do you like it?"

It was a two-door midnight blue roadster. It was the kind of car that had features the driver couldn't legally take advantage of, such as a top speed of 190 miles per hour. Seven reflected that this was the kind of vehicle he had been looking for back when he was trying to escape the city. A minivan it most certainly was not.

"It will do," said Seven with a smile. "But you did want to talk business, right?"

Danny's eyes widened as if a light bulb just lit up over his head. "Right! I wanted to ask about your mission last night. Get anything juicy I can use in the debate?"

Seven bit his lip. "Right. I've been meaning to talk to you about that..."

"What is it? Something bad?"

"I aborted the mission."

Danny's eyes widened and he leaned back in his chair. "What? Why?"

"I don't think it's right for us to spy on Susan Levi. I think it's hypocritical for us to condemn the Guard and then use their tactics to take down our opponent. We're supposed to be better than them. You have to beat her in the election by showing what you'll bring to the country that she won't."

"A positive campaign," mused Young, stroking his chin thoughtfully.

"If you don't agree," said Seven, "I'm going to have to resign. I'm sorry, but I just can't…I just can't do that kind of thing anymore. I'll do anything for the Underground–spy, fight, and even kill, but only if we maintain some code of ethics."

Young nodded. "I understand, and I'm not upset. I hired you to keep us honest, and that's exactly what you're doing. The smear campaign is off." He picked up his new political poster again. "Anyway, all I really need is this fantastic pun on my initials, right?"

"Exactly." Seven smiled. This had gone better than expected. He realized he liked Young. He didn't always have the best ideas, but he was willing to listen to anyone who made a good argument.

"By the way," Seven said, "I have to say I was a little… intrigued by how close my new apartment is to Levi's beach house."

Young responded with a cat-like grin. "That may have had something to do with why I suggested that particular apartment."

Seven laughed. "You know, you're actually pretty crafty. You'll make a good president."

Young laughed, but his expression soon turned serious. He got up from his chair and looked out the floor-to-ceiling window. "I don't know. My dad certainly would have made a good president. I…I'm only doing this because it's the only way to make things right. If I don't do it we'll get Susan Levi or someone like her, and all my dad's work will be for nothing. But I'm really not that great. I'm already failing on ethics, it would appear."

"No, you're selling yourself short," replied Seven, standing up to leave. "You know how to organize people and get things done. If it weren't for you, Drake would still be president and stuffing tracking chips down our throats."

"He never had much confidence in me," Danny said to the glass.

"Who?"

Something thunked loudly into the window, hitting so hard that it left two long spider cracks in the glass behind Young's head. At first, Seven thought a bird had crashed into the building, but as his vision focused on the object he realized a black disk had latched onto the glass. A red light on board blinked at an ever-increasing rate.

Seven jumped to his feet. "Danny, get away from the window! Now!"

Young froze. Seven lunged forward, grabbed the leader of the Underground by the arm and yanked him forcefully toward the exit. The force of the exploding bomb shattered the glass wall instantly and sent everything in the vicinity flying. Seven shut the door to the office just as the billionaire's chair shot at them like a red cannonball. It crashed loudly on the other side.

The two of them sat coughing and heaving on the hallway carpet outside the office. Ana came running down the hallway. "What happened?!" she shouted.

Seven paused for a few seconds to ensure things had settled, and then peeked into the room. There was a gaping hole in the wall and Danny's desk was on fire. Soon water was falling from the sprinklers.

"Give me a gun," he told Ana. "Get me a sight, too."

Seven felt a rush of wind from the now open windows as he slid behind the burnt remains of Danny Young's desk. It was toppled on its side, providing him with cover in case someone was still out there. Wiping water from his face, he laid the jet black sniper rifle atop the table and peered through the telescope sight.

The bomb must have hit the window nearly straight on, he reasoned, or it wouldn't have stuck. That most likely put the assassin in the skyscraper directly across the street. Seven scanned the building window by window but found nothing unusual.

Who was trying to kill Young? The assassin seemed like a

professional, but he or she couldn't be an Elite Guard–those guys were supposed to be on the Underground's side now. Seven considered the possibility that an Elite had disagreed with the changes and was acting alone. If that was true, he hoped to God it wasn't Eve.

"Seven, get down!" screamed Ana from the hallway.

Dropping behind the desk, he heard something smash into the wall behind him, and the sound of crumbling drywall. He turned back and saw the red dot of a laser. The sniper had his location–but now Seven had the sniper's location as well. The crimson beam refracted through the sprinkler water, and Seven could trace it back to an open window in the other building. Now he knew where to shoot, but raising his head above the desk wasn't an option with the assassin's weapon still likely trained over the table. He needed a distraction.

"Ana," Seven called. "Fire your gun."

"Where?"

"It doesn't matter, as long as the sniper sees it."

The tall brunette lined up a shot and fired at one of the sprinklers. The spigot burst and water exploded everywhere.

As the assassin's red target cut to the source of the disturbance, Seven popped up and quickly targeted the killer between the cross-hairs. It was a man dressed in a slimly cut black robe, leaning over what looked like a dining room table. Seven squeezed the trigger and watched the sniper's bearded jaw fall open in surprise. The man knocked his rifle askew and staggered away from the table. Seven took a final shot and the target crumpled to the floor.

"It's over," he announced, standing up and turning back for the hall. "Where's Danny? Is he okay?"

Ana nodded. "Think he's in a bit of shock, but Shaan's taking care of him. How are you?"

Seven shrugged and walked past her. He found Danny crumpled over one of the sofas in the lobby. He was alive but looked completely spent. Talia stood off to the side, arms crossed and with a look of worry on her face. Shaan, leaning over Young with a first-aid kit, waved Seven away.

"He'll be fine," he said. "Just needs some rest."

"What a day," moaned Young.

"You're lucky to be alive," Ana said. "I knew this building was a bad idea–we're too exposed, dammit. If Seven wasn't–"

A ghastly scream seemed to come from all directions at once. A classic guitar riff and a 1-2-3-4 drum beat followed.

"Sorry, that's my cellphone," explained Danny, tweezing the device from his pocket. He stared confusedly at the screen.

"Who is it?" asked Seven.

"Unknown number."

Seven snatched the phone from Young's hands. He hit receive and put the device on speaker.

There was only hissing static on the other end.

"Hello?" said Seven.

"Drop out of the race," said a garbled mechanical voice. "Next time we won't miss."

"Who is this?"

The static cut out. Seven looked at the phone and read the words, *Call Ended*.

The media caught wind of the attack quickly. Within fifteen minutes a small mob of reporters had surrounded the front entrance of the DAY Tower. They demanded to know what was happening. They said it was the people's right to hear directly from Young about where the attack had come from and what it would mean for his campaign.

Seven's immediate instinct was to tell them all to go away. He reasoned that Young was in no condition to talk publicly so soon after his brush with death. They needed time to consider what had happened and how to respond to the threat. No one wanted to bow out of the race, but the threat had to be taken seriously. Young's response had to be considered carefully.

POLITICS

Danny Young insisted that they let the reporters in. All of them. They could have twenty minutes to take pictures of the damage and then there would be a press conference with questions and answers.

"Are you sure about this?" Seven asked.

"I'm not going to hide," said Young.

And so in came the cameras. They didn't allow anyone inside Young's exploded office, but allowed pictures through the broken doorway. Seven hustled the reporters downstairs into a large conference room. The media chattered excitedly while they waited.

"I wonder if he was hurt?" he overheard one reporter say.

"Who cares?" said another. "All I want to know is if he's going to drop out."

"Probably will," said a third man with a deep set scowl. "Danny has always had more passion for women than politics. Can't have sex when you're dead."

Disgusted, Seven stepped out of the room to look for Danny in the hallway. He was standing out there already in a fresh blue suit. Talia was by his side, wiping a smudge of soot off his forehead with a handkerchief. Seven noticed something different about him. Rather than the slicked-back look he was accustomed to, Danny had parted his blond hair on the side. He actually looked kind of presidential.

"You ready?" Seven asked.

Danny forced a smile. "Always."

The candidate walked inside to meet the press. Talia looked hungrily at Seven before following Danny inside.

Seven stayed in the hallway. His phone was ringing.

"Ana," he greeted. "What have you got?"

She was in the building across the street investigating the scene of the crime.

"He's fucking gone!" she shouted with exasperation.

Seven blinked. "What do you mean he's gone?"

"The guy you shot. He's not here. There's not even any blood."

"Are you sure you're in the right room?"

"I checked the entire floor, just in case you blew up any other windows during your firefight. This is the room, I'm sure of it. The guy either got up and walked out, or someone moved his corpse."

Seven was sure he'd hit his target. He'd seen the black-robed man slump over. He had to be dead.

"Okay, do a full search of the area. Maybe something will turn up that will help us. I'm going to check with Shaan, see if he's found anything."

"Roger," she said.

Seven pulled the phone from his ear and dialed the engineer.

"Bit busy right now," Shaan complained.

"Have you traced that call?"

There was an incomprehensible mumble on the other end.

"What?"

"No," he said. "I've never seen anything like this. I still have a trick or two up my sleeve but I'm not optimistic. Will let you know if anything changes."

"Okay, well if you–" A beep stopped Seven from finishing the sentence. He looked at the phone and saw that Shaan had hung up.

With a sigh, he stuck the device in his pocket and entered the press conference.

"Fear has run this nation for too long," Danny Young was telling the media. "Well, it's not going to run my campaign, and it's not going to run my presidency."

CHAPTER TWENTY-EIGHT
Alone, Together

The keys slipped from Seven's hand and bounced with a jingle on the gray carpet. As he reached down to retrieve it, he felt a dull ache in his shoulder and groaned.

This bout of clumsiness wasn't the worst thing to happen today, he supposed. But what was that saying about the straw and the donkey's back? Well, at least he was home.

"Home," Seven muttered to no one. As he looked into the apartment the term seemed a bit of a stretch. Sparkling clean walls, glowing wood floors; he knew it was better than he deserved. He spent the past few months moving from place to place with only a few changes in clothes. It was weird to be in a place all his own with no plans for the evening.

Seven trudged into the living room and fell into a maroon leather sofa. He glanced at the television remote control but felt too tired to reach for it. He thought about going to the bedroom, but the orange sunlight streaming through the window indicated it was too early to sleep.

It occurred to him that he hadn't had supper and that this would not be easy to remedy. There was nothing in the refrigerator, and just about all the restaurants this close to the shore were still closed. People were still too scared to come to the site of the Enemy attack.

He thought about calling Talia, but decided against it. It was difficult enough dealing with all the memories by himself. Talia was good at distracting him from the past, but the bliss never lasted. Afterward he would feel empty and confused. For Talia's sake, he would try to force a smile, but Talia always saw through it. In the end, she would look just as miserable as he.

Picking up a pen and pad of paper from the coffee table, he began to write:

My name is Seven

He stared at the sentence for a long time, mouthing the written words over and over.

But Seven couldn't control the dreams. Last night, after falling asleep with Talia, he had seen Eve. He had seen her and he had felt her and he had wanted her.

"Stop it!" he snapped.

There was no point even considering trying to see Eve again. He was too different from her now. They believed in different things. Even if they had been in love, even if they had been engaged to be married, it was based on something that was no longer true. They had no foundation to stand on anymore. There was nothing there.

This isn't fair to Talia, he realized. He should stop seeing her at once. Maybe he would be better off on his own.

He needed fresh air. Seven grabbed his key from the coffee table and headed for the beach.

Eve felt terribly alone as she pulled into the lighthouse parking lot on the Luna Coast. She was driving a rugged four-wheel-drive vehicle that the Guard had given her as a sort of parting, "sorry-we-almost-dropped-you" gift. It was a machine built for off-road driving, and after bouncing up the war-torn coast, Eve was glad to have it. The once romantic road winding alongside the shore now was full of potholes. Vultures circled overhead, presumably surveying the area for fallen soldiers.

Eve had stopped for only a few minutes at her apartment. She hadn't been there since the attack, and now the place stunk of sour milk and rotting vegetables. Her first orders of business were to clear most of the refrigerator into a trashcan and toss the filth down the building's garbage chute. Discovering the stench lingered when she returned to the flat, Eve tore open a few windows and hastily walked out the door.

At first she didn't know where to go. Most of the stores, bars, and restaurants had been shuttered since the attack. All her friends were in the Guard, and she'd lost track of their whereabouts after the attack. She couldn't even call them because she'd lost the cell phone with all their numbers. Upon her release from prison, the Guard issued her a new one–a heavy old clamshell built for fighting outdoors–but she hadn't yet gotten around to rebuilding her contact list.

Still without any clear direction, she jumped in the buggy and just went. Eve found herself driving to the place she had gone her whole life to clear her head–the ocean.

The tall white beacon on top of Luna Coast survived the attack but was not unscathed. Eve touched a particularly deep bullet hole on the concrete exterior. Stepping back she saw many similar pock marks.

"Poor thing," she whispered.

The sculpture garden had fared worse. One statue she remembered in particular–a somewhat abstract man made of black wire–was missing its head. She found crumbled granite and twisted iron scattered around the grounds.

Eve stepped through the uncut grass toward the cliff's edge. She tripped over something hard but caught her balance, saving herself from a spill. Squinting into the vegetation she saw that her foot had caught on a marble-white hand. She guessed that it had broken off of one of the statues, but she couldn't figure out why so many flies were buzzing about. All at once she understood. It was not stone but bone, and the insects were eating the bits of human flesh that remained. As calmly as she could manage, Eve lifted her foot and pushed on toward the water.

In prison she had found peace with a number of things, including what had seemed to be her imminent death. She had even accepted that she would never have her fiancé back—that he would always, from now on, be Seven. For so long she blamed Seven for this, but she realized now that it was the Guard who had taken her fiancé. There was no point in being mad at Seven.

She had to admit, though, that it had been far easier to accept they didn't have a future when Death waited just around the corner.

No, she scolded herself. It's time to let go and to move on. They had been engaged, but they were not engaged anymore. They weren't going to get married, and that was final. Jon, for all intents and purposes, was dead. She would have to be okay with that.

Eve shivered as she looked down into the waves crashing blue-and-white into the rocks many meters below. She fell to one knee and began to pray. The ocean breeze filled her nostrils and she felt reinvigorated, like a weight was lifting. She was still alone, but now remembered how strong she had been on her own before she met Jon. She knew that she could be strong again.

In the corner of her eye she saw a man walking up the shore, but he was too far away to make out any features.

A sudden beep turned Eve's attention to her pocket. Tugging the thick phone from her snug jeans required some force, but she managed to get the device open and to her ear by the third ring. "Hello?" she said.

"Agent Parker?" said a man on the other end of the line. Eve could tell instantly by his tone that he was with the Guard.

"I'm here."

"I've got President Randall holding on the other line," he said. "Do you have a couple minutes to accept his call?"

Seven watched a seagull swoop down from the sky and dive into the sand. It shot back up into the air with a clamshell in its mouth. The bird rose high over a jetty and dropped the shell to shatter on the black rocks. The gull dove back down to retrieve it.

He had to be careful to avoid stepping on shrapnel and other remains of the battle fought here with the Enemy. It was strange to be here after the fact. Seven had only seen video and heard reports. While the Underground sent many of its members into battle, he had stayed back and watched from afar. Seven had volunteered to fight but Danny Young wouldn't allow it. The chairman of the Underground said Seven was too important to risk his life as a foot soldier. He was needed for bigger things.

Seven later helped to fuel the riots in Loganville, but when the revolution grew more violent, Danny again asked him to hang back on the sidelines. He hid with Young and the others while the protesters swarmed into the Capital.

Once, Seven tried to organize a rescue mission to save Eve. After all, she had helped the Underground—while she had done plenty of wrong, he didn't think she deserved to die. Young agreed with him and promised to help her, but asked for patience. They would not let her be executed, he said, but there were bigger things to deal with first.

It was frustrating to sit around doing nothing. Seven was possessed by the deplorable memories of Jonathan Wyle. He remembered arresting and killing "Heretics" for things that barely seemed like crimes at all: skipping church, questioning the government, defending friends and family who did either of the above. He tried to remind himself of all the good he had done since awakening as Seven. Talia told him the same, but he could not be convinced. The guilt pressed against him like a heavy boulder on his shoulders.

Seven looked far up the shore to the cliffs of the Luna Coast, and considered the white lighthouse towering above it all. He remembered Danny's advice about a path that wound up the hill.

He wasn't sure why he had come to the spot where he had first fallen for Eve. Why did he want to risk reliving that moment?

He went ahead anyway.

It was slow going on the sand but after twenty minutes he

found the trail, or what was left of it anyway. Someone's army had blown the mountainside to bits, and a huge rock blocked any hope of ascent. With a sigh, Seven moved back toward the water and sat down in the sand. He sank his hand into the earth, dug out a large clump, and let the warm granules fall gently through his fingers.

Eve found it difficult to believe she was actually talking to the president. He was only the interim president, of course, but he was still the president. Eve had never talked to a president before. This was—

"Are you still there, Agent Parker?" Randall asked politely.

"Yes, sorry, Mr. President. I've just been a little out of it since I've been back I guess."

"I understand perfectly," he replied. "You've had a hard month."

Eve suddenly remembered she was talking to the man who saved her life. "And I thank you so much, sir, for your pardon."

"You don't need to thank me. We are in your debt for helping us obtain the vital information necessary to expose the Patriot ID program. Young told me everything, including how you saved a young man's life."

She couldn't recall saving any boy. "Excuse me?"

"Young's aide. He is called Seven, I believe."

"Oh, him," she said. She supposed Seven was a young man compared to Randall.

"Now Agent Parker, I must ask if you are still willing to serve your country."

She sat down on the cliff and picked up a stone from the ground. She rolled it around in her palm. "I suppose it depends on who in my country I would be serving."

"I want to reform the Elite Guard," Randall said. "But it's going to take more than flipping a switch, and it's likely going to take longer than my short interim presidency will allow. If we're going to keep this thing going after I step aside, we're going to need someone in charge who understands what must be done."

Eve wound up her arm like a softball pitcher and flung the rock underhand into the sea. "Young?" she asked.

"Yes, Young," Randall said. "But he's in danger. About an hour ago someone–a professional–tried to kill him."

Eve blinked a few times. "What's his condition?"

"A little shaken up, but otherwise in good health. That Seven fellow saved him just in time."

"So what's this have to do with me?"

"Young got lucky this time," said Randall. "In the future I don't want an assassin to even come close to lining up a shot on the future president. That's why I want to put you in charge of his security."

"Me? I'm not a bodyguard. Can't you just surround him with a squad of Guard?"

"Yes, and we will, but putting up walls of defense will only stop the symptoms of the problem. You won't be a bodyguard– perhaps I phrased the contours of this mission poorly. What I want you to do, Agent Parker, is to find out who was behind the assassination. You will report directly to me."

"What about the Headmaster? I can't see him approving."

Randall paused awkwardly. "The Headmaster doesn't know, and I don't plan to consult him. Since this matter ties to the election, and the Headmaster has made clear his support for Susan Levi, I don't wish to involve him. I'm sure you understand the need for discretion?"

"Believe me, Mr. President–after my last meeting with his holiness, I would rather keep him out of it."

Randall laughed curtly. "I thought as much."

"Do we have any leads?" she asked.

"I can't afford to engage in speculation at this time. But the best place to start is Young's political headquarters. I want you to survey the crime scene and talk to the witnesses."

Eve saw where this was heading. She was going to have to deal with Seven again.

CHAPTER TWENTY-NINE
Heretics & Saints

The target had not seemed especially dangerous. A young clergyman, Paul Roland, taught a Sunday School class at the Northeast Capital Church. A clever cover, but not enough to slip past the all-seeing eye of the Guard.

It was communications records that finally flushed out Roland as a possible Heretic. The phone company reported several calls a week by Roland to people on the Watched list. After running the evidence by a judge, the Guard obtained the authority necessary to add Roland to the Watched list. The classification allowed the government to assign an Elite to the case.

Agent Jonathan Wyle got the job. He had another Watched on his plate already—a young reporter named Joanna—but it wasn't unusual these days for Elites to have more than one target. Things were moving slowly with the Joanna case anyway, and Wyle was glad for the change of pace.

Jon watched Roland off and on for about two weeks from an unmarked black van parked about a block from Roland's church. The Elite hung out for hours each day in the vehicle's roomy back cabin, spending most of his time staring at a laptop computer. He also had a small TV, but Wyle found it distracting and kept it turned off. A small coffee machine helped keep him awake.

Roland had a relatively new office computer with the latest version of Blue Wall installed, so it was cake for Agent Wyle to turn the workstation into a live television camera. Jon didn't even have to touch Roland's PC to commandeer its webcam and microphone.

The A/V feed flowed straight to the Guard's cloud network, which was accessible through Wyle's laptop and mobile devices.

A simple scan of Roland's web browser history alerted Jon to a violent plot. Roland was reading information about building explosives and comparing prices at online gun stores. The young priest had also entered a chat on a suspicious discussion group called <Fink_Net>. Jon hadn't personally heard of the network before, but he recognized the name Fink—a reference to a religious cult leader from the days of the Great War. A quick call to HQ revealed that the network was under investigation for possible ties to the Underground.

All of this was suspicious, but in the eyes of the law it wasn't enough to get a conviction. Rather, it was just another compelling reason to keep Roland on the Watched list.

Jon got his break on the Friday of his second week watching Roland. He had been thinking about his mission-turned-pizza-date with Eve when an unmarked truck pulled up to the church. A dusty-haired man in a brown uniform popped out holding a large cardboard box. None of this would have been particularly suspicious except that the guy's uniform didn't match any of the major national package carriers. After some deliberation, Wyle got out of the van and shadowed the courier through the tall wooden doors of the church.

Inside, the deliveryman approached a woman carrying a stack of books and asked for Roland. She pointed him down a corridor where all of this church's priests kept their offices. Wyle followed him part of the way there but stopped at a water fountain a few doors down from Roland's office.

Out of the corner of his eye, Jon watched Roland's door swing open. The priest greeted the courier. He took the package without signing and retreated into his room. Jon drank from the fountain and let the deliveryman pass. Then he followed him back to the main entrance.

A few steps from the courier's truck, Jon cleared his throat. "Excuse me, sir?"

The man turned halfway and looked at him with a sideways glance. Jon saw the name *Bob* written in cursive on his brown shirt. "Hi, Bob. Quick question for you. I was just a little curious which shipping company you're with? I don't recognize your uniform."

The courier smiled slightly. "DAY Shipping."

"Weird," said Wyle, staring him in the eyes. "I thought they wore blue."

"New uniforms," Bob returned with a menacing look.

"They got rid of the DAY logo, too, huh?"

"Glad to report you've got 20/20 vision," the man returned. "Look, man, I've got to run. I'm on the clock."

Jon reached into his jacket and pulled out a badge. "I'd rather that you wait here for a few minutes while I make a call."

That's when Bob bolted. He was a big man but got off to a quick start. Jon chased him for about a block before finally drawing a weapon and firing straight into the air. Cursing, Bob slowed up and raised his hands.

Wyle slapped a pair of cuffs on the courier's wrists. Then he dialed HQ and asked the Guard to send a couple officers and a car. Lowering the cell phone, Jon was surprised to see he had an unread message from Eve. He clicked it open and read:

Thanks for last night. Hope we cross paths again soon.

Jon felt his heart beating. He could think of nothing else until the police car pulled up to collect the package man. The whole thing took about ten minutes. Jon explained the situation to one Guard as another pushed Bob's head into the car.

It suddenly occurred to Jon that he should have immediately gone back to check on Roland and, more specifically, what was in the package.

He raced back to the church and moved straight to Roland's office. When the priest didn't respond to knocking, Wyle kicked the door open and entered with gun drawn.

The place was deserted. The box was on Roland's computer desk, opened and empty.

Jon flew out of the room. He asked a receptionist at the entrance if she had seen Roland.

"I'm surprised you didn't see him on your way in. He just left, but if you rush you might–"

The Elite was outside before she could finish. Immediately he saw Roland near the street several yards from the church. He was opening the door to a taxi.

The cab drove off just as Wyle was upon it. Gritting his teeth, the Elite raised his hand to hail his own transportation. After two passed him by, Wyle stepped in front of a red sports car and waved his badge at the driver. "Guard!" he shouted. "Step out of your vehicle!"

The driver, a slightly balding man with a paunch belly, shook his head pleadingly. Jon wrenched opened the door and tossed the middle-aged loser out onto the asphalt. A few seconds later he was speeding after Roland's taxi.

A blond woman walking down the sidewalk caught Jon's attention, and for a second he thought it might be Eve. But when she turned he saw that the woman looked nothing like her, and in fact was probably twenty years older at least.

Jon shook his head and looked back to the road. The cab was gone.

"Shit!" he yelled. He looked around desperately to gain his bearings and suddenly realized he was at the monorail station. Wyle parked the car in the middle of the street and got out. Ignoring the blaring horns and profanity of the other people on the street, Wyle located the taxi on the side of the road, but Roland was already gone.

"Your passenger, the priest," Jon screamed at the taxi driver. "Did he go in the station?"

The taxi driver looked flabbergasted but opted not to test the Elite's patience. "Yes, sir, he–"

And Wyle was off again. He had just begun wading through

the rush hour crowd when a gun went off. A woman next to Jon screamed and fell over. The rest of the commuters ran screaming in all directions. The clearing crowd left Paul Roland in plain sight, wielding a pistol and climbing the escalator to the Loganville train platform two steps at a time.

The escalator screeched to a halt before Jon was halfway up the steps. The force of the stop knocked Jon back but he managed to hang on to the railing. Gritting his teeth, he pulled himself to his feet and pumped his legs harder to catch up. At the top of the steps there was another bang and Jon heard a bullet whistle past his ear.

The whole world seemed to stop. Jon could see Eve's mysteriously alluring gaze. He was suddenly struck by the thought that he might not live to see her again.

Another shot woke him from his momentary delirium. Wyle fell into a roll and ducked behind a heavy brown trash can. They made the things strong enough to withstand a bomb blast, so he knew he'd be safe.

Things went dead quiet. Agent Wyle leaned over slightly to scope out his surroundings. They were parked on a narrow strip, with the rail on Jon's left and a dirty concrete wall on his right. A black sign hanging down from the ceiling displayed 6:11 p.m. in digital yellow.

Jon realized he had the Heretic trapped. The only way Roland could get off the platform was to make a dash back to the escalators behind Jon. There was in fact an elevator on Roland's side, but by now the Guard should have locked it.

Roland popped out from another armored trash can about three benches down the strip. Jon ducked back into cover just as the first shot was fired. Smiling, he pulled a kiwi-sized ball from a container in his belt, and in one quick motion lobbed it down the platform. The capsule bounced and skidded across the floor before bursting into a cloud of smoke. Taking a deep breath and holding it, Jon jumped to his feet and bolted toward the sound of choking coughs.

Roland, teary-eyed and wheezing, fired his gun but missed by a mile. Jon was on him in an instant. The Elite kicked the weapon out of the Heretic's hands and slammed a fist into his stomach. Lungs emptied, Roland automatically tried to suck in as much air as he could. Breathing smoke instead of oxygen, the target lost balance and fell unconscious onto the scuffed tile floor.

Agent Wyle shackled the Heretic's wrists and left him lying on the floor.

Breathing a sigh of relief, Jon strolled down the platform. Through the tunnel he could see a pink and orange sky.

Maybe, Jon thought, Eve might like to join him for a walk in the city park. He picked up his mobile and dialed.

"Hello?" said Eve.

"It's Jon," he said. "I need to see you."

The silence on the other end made his heart leap.

"Where?" she said finally.

Jon clicked the phone and turned back to deal with Paul Roland. To his surprise, he saw a man in a black robe leaning over the unconscious body.

"Who the hell are you?" Jon asked.

The stranger straightened up and a half-smile surfaced on his face. "I've been sent for Roland," he said.

"Excuse me? Who sent you?"

He was tan and his head was shaved bald. "This one here is a priest who has violated the rules of the Church. This one is a disgrace and he must be dealt with differently than the others. This one must come with me."

Jon was perplexed. "Are you with the Church?"

The stranger's brown eyes were empty. "I am with God."

Jon chuckled. "Can I see some ID?"

Just then, the Elite's phone rang. He picked it up and saw that it was the captain of his division.

"Sir?" asked Jon. "I was just about to call in. There's some wacko here who…"

"Walk away, Agent Wyle," the captain said. "This is bigger

than you or me. Walk away now and don't speak about this to anyone."

"But who—?"

"That was an *order*, Agent Wyle," his superior officer said. "When the Saints go marching in, it's best you don't ask any questions."

Jon was still thinking about the encounter as he waited for Eve by the rusted orange gates of the city park. He forgot about it the instant he saw her. As she approached, Jon pointed up at the two marble hawks perched on either side of the entrance.

"You know why they made them so big?" Jon asked when she approached.

"Why?"

"Originally they ordered something smaller, but the cameras were so bulky back then that they couldn't get them to fit. The sculptor had to start from scratch."

They looked together into one of the hawk's beaks and found a reflective black disc that was the lens of the CCTV device. "Think someone's watching us right now?" asked Eve.

Before Jon could respond, she kissed him hard on the mouth, letting her tongue dip momentarily into his mouth. When they finally pulled apart Eve winked at the hawk and said, "That one's for free."

Eve's hand fell into his and he led her through the gate. At this hour there were more people leaving than entering, but it was summer and the sun wouldn't set for at least another hour.

Eve peered into a dark cluster of evergreen trees. "So, aren't you even a little worried about getting mugged?"

"We're Elite Guard," Jon smirked. "I'd like to see someone try."

She squeezed his hand and they continued on.

"So how was your day?" she asked. "Tell me *everything*."

He thought about telling her about the mysterious man in black, but remembering the captain's warning, decided against it. "I nearly got myself killed making an arrest, no thanks to you," he said instead.

She tilted her head in question. "No thanks to *me?*"

"Yeah…" He looked at her but couldn't hold the gaze into her eyes for very long. "I couldn't stop thinking about you."

"You're such a cheese ball," she laughed, punching him lightly in the arm.

He gasped. "I'm serious! I…I guess I just get a little corny when I'm around such beauty."

There was a look in her eye that briefly made him fear for his life.

"What?" he asked nervously.

Eve pulled him off the paved trail and led him down a small hill. Jon tugged back and she fell into his arms. After a breathless minute they disappeared into the tall grass.

CHAPTER THIRTY
Evidence

Seven woke to the staccato buzz of his brand new cell phone. Keeping his head planted firmly in the pillow he reached blindly to the side table. After many seconds his fingers located the device.

"What is it, Danny?" he asked groggily.

"Sorry to call so early," Young apologized with alarm in his voice. "But I need you over here right away."

Seven bolted upward. "What's wrong? Another attack?"

Talia, draped topless over the other side of the bed, opened her eyes briefly.

"Everything is fine," Danny said. "But there's...a new development. I can't explain over the phone. Just come as soon as you can."

"Okay, I'll–"

The phone beeped.

"–be right over."

Seven looked at the screen and saw that it was 5:27 a.m.

"What is it?" Talia yawned.

He stroked her soft black hair and whispered, "Go back to sleep."

Talia's heavy eyelids fell slowly shut, and in less than a minute her breathing grew slow and measured. Carefully, Seven lifted himself from the bed.

Eve felt a lump in her throat as the door opened.

"Danny, you really need to do something about that elevator," Seven grumbled as he stepped inside. "The stupid thing almost just called..."

His eyes connected with hers.

"...the Guard," he finished.

She tried to compose herself. "Hi, Seven."

Danny Young, standing by her side, waved his right hand as if to conjure up something appropriate to say.

They looked at him.

"Um," said Danny, "surprise?"

Eve grimaced.

"What is *she* doing here?" Seven sneered. "Why didn't you tell me on the phone?"

Danny opened his arms helplessly. "I didn't think you would come if I had."

Seven's laugh was icy. "You're right!"

Eve brushed Danny aside and engaged Seven's attention. "Look, I don't like it either. But the president ordered me to come. I'm just here to find out who tried to kill Young."

His eyebrows shot up. "What? You mean it wasn't you? I guess I forgot again which side you were on."

Cackling, Danny pointed at Seven. "Hey, maybe you've got the amnesia chip back in your head!"

Eve shot the leader of the Underground a look that she hoped conveyed deadly revulsion. She noticed Seven joining her in the expression.

Danny held up his hands and whistled. "Well then, I'm going to let you two kids work things out. In the meantime, I'm going downstairs for some coffee. Those political whiz kids just installed a cappuccino machine. You've got to try it. It's *out of this world!*"

The presidential candidate began to saunter out of the room, but turned back at the last minute. "Oh, I almost forgot, we're having a dinner kind of thing tonight for V-H Day. Turkey, champagne, the works. It would be an absolute blast if you could make it, Eve."

Seven stared helplessly. Finally he made out, "It's V-H Day?"

Eve couldn't believe it either, but for a different reason entirely. "You...*celebrate* Victory Over Heretics Day?"

"Of course!" Young shot back with an enigmatic grin. "I'll explain at dinner. Right now I need to get my coffee on. Laters, players."

And like that, he was gone, leaving the ex-lovers alone to consider each other.

"Is anyone else here?" Seven asked without any attempt to hide the hope in his voice. "Shaan, maybe?"

Eve shook her head. "Not unless he's hiding."

Seven glanced out the window.

This, realized Eve, was going to be exactly as difficult as she expected.

"How's your arm?"

"Better. A little sore sometimes."

The silence returned.

"Look…Seven…what I did to you at Facility B, I–"

"Whatever–I guess the chip had to come out of my head sometime. Sure I would have appreciated an approach that felt a little less like a stab in the back, but–"

"I'm sorry. I really am."

Seven nodded.

"Do you remember…anything?" Eve asked.

He looked away. "Certain things. Some good, some bad. It feels…almost like I'm watching a movie, but in first person."

She nodded slowly.

"I did a lot of awful things," he said. "I remember killing some people and making others wish they were dead."

She laid a hand on his shoulder. "You're a different person now."

He jerked away. "Are you?"

"I don't know," she said, her hand lowering slowly back to her side. "Prison was hard. I don't mean the living situation, though that wasn't exactly sunshine and lollipops, either. It was more the realization that after all the service I had done for the country, this was how they repaid me. The minute I did anything for myself–because I thought it was right–they put me on death row. Do you know how hard I worked to get where I was?"

"I remember."

"Things have gone too far," said Eve. "I still believe there's a need for the Guard to protect and serve the people. But at some point we took a wrong turn and became more concerned with conformity than justice. Hell, they wanted to have a computer doing our jobs. A cold machine that could only understand two functions: Patriot and Heretic." She held out her hands. "I wasn't going to come back to the Elite Guard. I didn't want to come back. But Randall promised me change."

Seven nodded as if he understood.

"Well, if you will have me, I want to be part of that. I know it's going to be hard, but I really hope we can put aside our past, and…and…"

"Create a better future?"

She had to smile. "Yeah, that's what I was going to say. I guess I was searching for something that didn't sound so corny."

He chuckled and stepped thoughtfully toward the window. "So have you already seen Young's office?"

Seven couldn't help but notice the small of Eve's back peeking under the bottom of her shirt as she bent to sift through a pile of rubble. The room was still black and covered with broken glass and other shrapnel.

"Aha," said Eve, lifting a piece of gun metal from the floor. "A fragment of the bomb. And I think it's one of our ours."

He couldn't say he was surprised. "Someone in the Guard did this?"

"Or possibly someone who *was* in the Guard and still has access to our supplies," she replied. "I'm going to see if I can find any more shards and then take them back to the lab to run a few tests. We keep pretty careful track of all our weapons. With some luck we might be able to find out who last had possession of this one. You didn't happen to get a look at the killer, did you?"

Seven nodded. "Briefly. Tall man with a beard, wearing something like a black robe. He's dead, but someone got to the body before we could."

"A robe?" she asked. "Doesn't sound like standard-issue equipment for the Guard."

"No," said Seven. And then, suddenly, everything clicked. He had seen someone like this before, in a dream. Or—more accurately—a memory.

Eve seemed to read the realization in his face. "What is it?"

"I remember meeting someone like him before, a long time ago, when I was still working with the Elites," he said. "I was told not to ask any questions. He was called something I'd never heard before—a Saint, I think."

Eve crinkled her eyebrows. "A Saint?"

"The one I encountered told me he worked for God. Any of this ring a bell?"

Eve shook her head. "None of it."

"There's more," Seven said. "I'm not entirely sure, but the man in my dream—the Saint—I think he looked familiar."

"What do you mean?"

"Those empty brown eyes…Eve, I think it may have been your old partner."

She gasped. "Rodriguez?"

He nodded. Seven saw the face of Rodriguez as clear as day.

"I'll see if I can find anything out," Eve said. "If Rodriguez was working for some secret religious clan, well, it certainly would explain a few things."

"I'll see if Danny's heard of them," said Seven, turning to the door.

"Wait!" Eve called after him. When he turned back she was holding a diamond ring in the palm of her hand.

The memories flooded back. Seven remembered the way Eve's cheeks glowed when she slipped it on her finger for the first time.

"I cried when they took this from me in prison," she said. "But when I got it back, I couldn't bring myself to wear it. I guess I realized it didn't belong to me anymore. Not really."

She opened Seven's palm and closed his fingers over the ring. "I think you should have it back. One day…one day you'll fall in love again."

Seven felt a vibration in his pants; Talia was calling him. He placed the ring carefully in his jeans pocket. "I should take this," he said.

Eve smiled and turned back to the rubble.

He took the phone into the hallway.

"Where did you go?" Talia demanded.

"I had to come into the office," he said quietly.

"Why?"

Seven wasn't sure how to explain. "Eve's here."

"Excuse me?"

"It's a long story. Randall wants her to help protect Danny."

"And like, you're just going to trust her? After what she did to you?"

"We talked about it."

"Oh did you?"

"C'mon, Tal," he said. "I mean, she is the Elite's best."

"Are you seriously defending that bitch right now?" seethed Talia. "You know, when you and I started…Like, I know we said it wouldn't be serious. But…I want you to be honest with me. Do you still have feelings for her?"

Seven sought the ceiling for the answer.

"It's still 'complicated,' isn't it? That's what you told me back in Loganville and I guess it's even truer now."

"Talia, I–"

"Maybe we should let things cool off for a little while," she snapped, "until you figure out what you want."

The phone beeped.

CHAPTER THIRTY-ONE
V-H Day

This was weird, thought Eve. She was sitting at a mahogany dining table in a room that looked like it belonged in a hunting lodge somewhere deep in the mountains. But this was only another floor of the extensive DAY Center. From the maple-wood paneling to the sullen moose head hanging over their heads, Eve was beginning to think Danny Young's father had been something of an eccentric.

Stranger still was the occasion for the dinner. Eve had come here to celebrate Victory Over Heretics Day…with the Underground. She could think of several reasons why that was wrong, not the least of which being that she hadn't exactly been the rebels' strongest ally. Why, if Interim President Randall hadn't ordered her to help Danny Young and his crew, she probably would never have even seen them again. And yet, here they were like a family, passing dishes around for a holiday feast.

It wasn't all smiles, of course. Talia, positioned directly across from her, had been giving Eve the evil eye since she sat down. Talia had never been very kind, but today something in her body language had intensified. Eve couldn't figure out why. After all, Talia had known about Seven and Eve's history since before the mission at Facility B. The only thing that had changed was that Eve had given her engagement ring back to Seven. If anything, thought Eve, Talia should be nicer to her now.

She noticed Seven looking sharp in a black dress shirt. She hadn't seen him in something so clean since he went by another name. She smiled a polite kind of smile at him, but Talia–sitting next to him–immediately intervened.

"Like, who invited you anyway?"

"Danny did," Eve replied.

"Messed up."

"Honestly? I agree."

Talia rolled her eyes. "You *would* agree."

Eve decided to let the girl have the last word. Instead, she turned left and tried small talk with Ana. It was a challenge to get her attention; the slender brunette appeared more interested in giggling at Danny's jokes.

"Crazy how empty the city is," Eve tried.

"I know," Ana replied. "I would just kill to go dancing, but I haven't seen any clubs open, and even if they were they'd probably be dead, you know?"

Eve wasn't much of a dancer. "I suppose that would be true," she replied.

Ana turned closer and in a low voice said, "By the way, I wanted to apologize."

At first, Eve thought the other woman was joking. "What?"

The brunette sighed. "I know I was an absolute bitch to you last month."

It was true, but Eve had already heard the reason. Ana had been upset, rightfully so, over the Guard killing her boyfriend at the blockade. "No, you explained it to me before, and I completely understood," Eve said. "Anyway, I wasn't exactly in the best frame of mind either."

Ana shot a furtive glance at Seven, who was engaged in conversation with Danny. "The truth is, I don't know how you can stand it," she said. "You think you know somebody and then they just go and change on you. If you ever want to talk…"

Eve smiled warmly. "Thanks, Ana. I really appreciate that."

Shaan entered the room with a large silver dish and a golden-brown turkey. He was wearing a white chef's hat that was stained in multiple spots. Gently, he let the bird down in the empty spot between Eve and Talia and sat down at that end of the table. The turkey looked glorious–juicy with a crispy skin slathered in butter. Eve knew from her history watching the man that he was a gourmet chef in the kitchen. She'd always meant to investigate where he learned how to cook, but never got around to it. She was salivating at the chance to finally eat one of his creations.

Eve couldn't help but notice a certain sadness in Shaan's demeanor. It was in his eyes, mostly. She wondered why.

A light ding brought Eve's attention instinctively to the head of the table where Danny Young was positioned. He was holding a glass of red wine in one hand and a spoon in the other. "I'd like to offer a toast," he announced. "Thank you all for coming. You five are the team that exposed Patriot ID and toppled the presidency of William T. Drake. Thanks to all of you, this country has a future again. And that's what I would like to toast–the *future*."

They held their glasses high. "To the future!"

Ana added, "Let's not forget that Danny has his first big debate tomorrow with one Susan Levi. Danny, I think it's safe to say we all wish you the best of luck knocking that bitch down a few pegs."

"I'll cheers to that!" burst Seven.

They clinked glasses and then Shaan stood to carve the turkey. Eve found herself hypnotized by the pieces of meat falling delicately onto the serving plate.

The excitement on Eve's face as she thrust her plate forward amused Seven. A vegetarian she clearly was not. As he looked around the table, Seven realized he was surrounded by friends. He didn't have any when he woke in the forest so many weeks ago, but now here he was breaking bread with five people he actually trusted. Well, four. Four and a half, maybe. Eve was in trial mode.

Okay, so he wasn't on the best terms with everyone, Talia being the main example. But she still sat next to him, didn't she? That broken friendship didn't seem beyond repair.

He worried about Shaan, who was finally sitting down to his own meal. Seven wondered how the man would act toward him if he knew the truth about Seven's past, if he knew that Jonathan Wyle had actually smiled when Joanna was dropped. Seven felt the memory tear into him every time he looked at Shaan. He knew he had to tell him, but it never seemed like the right time. Then again, would it ever feel like the right time?

He also hadn't ever told Shaan that he was sleeping with his little sister. But Seven listed that little truth somewhat lower among his priorities.

"So can somebody please explain why the Underground celebrates this holiday?" asked Eve. "You all do realize that V-H Day celebrates the day the government defeated the Heretics in the Great War, right?"

Seven remembered the last V-H Day. He was still Wyle and had taken Eve out for dinner. They celebrated it because everyone did. Not once did he remember the two of them talking about what the day actually meant. Details like that had never seemed all too relevant when they were out together.

Danny laughed. "The reason for celebrating is simple really. I mean, you're absolutely right. Today is a day celebrating the loss of religious freedom in this country, the day the government and the Church decreed once and for all that the people would place their allegiance and faith exclusively in them and no one else. V-H Day celebrates the day that *fear* won."

Eve laughed. "You're pretty much doing the opposite of answering my question."

"But I am answering it!" he countered. "Think of it this way. How do you beat fear? Do you run away? No, that's what fear is supposed to make you do. To defeat fear, you have to confront it head on. More than that, you've got to laugh in its face!"

Eve half-smiled. "So, what you're saying is, you celebrate V-H Day…ironically?"

He pointed at her excitedly. "That's exactly it!"

"Huh," she said, munching thoughtfully on a piece of broccoli rabe. "You rebels sure are a sarcastic bunch. Well, happy V-H Day I guess."

Danny grinned and lifted his glass. "Happy V-H Day!"

Seven joined him and downed the rest of his wine. Seconds later, his glass was full again.

He stole a glance at Eve and saw her laughing merrily to some joke he'd apparently missed. He had to fight his eyes from falling to the curves that seemed ready to burst from her navy blue blouse.

Eve saw him looking.

He turned away fast, cursing the wine.

The alcohol continued to flow after dinner, and despite her best excuses Eve was unable to avoid her cup being refilled time and time again. She was having trouble remembering when precisely they had moved from the dining room to another chamber full of books and couches. No one was sitting. Eve was sipping her wine when, unprovoked, Shaan came up to her and pointed a finger in her face.

"You killed her!"

She thought she knew who he was talking about but asked anyway.

"Joanna," he growled.

"God, Shaan," she said. "No, I didn't."

He kept pointing at her but seemed to be at a loss for words. Eve wondered how many drinks he'd had. She wondered how many drinks *she* had had.

"You were my Watched," she tried to explain, "but Joanna was watched by…someone else. I remember Joanna, yes, but I never had anything to do with her arrest."

Shaan looked unconvinced. "You know, when it happened, when she was dropped, I really did think about killing myself. She was my…I was going to propose…We would have been…"

"I'm so sorry," Eve said. "I wish I could have stopped it, but I didn't have the power. We were all under orders. And the agent who did watch Joanna…well, he's dead now."

"Dead?" Shaan appeared confused. "How?"

"He, uh…" she struggled.

"His name was Jonathan Wyle."

Eve turned to see Seven approaching.

"Joanna was my Watched," he confessed, "and I reported her as a Heretic."

Shaan stared at him cold and hard. "Don't fuck with me, Seven," he said.

Eve spoke up. "It was a long time ago. He was a different person."

Shaan ignored her. He looked like a bull upon noticing the man with the red flag.

"I'm sorry, Shaan," said Seven. "I didn't know until I got my memory back. I've wanted to tell you for a long time now, but was worried how you'd respond."

"You were *worried* how I would respond?" Shaan yelled with incredible volume. "You killed the woman I loved and you were worried how I would *respond?* Do you have any idea what it's like to be Watched, what it's like knowing your emails are being read and your phone is being tapped? Every time you open your mouth, you think, what if this is the time I slip up and say something I shouldn't? What if I lose control and all the anger comes bubbling out? Jo… she just had *one* bad day. One bad day and you had her dropped!"

All at once, Eve got why so many had protested alongside the Underground. She had been baffled before because these were the same people who had seemed to accept government surveillance and who went to church every week and who even tipped off the Guard to Heretic activity. The nation had appeared stable and patriotic. Now Eve understood that anger had festered below the surface, and just because the people played by the rules didn't mean they liked the rules. They were all prisoners, and Danny Young was showing them the way out.

Talia jumped between Seven and Shaan and held her brother by the shoulders. "Shaan, calm down. He's not Jonathan Wyle. This is *Seven*."

Shaan shook his head. "He looks like Wyle. He talks like Wyle. And he has the memories of Wyle."

"But he's Seven."

He looked at his sister suspiciously. "You knew about this, didn't you? He *told* you."

"No, I..." she started, but then she hung her head. "Yes, he told me."

Shaan gesticulated wildly at the party. "I guess all of you knew, right?"

"I didn't know," mumbled Ana. But Shaan didn't seem to hear her.

"Fantastic, just fantastic," he grumbled. He turned away and stepped heavily to the door.

Seven called after him, "Shaan, wait!"

He kept going. Bitterly, the broken man called back, "Happy V-H Day!"

Seven felt miserable. The confession had gone just as poorly as anticipated. Maybe worse. He hadn't expected it would come out that he had confided in Talia. But he had to tell someone and she was always so good at listening.

"What the fuck?" Talia screamed in his ear.

He turned. "Huh?"

"You chose *tonight* to tell him? Couldn't you see how miserable he was all night?"

He hadn't noticed.

She shook her head. "Shaan was going to propose to Joanna on V-H Day. During the fireworks."

"I…I didn't know."

Eve looked uncomfortable. "I should probably go," she said.

Talia laughed viciously. "Uh, yes please?"

Eve grimaced. "Tell Danny for me that I wish him good luck at the debate tomorrow. I'll have a team in place to make sure the event is secure. But we can talk more about it tomorrow."

Seven wondered why Eve couldn't tell Young herself. He looked around the room and realized that Danny had already stepped out. In fact, so had Ana. With great horror, Seven realized that he was about to be left alone with Talia.

"Bye, Seven," said Eve with genuine empathy. She tried to make eye contact with Talia but was rebuked. The younger woman kept her eyes trained on Seven until Eve had gone.

"It's not really the thing with Shaan that you're mad at me for, is it?" he asked cautiously.

"Wow, like you should really open a detective agency." She held her hands up to mime the sign on the door. "Seven No-Last-Name, Private Eye."

"Tal…"

"Stop calling me that. I hate it! I don't call you Sev."

He was completely stymied. He didn't see any other way out but to apologize.

"You don't even know what you're sorry for," she replied sourly.

"No, I do know. I haven't been fair to you since I got my memory back. It's been very confusing for me. It was easy before because I didn't really remember Eve. Or what she had meant to me."

Talia sighed. "Do you love her?"

He had been asking himself the question for days. "Yes," he said finally. "I don't want to, but…"

He trailed off when he saw tears in her eyes. He hadn't expected Talia to cry. She was usually so tough, but that hard exterior seemed to have completely eroded. "I guess the procedure worked after all, huh?" she whimpered. "Eve's plan worked."

"No," he said. "You have to understand…The thing is I realize now that I loved her as Seven even before I got my memories back. When I met her for the first time as Seven, I fell for her right away. When I found out she was with the Guard, I thought I hated her and I thought I could make a clean break. But now I realize I just hated myself for still wanting her, even though she was on the other side."

Gently, he lifted Talia's chin. "And then you came along and you seemed to understand me. I was drowning and you were there to pull me out. I needed a friend and you were a great one. When things went beyond friendship, I felt like everything was falling into place. I felt like I could put that chapter with Eve firmly in the past. But I can't. Now every time I see Eve I think of how we used to be."

Talia nodded glumly and with a sniffle sat down on one of the sofas. Seven sat next to her and placed his arm around her shoulder.

"You're my best friend, Talia," he said. "I should have told you all of this before. I'm really sorry."

She smiled a little. "Some friend I've been. I knew you were still messed up about Eve, but I still took advantage of you."

Her sudden maturity surprised him.

"I didn't mind," he said.

She snickered.

They sat there for a while saying nothing.

"So do you think she's really changed this time?" Talia asked.

"I don't know," he said. "I want to think so. She did help us at Facility B, but she was a mess about me being a different person and was desperate to turn me back. She saw an opportunity and took it. If I was in her shoes, maybe I would have done the same."

She looked him in the eyes. "Just promise me you'll be careful. And I'm not talking safe sex here."

He knew what she meant. "I promise."

"And don't worry about Shaan," she said. "He'll come around. He likes you a lot. Just don't change sides on us."

"I won't."

She took a deep breath. "God, that was a lot of wine. I'm going to have one hell of a headache tomorrow."

Seven felt it, too. "Yeah, I'm not sure how I'm going to get back to the apartment."

"Are you coming on to me?"

He scowled.

"Joking, joking," she laughed. Talia shoved him off the couch and stretched out. "Think I might–" The sentence was interrupted by a yawn. "Think I might just stay here tonight. Pretty comfy actually."

The yawning was addictive. "Not a bad idea, really," he said.

"Plenty of couches…" she lilted. "Don't forget…to water the goddamned plants."

That was it for Talia. Seven lay down on the couch across from her and closed his own eyes. For the first time in a while, he had little trouble falling asleep.

CHAPTER THIRTY-TWO
Commitment

Seeing Eve with boxes stacked up to her eyes made Jon smile. It was *finally* happening, he thought.

The double doors to the freight elevator opened and the two of them stepped carefully into an off-white hallway with floral-print carpeting. When they reached Jon's apartment–now theirs–he put down the two dining room chairs he was carrying and ran ahead to hold open the door. As Eve waddled by, a corner of the box in her arms caught Jon's hand and tore into his skin.

He yelped.

In lieu of an apology, Eve rolled her eyes. "Well maybe you should have taken this one…"

His hand was cut and oozing crimson.

"I'm bleeding!" he screamed, darting to the bathroom.

He flipped on the cold faucet to full blast and let the jet stream of icy water numb his wound. Jon thought he may have heard Eve's voice but decided whatever she was saying could wait. Regarding himself in the mirror, Jon noticed dark bags under his eyes.

"Snap out of it," he told his scowling reflection. "Your girlfriend is moving in with you. It's just a cut."

He splashed his face with water, took a deep breath, and reached for the door. Returning to the living room, he found Eve engrossed in her phone. He wasn't surprised.

Jon cleared his throat to get her attention. "Aren't you going to unpack?"

"Oh," she answered enigmatically. Her attention was still on the device.

"Eve?"

"Think I've got to go to work."

"What? Now?"

"One of my Watched just got on a bus wearing a backpack."

He shook the water from his hands with vigor. "So what?"

"She hates the bus and I've never seen her with a backpack. Could be a bomb."

Jon shook his head in disbelief. "But…we're in the middle of moving, and you already told everyone you were taking the day off."

Eve looked down at the phone and then back up at Jon. "Look, I mean, we got a lot done already today, right? I just think I should check on this, and then I'll come back, and I promise we'll do more."

Jon opened his mouth to speak, but sighed loudly instead.

"What?"

"It's just…" he said. "Never mind. Go."

She started toward the door but turned back. "Look, I'm sorry I have to go out and save lives," she whined. "And anyway, you do the same thing when your phone rings. Yesterday, in fact."

"That was just dessert!" protested Jon. "This is different!"

Eve's jaw dropped. "How does having pie in front of you make it any different? Is there some kind of pastry exemption I don't know about?"

"You're in the middle of moving in with me!" he cried. "Stop trying to get out of this!"

Her eyes widened. "*Get out of this?* What are you talking about?" Now she was shouting, too.

Jon shook his head in disbelief. "Maybe we did this too soon. Do you even want to live with me?"

"Of course I do! I think you're blowing this *way* out of proportion…"

He looked at his feet and spoke somberly. "You know, part of the reason I wanted you to live with me in the first place was because I felt like–with our jobs and everything–we barely had any time to see each other. And I figured, if we had the same home, then we'd be guaranteed at least a little time every day."

She sighed deeply and approached him. "I know…that's what I want, too."

"Do you?" Jon shook Eve's hand away and walked to the window. The sky was growing red.

"I just don't get why…" Jon said eventually. "…why you're actually encouraging me to take the mission."

Eve's face fell. "Is that why you're so upset?"

He didn't respond.

"I told you before," she said. "I think it would be good for your career."

He glared at her in exasperation, and his palms shot out to his sides. "And what if I don't come back?" His face sank to the floor as he added meekly, "Would you even care?"

She scowled. "Why wouldn't you come back?"

"You heard the risks. They're going to do something to me that might–what if I'm different afterward? Why doesn't that matter more to you?"

"I–" she started and then stopped, her eyes flitting back to her cell phone.

"Just go!" Jon roared. "I know you want to go, so just do it. Good luck on your backpack patrol."

She shot him a pained look. The next thing he knew the door slammed shut and she was gone.

Dusk turned to night and still Eve had not returned. Jon hadn't had dinner yet–he had been waiting for her. But she didn't even call. He had tried her once and gotten a voicemail. That was an hour ago and she hadn't even texted him back. That was suspicious. Eve could barely go ten minutes without looking at that damned cell phone.

Jon tried distracting himself with TV, but an invisible, vice-like grip dug into the back of his neck and shoulders. Eventually, he decided the windows weren't providing enough fresh air and he stood up to leave. He didn't turn off the TV or any of the lights on the way out.

A cool wind cut through the night air, the first warning of autumn. Jon liked the feel of it as he marched forcefully down the block. He used to go on walks like this all the time, before he met Eve. It was how he learned his way around the city. There on the left across the street was the burger place he used to go to all the time, before Eve made him feel guilty about the calories. Over on the right was the comic book shop he used to frequent before Eve had made him feel embarrassed about the hobby.

Jon turned right around the corner at the end of the block. Across the street to his left were the big green grounds of the local church. The over-sized glass pyramid, lit from within with blue and yellow, sliced through the black sky. He paused to take in the dramatic sight, but his brain flitted back to the blonde who was supposed to move in with him, but now wanted to leave him behind.

A shattering of glass interrupted Agent Wyle's thoughts. Jon's head snapped toward the church gardens where a teenager was readying another rock to launch into the side of the holy building. Jon yelled at the kid and raced across the street to stop him.

A car screeched on the brakes, missing Jon narrowly.

"Hey!" yelled the driver.

The punk kid turned in surprise, caught a glimpse of Jon, and darted away like a frightened squirrel.

Jon wasn't about to let this go. "Stop!" he yelled, taking chase. "I'm with the Guard, you goddamned Heretic!"

The kid reached the city street, and halfway down the block turned into a tight alley. He was quick, but Jon gained ground with every stride. Soon he found the delinquent struggling desperately to climb over a great green dumpster blocking the path through to the next street.

COMMITMENT

"Hold it, Heretic!" Jon roared.

The kid stopped, took a deep breath, and turned back around to face Jon. His eyes were filled with fire.

Scowling as he advanced, Jon reached into his jacket and pulled out a standard issue silenced pistol.

The delinquent laughed at him. "What are you going to do, kill me? For throwing a rock? You fucking cops."

That insubordinate brat, thought Jon. He was about a foot away now. "No, I'm not going to kill you," he growled. But then the hand holding the pistol whipped around and struck the boy across the face. Immediately, blood began gushing from his nose. Jon kneed him in the stomach and the delinquent crumpled forward. Finally, he landed a sharp, plummeting elbow that left the child whimpering.

The boy's tears mixed with the asphalt on his cheek, making Jon feel completely disgusted with himself. The kid had learned his lesson. Deciding not to make the arrest, Jon turned back for the street.

Jon grew angrier the more he thought about the mission that Eve said would be good for his career. The Guard were asking him to give up his identity in order to conduct a covert investigation of the Underground. So covert, in fact, that not even he could know he was on a mission. He had to be a blank slate, his superiors told him. That was the only way it would work.

Here Jon and Eve had just moved in together and his job was already forcing him to give it all up. They were asking him to forget this girl who just might be the love of his life. And she didn't even seem to care!

Sure, they promised that they would restore his memories, but after how long? What if Eve got tired of waiting? What if she fell for someone new? Jon thought he could prevent that by having her move in, but now he wasn't sure that would be enough. He needed to find a way to guarantee she would wait for him. He needed to find a way to show her how much he needed her to wait. Something to prove to Eve—and perhaps to himself—that they would have a future together, no matter what happened.

On and on he walked, thinking too hard to see anything around him. The hopelessness of night closed in upon him. He hadn't felt like this since…before he met Eve. All he wanted was to keep her and tonight he had lost her.

Suddenly Jon was overcome by sharp fear that she was back at the apartment taking back her boxes. She hadn't unpacked—with a friend or two she could have her stuff out in less than an hour, he realized. She could have come and gone already. She could have—

His phone rang.

"Jon?" Eve said meekly on the other line. "Where are you? Why aren't you home?"

"I went for a walk," he said coldly.

"I tried calling you."

He stopped short. "What? I didn't hear my phone ring."

He pulled the device from his ear and checked the screen. Sure enough he had three missed calls, two voicemails, and a text message. How had he missed them?

"Shoot," he said, turning around in the direction of his apartment. He looked at a street sign and realized he was at least three miles away. "I'm not sure what happened. I thought you were…I don't know. You're home now?"

"Uh huh," she said. "You were right—I shouldn't have left to check on my Watched. It took all day and ended up being a total bust. I guess I just don't like moving very much."

He stopped again. "Having regrets?"

"No, no!" she protested. "Jon, I love you—of course I want to live with you. Moving is just so…boring…and sweaty. I just got irritable."

"It's okay," said Jon, resuming his walk. "I'm heading back now but I might not be there for a little while. I walked…a lot further than I thought I was going to."

COMMITMENT

"Okay, I'll do some unpacking. Don't take too long. Don't forget we've still got some celebrating to do tonight."

Jon's mouth parted slightly. Suddenly all he wanted to do was touch her warm body again. "I love you, Eve."

"And I love you."

As Jon put the phone away, bright lights rushed upon him. He realized he was in the jewelry district. Jon pulled in close and peered into one of the store's displays. A single diamond caught his eye.

He stood there considering the ring for some time. Finally, with a smile on his face, he stepped inside the shop. He had his answer.

CHAPTER THIRTY-THREE
The Debate

The pounding of war drums quickly suppressed the auditorium chatter. The lights lifted, revealing a grinning man with grey wisps running back through brown hair.

"And we are live inside the Wellor Theatre," he said, "in the heart of the Capital, where two candidates for president will soon begin a one-hour debate about the future of our fair nation."

Seven and Ana had front row seats. They were there to lend Danny some moral support and, if necessary, protection. Both Underground agents carried pistols on their ankles, just in case someone made another attempt on their boss's life. Seven was also armed with a pen and small pad of paper to take notes on the debate.

"I am your host and moderator Bob Santos," the announcer gushed. "Let's welcome Susan Levi and Daniel Alexander Young to the podiums!"

Levi strolled out from stage right blowing kisses to the audience. Halfway to the stand she blushed and pointed in the vague direction of the audience. Young appeared and took several long strides toward his own podium. Momentarily distracted by the crowd and cameras, Danny nearly crashed into Santos' moderator desk.

"He looks nervous," commented Ana. "C'mon, Danny, pull yourself together."

When the clapping died down, Moderator Santos took up the mike and spoke. "Thank you, Mr. Young and Mayor Levi–"

"Please, call me Susan," she interrupted. "And it's my pleasure."

Young squinted perplexedly at the glass of water on his podium. "I guess you can call me–"

"–This is perhaps the most difficult time we have ever faced as a nation," interrupted Santos, "and this is certain to be one of the most important presidential transitions in our history. So, if you don't mind, let's get right down to business."

Danny offered a thumbs up.

"God," groaned Ana. "Does he have to act so…so…Danny?"

"Here is your first question, and I'm going to ask Mayor… er, *Susan*, to respond first."

Santos cleared his throat.

"Former President Drake resigned amid controversy over what appeared to be an illegal surveillance program. If you are elected president, what role should surveillance play and how will you balance that against the people's right to privacy?"

Levi smiled. "Well, that's a great question, Bob. But first I just want to thank you again for moderating this super debate. I'd also like to thank everyone in the audience for having the courage to come back to the Capital after the Enemy's simply devastating attack. It's wonderful to be here in the beautiful Wellor Theatre. This place is positively glowing! And a final thank you to all of you tuning in on television. It is so very important that the people of this fine nation be engaged in this critical transition. I cannot stress enough how critical that is."

Seven glanced at his watch.

"Bob, your question is a very important one. The president's number one job is to serve the people. She must protect their security, and she must protect their privacy. As you said, there is a definite balance between those two vital, absolutely critical rights that must be found if we are to keep the people safe and simultaneously, just as importantly, protect their privacy.

"It's a tricky issue. The goal of surveillance is to keep people safe. But people are skeptical, and they have every right to be skeptical, because it does mean they are being filmed, watched.

But they are being watched by a government whose job is to protect them—that's what it's all about. So I firmly believe we can find a balance that gives greater privacy protections to the people, while also ensuring we promote national security. We owe it to the people to keep them safe while also making them feel as cozy as a bug in the rug."

Some in the audience chuckled at the cute ending. "She's great," commented a lady behind Seven. "She reminds me of my neighbor."

Seven glanced at his notebook and tried to figure out what to write. Finally he scrawled:

Levi says balance b/w privacy and nat'l security needed, otherwise dodges Q.

"Mr. Young," prompted the moderator, "what's your take on all this?"

Danny nodded slowly and took a deep breath. "Well, as my opponent said, the government's responsibility is to the people."

He paused again for what Seven felt was an excruciatingly long time.

"But if a government is to be effective, the people must trust their government. Trust is not a one-way street. The former president's failure, I think, was that he did not trust his people—he was inherently suspicious. So much so, in fact, that he felt that he had to watch everyone. Drake thought he could avoid rebellion by catching it early. As if it was some kind of cancer."

Young shook his head. "My father, rest his soul, taught me that revolution is not a disease. Revolution is a mere symptom of a broken government. Instead of trying to stamp it out, Drake should have worked to reform the government and make the changes that were absolutely needed. If I'm elected president, I'm not going to have the Guard watch a citizen's every move for signs of independent thought. I'm not going to say free thinking is heresy. If someone has a valid complaint against the government, I'm going to listen and I'm going to make the changes needed to solve the problem.

"I have not kept secret my reservations with the level of surveillance under the previous administration. If we are to reestablish trust with the people, we must completely reevaluate this program. When I am elected, my first step will be to reform the Guard. We will go down the Watched list name by name and reassess whether the people on the list should really be there. My guess is many of them are not really Heretics at all."

From a rooftop across the street, Eve scanned the Wellor Theatre for suspicious activity. Someone out there wanted Young dead. What better night to strike than his first presidential debate?

"Anyone got anything?" Eve asked her headset radio.

"Negative," a gruff voice responded

"All clear," said a feminine one.

Eve had Elite Guard set up with sniper rifles on other buildings around the block. They were seasoned veterans, men and women who she had worked with and trusted for years. No one could get into the Wellor Theatre, not without a fight.

"Good evening, Agent Parker," said someone new on the radio. He sounded familiar. Eve checked her phone, but the device couldn't locate the source.

"Who is this?"

"I'm insulted. Do you not remember thy former partner?"

Now she recognized that flowery timbre. "Rodriguez."

She reached for her phone and sent a text message out to the team:

Someone is here. Get visual and take down.

"Excuse me a second," said Rodriguez. "One of your soldiers just received a message."

She was overcome by a horrible sense of dread. "What did you do to him?"

"The will of God."

THE DEBATE

"You're insane. God would not seek the death of innocents."

"They are not innocents who would harbor a Heretic. That includes you."

"I won't let you kill Young," Eve growled. "You tried and failed once. And this time we're ready."

He clucked his tongue. "If we had wanted to kill the Heretic Young then, he would already be dead. At the time, we sought merely to scare. A more sensible man would have bowed out of the race immediately. It appears, however, that this one requires more…encouragement."

"I won't let you–"

"We must say we're disappointed, Eve. After all, you grew up in the Church. Whatever happened to Daddy's little girl to make her turn Heretic?"

"I'm not a Heretic," growled Eve. She could feel her cheeks ignite. "And you're not getting inside the building."

"What makes you *so sure* I'm not inside already?"

Eve's eyes widened into blue lakes. She had to get into the Wellor Center immediately. When she spun toward the stairwell, however, a hooded man in a black robe was standing in her way.

"Dust to dust," said the Saint, leveling a pistol to Eve's chest.

The moderator Bob Santos shuffled through his papers. "His holiness, the Headmaster, has expressed his support for Mayor Levi. Mr. Young, can you tell us why the Church opposes your bid for president?"

Ana squirmed. "That bastard! What kind of one-sided question–"

"It's okay," whispered Seven. "We prepared for this."

"That's a very good question and it definitely deserves an honest response," Young said. "But before I do, I would like to point out that Interim President Randall has endorsed me for president. Randall, as you know, was the member of Congress who listened to our complaints about ex-President Drake and led the charge to oust him. Randall built the foundation for real change in this country, and it's my plan as president to fulfill that vision of change.

"With all due respect to his holiness, the Headmaster has largely kept out of our effort to turn this country around. The Headmaster worked side by side with President Drake, and I have reason to believe he had a powerful influence over Drake's policies. I do not think he has any interest in the changes sought by myself and Interim President Randall."

"Do you envision a new relationship between Church and State?" asked Santos.

"Yes," he said. "I believe that they should be separate."

"Heresy!" burst Levi.

"Mayor," Santos broke in. "You will have your turn to respond in a minute. Please continue, Mr. Young."

"It's my opinion that President Drake, working together with the Headmaster, exploited the people's fear of God to keep them in line. They made people believe that free thinking was heresy and a sure path to imprisonment and Hell. But fear is not how you run a country. And the only solution I see is to keep the Church completely separate from the affairs of the government. I do not anticipate the Headmaster will support me. But I think it's a key change if we are to come out of the dark ages in which we are living."

Santos pointed to Susan Levi. "Mayor?"

"I have never heard such heresy," she said. "The president and the Headmaster have always worked together, long before the Drake administration. Nobody has ever questioned this before. It's only logical that the president would consult with God's representative. How else can we be sure we are on the path to Heaven? What my opponent is suggesting would take us off the path and send us right off the cliff into Hell's bottomless pit."

Young laughed. "You see? This is exactly the kind of fear-mongering I'm talking about."

"You are trying to destroy the foundation of our law-abiding society," Levi spat back. "Why don't you tell everyone your policy to improve church attendance?"

THE DEBATE

Young glanced at the moderator, who nodded his assent.

"Well, I would not require church attendance," Young said. "I would allow people to practice any religion they choose, or if they would rather, not practice any religion at all."

"Don't shoot!" exclaimed Eve, edging backward. The building was at least ten stories and the street looked a long way down.

Tilting his head, the Saint grinned and mumbled something incomprehensible. At first she thought it was Rodriguez himself, but now she could see that this face was pale and bearded.

The tweedy voice of her former partner returned to her headphones. "Truly, it would be a shame for your skills to go to waste, Agent Parker. You were meant to serve God."

"Is it too late?" she asked the radio.

C'mon Eve, she thought. Keep him talking.

"Interesting, interesting, interesting," sang Rodriguez. "So the prodigal *daughter* wants to return."

Eve felt the roof's brick railing come up against her lower back.

"Here's what we'll do," Rodriguez said. "Empty your pockets and lay face down on the ground. My partner will bring you to a holy place. There, God will decide if you deserve redemption."

As he issued the command, the Saint on the rooftop relaxed his gun's aim. Immediately, Eve flipped backward and over the side of the building. Her hands held onto the brick wall as she did so and it took all her strength to hang on.

Eve could hear the pounding footsteps above of the Saint moving in for the kill. She squinted downward to confirm she was just a few inches above a window ledge, and then, holding her breath, dropped lightly onto the platform. Eve lost balance instantly and nearly fell backwards, but she caught the edge of the window frame with a flailing right hand and pulled herself in tight to the wall. With a free hand, she took her pistol and aimed for the sky.

The Saint's black hood dipped over the edge and Eve fired. The dark figure fell forward and slid over the edge of the building. A piece of soft cloth brushed against her neck as she pressed against the window. A few second later, she heard a crash and the screams of bystanders.

"We offer you Forgiveness and this is how you respond?" sneered Rodriguez. "How disappointing."

Eve pulled off the headset. "I already missed my chance at redemption," she said.

She dropped the radio and watched it fall toward the bloody, black heap on the sidewalk. Balancing carefully on the ledge, she got out her phone and dialed Ana.

Seven noticed Ana listening to her cell phone. He scowled at her and whispered, "You didn't turn that off?"

She grabbed him by the arm.

"What?" whispered Seven.

"That was Eve. Rodriguez attacked her team and she thinks he may be inside."

Seven turned sharply to the stage. Instead of Danny he saw his friend Adrian. A red laser dot appeared in the middle of the rock singer's forehead. The electric guitar fell out of his hands, hitting the floor with a sonic boom.

Ana prodded him. "Seven?"

He fell out of his dream and saw Danny behind the podium again.

"Let's spread out," Seven ordered. "Go up to the balcony and scan the crowd. I'm going to check backstage. When the show ends, we're getting out of here immediately."

Ana nodded and they dispersed.

Santos cleared his throat. "I was planning to ask a question about how each candidate plans to handle our ongoing war with the Enemy. However, just prior to the show, an anonymous viewer submitted a shocking tape that we believe requires answers first and

THE DEBATE

foremost. We'll play the tape, and then I will ask the candidates for their responses. Mr. Young will probably want to answer first."

After a few moments pause a deep, heavily accented voice filled the auditorium. The familiarity of the recording stopped Seven short at the door leading backstage.

"Our intelligence indicates that you lead a rebel movement in your nation known as the Underground," said the voice on the tape. "We would like to make our intentions known to you, because we believe our interests may align. In one hour, we will launch a 'shock-and-awe' attack on your Capital. We then intend to come to shore and take it.

"You refer to us as the Enemy, but we are not the Underground's enemy. Our mission is not one of destruction, but rather salvation. We are here to free your nation from the tyrant William Drake and his wholly oppressive government. We are here to install you, the Underground, as leaders of this new, free republic."

The message set off a clamor in the audience. Even behind his makeup, Danny Young looked frightfully pale.

Santos turned to him. "Mr. Young, did the Underground assist the Enemy in its attack on our nation?"

Young gaped. "What? No!"

Seven saw Susan Levi grinning like a cat who had just bitten the head off a mouse.

Santos pressed, "Do you or do you not recognize this audio message?"

Danny looked helplessly at the seat where Seven had been sitting. He spluttered, "I–I recognize it."

Everyone gasped.

"Wait, hear me out!" he shouted. "Yes, we did receive that message from the Enemy, but we did not respond and we certainly did not help them."

"Did you alert the Guard?" grilled Levi. "To warn them of the impending attack?"

"No," he said to more gasps. "But I didn't even know about the tape until after the attack. We–"

"So, here's what I'm hearing," Levi interrupted. "Danny Young could have stopped the Enemy from destroying the Capitol Tower. Danny Young could have stopped the Enemy from blowing up our city's churches. Danny Young could have prevented the evacuation that cost even more lives and brought this country's economy to a screeching halt. But he didn't. He stood by and let it happen."

The speech sounded prepared, Seven remarked to himself.

Susan Levi shook her head disparagingly. "Is that the kind of person we want to be our next president?"

The crowd began to boo and Seven heard cries of "Heretic!" and "Traitor!" A water bottle lifted from the audience and slammed into Danny's podium. He ducked as more debris came raining down.

Seven jumped to the stage and helped Danny escape. With horrifying clarity, he realized that the Saints had struck, accomplishing exactly what they had come for. Seven, Eve, nor anyone else, could have stopped them. The only thing to do now was regroup and hope the damage was not irreversible.

CHAPTER THIRTY-FOUR
Life Support

Eve wondered about the fate of old Bill's flowers as she approached the ruins of the church. On this night she saw only mud, broken concrete, and twisted metal. The great sheets of glass that once defined the modern structure were now just color-stained shards on the ground, easily mistakable for the remains of broken beer bottles. The Enemy had come and wrecked this holy place beyond repair. For now, at least, all the Guard could do was erect a barbed-wire fence to contain the mess.

She was walking toward a circus big top on the other side of Ground Zero. It floated like a ghost above the wreckage, with white nylon skin flapping loudly in the wind. Eve glanced over her shoulder but didn't see a soul. She was still feeling a little freaked out that the Saint who attacked her–the Saint who should be dead–had seemingly vanished into thin air. When Eve got down to the street, the black-shrouded body was gone. There wasn't even any blood on the sidewalk.

Somewhere, a hound howled at the moonless sky. Eve couldn't locate the animal but guessed it was another stray. There were so many of them now.

There was no way the Saint could have survived the fall, she told herself. The only rational explanation was that someone had dispensed of the body while she was still inside the building. Someone with a squeegee.

Eve moved on toward the big top. She wouldn't have come here but she needed answers. Randall told her the Saints were just an urban legend. But he couldn't explain who Rodriguez was–checking the Guard's database turned up no results

Based on the Saints' agenda so far–destroying Young's campaign for president and punishing Eve for "heresy"–it was pretty clear they had a religious bent. What Eve wasn't sure about was if they reported directly to the Church or if they were just a gang of reactionaries–some kind of ultra-conservative Underground. Randall suggested that she ask the Headmaster himself, but Eve didn't want to confront the high priest just yet. No, first she needed to talk to someone she could trust. Or, at least, used to trust.

She hoped to God the Saints didn't come from the Church. Eve grew up in a church. She had studied the Bible and listened to sermons every week of her life. Church was where she learned the difference between right and wrong. It was where she became inspired to join the Guard and make a difference. The Headmaster had been in charge of the Church as long as Eve could remember. How could a man she had respected and bowed down to her entire life be evil?

Okay, so he had sentenced her to death. He was still the Headmaster.

It started to rain, a cold sprinkle that felt like the harbinger of a great storm. Eve didn't carry an umbrella–it would only get in the way–so she sprinted the rest of the way to the tent. She passed a sign that read *INTERIM CHURCH* in big block letters. Below that was a message: *What appears as punishment is truly a test.*

Inside she found rows upon rows of plastic folding chairs, separated into sections by a wide walkway and pointed at a great podium on the other end of the tent. The makeshift pews were empty except for a man with short gray hair, sitting in the front-row aisle seat of the right section. Eve called out to him but her voice failed to break through the rain thumping against the top of the tent.

She touched the old man on the shoulder. "Dad."

He started with a yelp, spinning sharply to Eve.

Eve smiled lightly. "It's just me."

"My daughter, you're alive!"

"I was pardoned."

He stood up and hugged her. "Oh, Evey."

Remembering the callousness with which he had treated her in prison, she pushed him away. "I'm here on business."

"Oh," he said, backing off.

"I was just wondering," began Eve, sounding a bit too much like Daddy's little girl, "have you ever heard of a group called the Saints?"

His eyes widened as if stabbed in the belly.

Eve smirked. "I'll take that as a yes."

He closed his eyes in assent. "They are bodyguards for the Headmaster. That's all I can say. I'm sorry. I shouldn't even tell you that much."

She looked at him closely and realized he was shivering. This was not the man she remembered from when she was young. He seemed so frail.

"You have to help me, Dad. The future of this country depends on it."

"It's not up to you to decide the future, Evey. The Headmaster has already seen it."

Now she was irritated. "And who exactly is the president in the Headmaster's vision of the future? Susan fucking Levi?"

Dad looked appalled. "How can you use words like that in a House of God?"

Eve laughed. This circus tent?

"It's not up to us to judge Susan Levi," her father continued. "He has chosen her."

"Are you talking about God or the Headmaster?"

"These questions are blasphemy! What's happened to my–?"

"You left me for dead!" Eve screamed, not able to contain her anger any longer. "The Headmaster sentenced me to death. No one told you why, but because the Headmaster said I was a Heretic, you–my own father–believed that I was. And now you're still on his side. Dad, just because he's the head of the Church doesn't mean he's doing God's work!"

They were interrupted by a loud crack. At first Eve thought it was thunder, but then a second bang made the folding chair next to her father fall forward.

"Get down!" she screamed, tugging her father by the collar.

Eve lifted a gun from her holster and aimed it back toward the tent flap that served as the church's entrance. A rifle and the hooded head of a Saint poked out into the open. Eve ducked just in time to avoid the bullets.

The Saint dipped back into cover behind the entrance to the temporary church. Eve fired straight into the nylon wall. The Saint staggered back into the tent and fell dead in the aisle

Eve muttered, "Taking cover behind a tent–what an idiot."

Her father didn't respond.

"Daddy?"

He was lying on the floor in a growing pool of red.

"You're going to be okay," Ana told Danny as they stepped off the elevator on the 114th floor. "Right, Seven?"

"Huh?" He was mesmerized by the flurry of activity. Young's political whiz kids were running every which way and the phones were ringing off the hook.

"Danny's going to be okay, I said."

Talia emerged from the crowd of frantic politics to meet them. "Okay, as in alive, maybe," she said. "But like, probably not as president."

Danny Young frowned miserably. "What are the damages?"

"Channel 3's headline right now asks, 'Is Young a Heretic?' Channel 5's headline is, 'D.A.Y. Traitor?' And Wolf News asks, 'Is Young's Campaign on Life Support?'"

The presidential candidate looked like a balloon someone had stuck with a needle. "This is my fault," he sulked. "And they're right. I should have done more."

"You didn't hear the message from the Enemy until it was too late," reminded Ana. "It was just bad timing, babe."

Talia grinned ironically. "Yeah, well so far all of the networks have pretty much washed over that whole argument. And like, anyway, every five minutes they play that evil-sounding voice interspliced with footage of the burning Capitol Tower. No matter how much you try to explain it away, that image is going to be the main takeaway here."

Ana looked annoyed. "What makes you such an expert anyway?"

"I'm a public comm major," she replied sweetly.

"Wow!" burst Danny, seeming to forget his current plight. "That's very cool! I didn't know that! You should have said something about that before!"

Ana scoffed, but Seven had stopped listening. He was thinking about the way Talia had described the Enemy's voice. And then it occurred to him. "Do we know who's talking on the tape?"

They looked at him skeptically. Talia asked, "What do you mean?"

"Is that the Enemy's leader? One of their generals?"

They all looked stumped.

Seven shrugged. "All I'm saying is, maybe we should try to confirm the authenticity of that tape before we let Susan Levi steamroll us."

Danny's eyes lit up. "Talia!"

"Yes?" She sounded excited.

"Could you ask your brother to check on that?"

Her face fell. "Yeah," she said without enthusiasm. "Sure."

Danny seemed to pick up that she might be feeling left out. "Talia!" he exclaimed again.

Her eyes narrowed. "...Yes?"

"From a public comm standpoint, how much longer do you think we can stall the media?"

Talia glanced at her hot-pink wrist watch. "Well, ideally

we'd have cleared your name already. But it's a little after ten already, and in a few hours everyone we want to get the message to is going to be asleep. So like, first thing tomorrow morning, I guess, at the latest?"

Ana gasped. "That's not a lot of time."

"The longer we wait, the worse Danny is going to look."

Their meeting was over. Talia excused herself to ask Shaan about the tape. Danny, seemingly aware again of what he'd stepped in, staggered toward a big blue sofa by the receptionist's desk.

"Someone should check on Eve," Ana said to Seven. "She sounded like she was in trouble when she called."

That's weirdly sympathetic of her, thought Seven. But she had a point–Eve had been up against the Saints tonight by herself. He knew she could take care of herself, but these shadowy soldiers seemed somehow beyond human.

The phone rang three times before Eve picked up. "H-hello?" she stammered.

"It's Seven. We got Danny back to HQ. Have you seen the news?"

"Just saw it," she said. "Doesn't look good."

Her voice seemed quieter than normal–weaker.

"Are you all right?" he asked. "Where are you?"

It went quiet on the other end and Seven worried there was something terribly wrong. "Eve? You there?"

"I'm at the hospital," she said. "I visited my dad tonight because I thought he might know something useful about the Saints. I was careless…and I guess they followed me. They–they shot him."

For Seven, the clamor on the 114th floor seemed to dissipate suddenly. He saw himself, Eve and her father sharing a bowl of chips and drinking whiskey in front of the television. Football was on and outside the snow was falling.

"Which hospital?" Seven asked.

Eve sat next to her father with her head in her hands. One

hundred tubes and wires held the old man down in his sick bed. The doctor had stopped the bleeding and removed the bullet. Daddy was going to be okay but needed some rest. That's what he was doing now–resting. Maybe he was asleep, Eve wasn't sure. But she couldn't pull herself away from the bed. She just felt so damn guilty.

There was a knock at the door but Eve couldn't bring herself to look up. "What?" she croaked.

"How is he?" she heard her former fiancé say.

Eve looked up. "Seven?"

He was standing at the door with a potted daisy. "It's for him," he explained. "I wasn't sure what would be appropriate–"

"–for a man?" she snickered.

"For a priest, actually."

"Oh." She smiled. "Well, I think that's a very appropriate looking flower you bought."

Seven placed it carefully by his bedside and turned awkwardly to Eve.

"It was nice of you to come," she said. "I wasn't asking you to."

"I know," he said. "But I think I remember liking your dad."

She looked confused. "I don't remember that."

Seven shrugged. "Maybe I didn't show it. I also remember being somewhat of a dick."

She laughed. "I don't remember that, either. But you *were* different."

After some hesitation, Seven sat next to her. He dragged his chair a few inches away from hers and looked thoughtfully at her father's blanket.

"I had to turn it off," she said, indicating the small TV hanging over her father's feet. "How's Danny taking all this bad press?"

"Well, it's going to be tricky to win back the public, but I think we might have a shot at clearing his name," Seven said. "Shaan's analyzing the tape–no one had bothered to check its authenticity."

Eve's eyes widened. "You think someone could have made the whole thing up?"

He shrugged. "I think it's worth checking out, don't you?"

As she agreed, her father groaned and kicked at his blanket. "Evey?" he rasped.

She sprung up and went to his side. "I'm here, Daddy."

He looked at her bleary-eyed. "It's not true."

"What's not true?"

"I don't want them to hurt you," he said. "Why are they trying to hurt my little girl?"

The concern seemed genuine and Eve choked up.

"I already lost your mom," he went on. "When I found out I was going to lose you, too–they said it was heresy if I tried to help, if I even felt bad for you. I didn't know how I could see you under conditions like that. That's why I waited so long to visit you. Finally I realized that I had to see you–I had to just do the best I could to…"

"It's okay, Daddy," she said. "I–I forgive you. I'm the one who's worried about you now."

He nodded slowly. "Well, I feel like I've been hit by a truck. Other than that, I think I'm okay, dear. God didn't see fit to do away with me just yet."

Eve smiled. She thought he was starting to sound a little more like his old self.

"You get me that big ol' flower over there?" he asked, indicating the pot on his bedside table.

"No," said Eve, glancing tentatively over her shoulder at Seven.

He got to his feet in a hurry but practically tiptoed to the bed. "I did."

"Well, I'll be," said Eve's dad. "Jon, it's been a while since I last saw you, boy! You still treating my Evey right?"

Oh God, thought Eve. She felt the blood rushing to her cheeks and looked apologetically in Seven's direction.

"As well as I can," Seven replied cheerily, not missing a beat.

Daddy beamed. "Have you kids settled on a date yet?"

"–No," Eve broke in, perhaps too enthusiastically. She tried to laugh off the anxiousness. Second guessing herself, she covered her mouth with her hand. Realizing she didn't have her engagement ring on, she slapped the hand down and hid it behind her back. "Just been so busy, you know?"

"I would imagine trying not to get shot would get a trifle distracting," Daddy replied thoughtfully. "Maybe I can help. Tell me what you want to know about the Saints."

She placed a hand gently on his wrist. "Are you sure? Talking to me has already landed you in the hospital…I don't want to make it worse."

"The Saints shot me; you saved my life," he said. "Don't pretend it was the other way around."

She smiled lightly. "Okay. Well, you were saying the Saints worked for the Headmaster."

"The Headmaster has always had bodyguards," Daddy said. "The Saints take care of matters that the Guard won't. It's the Headmaster's view that the Guard are constrained by the law of the nation. The Saints, on the other hand, follow only the commandments of God."

Seven smirked. "Which I imagine are pretty flexible when the Headmaster is the one interpreting them."

"Maybe so," he said, considering. "Look, I will teach and follow the lessons of God until the day I die. But if I'm being honest, I've never felt right about the Headmaster directing his own small army. I believe in God, but I also believe in laws and the need for them in our country."

"Are there other priests who feel that way?" Seven asked.

"Yes, I think there are at least some. But no one has ever had the strength to stand up to the Headmaster. I've always known that questioning him would be the end of my career and maybe my life. I couldn't do that to Evey."

She kissed him gently on the cheek. "So Daddy, where do the Saints go marching in when they're not breaking the law for God and country?"

"The Saints go where they are most accessible to the Headmaster."

※

"Thanks," said Eve, closing the door to her father's room.

Seven felt absorbed by the blond girl's smile. "For what?"

"For playing along," she said. "I haven't told him yet, obviously. About us, I mean—or rather, that there is no 'us,' anymore."

"Aha," he said. Even though he knew it was true, he felt somewhat let down hearing her say it.

"There just hasn't been an ideal time to tell him. Tonight was especially non-ideal."

"Don't worry about it," he said. "I'm not worried."

That was a lie. He was very worried. Why was he being so nice to her, considering everything that she'd done? Did he really love her, or was it just Jonathan Wyle? He felt like he needed to add something malicious just to balance things out. "I played along for him, not you."

Eve's smile vanished and he felt pained to see it go.

Seven's phone buzzed. He picked it up quickly.

"Seven, it's Shaan," he said.

"Shaan!" he repeated for Eve's benefit. "What have you found out?"

"The Elite Guard keeps an extensive audio database containing speeches and other recorded communications of the Enemy. So I ran the recording we received against all of those."

"And?"

"There were no matches."

"No matches? Could it just be someone the Guard doesn't have a recording for?"

"I thought the same thing, so I expanded the search to include people in this country. No results again, but then I remembered there was someone we met who's not in the database."

"Rodriguez," guessed Seven.

"Bingo. So I grabbed an audio clip of his voice from when he was our prisoner and compared it to the Enemy's tape. And guess what? It was a perfect match. His voice was scrambled to sound like someone else, but it was easy enough to break through."

Seven gasped. "Well done, man! I think this might be a good occasion to yell, 'Stop the Presses!'"

"No, Seven," said a new voice on the phone. It was Danny Young–apparently they had Seven on speaker. "I'm tired of playing defense. I want to do more than just clear my name. Talia says we have until morning to respond. That gives us about eight or nine hours to find as much evidence as we can to nail these bastards once and for all."

CHAPTER THIRTY-FIVE
Once & Future

Eve touched the doorbell just lightly enough to make it ring. Seven looked at her oddly, as if recognizing this was unusual behavior. When the tap resulted in an electronic version of the national anthem, Eve wished she had gone with her instinctive approach of pounding the door.

It wasn't the song that annoyed her–Eve considered herself as patriotic as the next girl. What really irked her was the *person* using it as her doorbell chime. Eve couldn't place her finger on exactly what it was about Susan Levi, but everything she did seemed fake, forced, and phony. Levi didn't likely have the national anthem playing because she loved her country. She just wanted people to *think* that she loved her country.

Then again, maybe she was just jealous of Levi's house. The stone siding, big picture windows, and round-cut bushes made it look like something out of a holiday catalog. The ocean literally roared from the backyard. People bought overpriced alarm clocks from airplane catalogs to hear sounds like that. If you lived here, all you had to do was crack a window.

The door clicked and swung inward. A heavy man who looked like a club bouncer appeared in the open space. He didn't say anything, so Eve introduced herself with a flash of her badge. "We'd like to have a word with Ms. Levi," she said.

"She's sleeping," said the bouncer, closing the door.

Seven suddenly charged, slamming door into man with a heavy thunk. The bouncer staggered backwards, giving Seven an opening to strike. But the punch was consumed by the fat man's belly and the bouncer got a tight grip around Seven's wrist.

"Boys," remarked Eve, pulling a silver pistol from the inside of her short black jacket. She aimed it at the bouncer's head. "Please let go of my partner and wake up your boss."

Startled by this latest development, the bouncer let go of Seven and froze.

"Now," she prodded.

The bouncer was only halfway up the stairs when Susan Levi began to step down. It was obvious that she had not been sleeping. Levi was dressed in a pants suit and her hair was up in the same prim fashion as it had been at the debate. Eve concluded she had been waiting on the top of the steps the whole time, like a child listening in to a fight between her parents.

"Nice to see you," Levi said as if she was greeting guests for dinner. But her eyes appeared strained beneath all the makeup. "I don't believe we've met."

"Good evening, Ms. Levi. My name is Eve and this is my… uh…partner, Seven. We're with the Elite Guard. Sorry to visit so late, but we have a few questions about tonight's debate."

Levi nodded more times than necessary before waving at a pair of sofas. "Why don't you have a seat?" she suggested. "Larry, get us some coffee, would you?"

The bouncer named Larry shambled off to the kitchen. Not wanting Susan Levi's henchman out of her sight, Eve pointed the gun in his direction again. "I'd prefer it if Larry would stay with us. We won't be long."

The four of them took seats, with Seven and Eve on one side and Levi and her lackey on the other. Between them stood a coffee table smothered in magazines. They covered a variety of interest areas. Eve observed that they were in impeccable condition, and in fact several were still in their original plastic sleeves. Seven dropped a digital tape recorder on a magazine called *Church and Garden*.

"Here's what's going to happen," said Eve. "We're going to ask you some questions, and you're going to answer them truthfully. If I think you're lying to us…well, let's just say we'll have a problem."

"I haven't done anything wrong!" protested Levi suddenly over the surprise of the encounter. "You can't do this to me! When I'm president, you're going to regret this!"

Eve pointed the gun at Larry and fired. The bouncer howled but the only damage was a hole in the sofa inches from where he was sitting.

"Are you insane?!" screamed Levi. "Do you have any idea how much that will cost to reupholster?"

"I have an idea," smiled Eve. "I bet you've got a lot of rare, expensive furniture in here, don't you? Would be a shame if any more of it was damaged."

Now she took aim at a crystal chandelier above the foyer.

"Stop!" cried Susan Levi. "Ask me your questions."

"Did you know about the audio tape of the Enemy before the debate?" Eve asked.

"It was played to me, yes," Levi said. "And I'm glad it got out. We don't want an ally of the Enemy running our nation."

"Did you know it's a fake?" Seven interjected.

"Excuse me?"

"We ran an analysis of it. The Enemy didn't make the recording."

Levi appeared skeptical. "Then who?"

"Have you heard of the Saints?"

"…No," said Levi, but Eve caught the hesitation and brought her weapon back to the chandelier. The bullet cut through the wire holding it to the ceiling and the whole thing crashed tragically to the floor.

"I've heard of them!" Levi squawked. "They were with him when he convinced me to run."

"Who convinced you to run?" snapped Eve.

"The…the Headmaster," Levi said. "He told me that if I ran for office he would make sure that I won. I didn't want to run—I didn't think I was ready for at least another four years—especially not with the attack and everything else that had just happened. But then these men with him, they said I *had* to run, that it was God's wish and that I couldn't say no. They said refusing God was heresy."

Seven asked, "How did you hear the tape for the first time?"

"One of the Headmaster's men brought it to me. I wanted to send it to the authorities right away, but the man with the Saints told me it wasn't in God's plan. He said that God wanted the tape to come out in front of the public on national TV so that everyone could hear the truth about Danny Young."

Their next stop was Old Town. Eve had always thought it was the most beautiful neighborhood of the city, but unfortunately it was too expensive to buy a home there. At this late hour it was quiet and the lights were out in most of the houses.

Walking with his black labrador in the dim, flickering light of street lanterns, the former President William Drake looked like a shell of himself. Eve thought his hair looked grayer, as if he'd aged many years since resigning from office.

He never saw them coming, but the dog did. When they were a few feet away the animal spun around, barked and gnashed its teeth.

Eve gasped and backed away, but Seven stood strong. "Drake," he called.

The former president bent down to stroke his pet's neck. "Whoa, Hoover," he said. "It's okay, boy."

The dog woofed uncertainly. After a few more strokes, the animal began to lick his master's hand.

"Good boy," said Drake, ruffling the fur on Hoover's head in such a way that it pulled back the dog's eyelids. "Now sit."

Hoover sat. When the animal was sufficiently calm, Drake stood up and met his pursuers' eyes. He had bags under his eyes but the man was still strikingly handsome, and tall enough to make Eve feel like a child. She wasn't sure what to say.

"Who are you?" Drake asked with a trace of exasperation.

Seven did the introductions this time. Eve felt thankful he was taking charge. Speaking to the president–even though he was now the former president–was…well, it was weird.

"I'm done talking to reporters," Drake said.

"We're not reporters," Seven said. "We're much worse than that."

Drake narrowed his eyes. "Are you threatening me?"

Seven smirked. "I guess it depends on what you have to say."

Eve fought back a giggle. She liked the confidence in his voice.

The president shuddered heavily. "I've had enough of this," he said. "It was never supposed to be like this. I'm the goddamned president!"

Interesting choice of words, thought Eve.

"We spoke with Susan Levi earlier tonight," Seven continued. "She said that she was chosen by God to run for president. Were you chosen by God, Drake?"

He scratched the stubble surrounding his frown. "I thought so once."

"And did someone tell you that?"

"I-I don't understand what you mean."

"Who chose you, Drake? Was it God? Or was it the *Headmaster*?"

Upon hearing the name, a peculiar expression appeared on Drake's face. It turned to one of incredible pain. Suddenly he was gripping his chest with a shaking, white hand.

"Oh, my God," gasped Eve. "I think he's having a heart attack!"

Seven caught the former president and brought him gently onto his back. Hoover started barking again, louder than before. One by one, lights went on in the houses.

Seven got out his phone. "I'll call for an ambulance."

Eve bent down to help the president. Drake was shaking. "He… told me I had to resign, said it was the only option. But then the people…my own family…everyone hated me…It wasn't fair!"

He gasped for air. "I'm so *sorry*. Please tell them it wasn't my fault."

"What wasn't your fault, Mr. President?" Eve asked as nicely as she could.

"The surveillance...The executions...The war..." he rasped. "They were always *his* ideas. I was just...the man in front of the people."

He said no more. President William T. Drake died right there on the pavement, with Hoover whimpering at his side.

Seven clicked off his tape recorder.

Eve felt disturbed and upset as they walked back to Seven's car. She was having great difficulty accepting that the President Drake had just died in her arms. She knew now that he was not a good man, but still, Drake had been someone she looked up to for so many years. It was hard to let go of that image in her head of the brave and handsome leader who would not stand down to anyone.

Now she saw it was all fiction. Drake was a puppet and his strings had been cut. The paramedics told Eve that Drake's heart attack was likely induced by an overdose of painkillers and anti-anxiety medication. Whether Drake intended to kill himself was an open question; what was clear, though, was that he had been in agony and had tried to make it all go away.

The good news was that Eve and Seven got what they came for. They had recorded everything Drake said. Combined with the Susan Levi interview, the Underground now had enough material to raise a pretty fair amount of questions about the legality of the Headmaster's involvement in national affairs. The only thing left to do was to take down the Church leader and his Saints once and for all.

Eve watched for cracks in the concrete sidewalk. She realized she hadn't played that game since she was a little girl. How many cracks had she stepped on since then?

"I need to ask you something," she said. "How is it you can be so sure you're doing the right thing?"

Seven looked at her curiously. "What do you mean?"

"Somehow, you've seen through the president and the Church from the minute you became you. You always seem to know what's right and what's wrong, who's good and who's evil. You see it more clearly than anyone else. How do you do it?"

"I don't see good and evil," he said. "I just see a divided nation. The Patriots are completely bent on ridding the country of the Heretics, but for every Heretic they arrest or drop they unwittingly inspire more people to *become* Heretics. It's this never-ending, masochistic cycle making the country weaker and weaker.

"So I guess I decided that the bad guys are the people who perpetuate division in our country. People like the Headmaster, who use fear to make people worry about every little thing they say or do. People like Drake, who got away with invading his own citizens' lives by citing this blanket authority to protect national security. Those are the bad guys."

"I spent my whole life believing in the bad guys," said Eve. "I was the bad guy."

"So was I," said Seven with a reassuring smile. "But people can change. We can unite the Patriots and the Heretics. It's already begun. That's how we're going to win."

She was stunned by how much he had changed. Jon had been the ultimate Patriot. Never once did she remember him questioning a superior's commands. He *enjoyed* his work hunting Heretics, enjoyed it so much that it scared her sometimes. He didn't blink an eye when they dropped Joanna. He discussed it at the dinner table like any other trivial event that had happened in the work day. When Shaan had seemed to commit suicide, Jon barely seemed to care.

"I hope the dog will be all right," Seven said with surprising apprehension. "What do you think will happen to the boy?"

Eve snickered. "You're worried about the dog?"

Seven shrugged. "He seemed nice."

"Drake had a family, right? I'm sure they'll take the dog. Shouldn't we be worried more about the family?"

"Oh, yeah, you're right."

She couldn't help but laugh.

After a few more paces, he looked over again like he had something to say.

Eve bit. "What's on your mind?"

"So, would we have gotten a dog?" he asked.

"What do you mean?"

"If we had got married, would we have bought a dog?"

"No way. Sorry, but no."

Recollection rushed through Seven's face. "Oh, that's right! You're afraid of dogs, aren't you?"

She sighed. "We can get a kitty if you want."

Realizing with some shock what she'd just said, Eve blushed and corrected herself. "I mean, we could have gotten–"

Seven waved her off calmly. "I know what you meant."

She shook her head and focused her attention on the horizon. At the top of the street a police car was approaching, probably on its way to the scene of Drake's collapse.

"They're a little late," she commented.

"Take cover!" shouted Seven. "It might be the Saints!"

The two of them jumped a white picket fence and fell into the yard of a darkened house. Eve peered over the top as the vehicle cruised by. She got a look at the driver and…he looked pretty ordinary. A run-of-the-mill, buzz-cut Guard. He was even chewing a donut.

Seven shut his eyes and grinned. "So…I think I might have overreacted."

She laughed. "Hey, I'm the one who followed you over the fence."

"At least this time it happened after we accomplished something. Do you remember our first stakeout together?"

Eve felt the blush return as she recalled that golden evening on the Luna Coast. "I remember."

She felt acutely aware how close his face was to hers. She couldn't hold her eyes on him and looked at the grass instead.

She hated herself. She was sorry she let Jon get away, but even more disgusted with herself for the way she'd tried to get him back. That wasn't her. How could that be her?

The change had been good for Jon. She could see that now. Seven was the better man. And yet she had treated him like a virus.

"Seven," she despaired softly. "I've been so selfish."

Eve felt his hand on her cheek and then the firm grip of his lips against her own. Her heart beat like it was trying to break out of her chest. She bit Seven's lip gently and let him take her down into the grass.

CHAPTER THIRTY-SIX
Attack!

The guns rattled against the inside walls of the trailer as the eighteen-wheeler started its ascent up Heaven Hill. Seven felt a bit like he was sitting inside a dryer. They were in a box made for cargo, not people. The closest thing to seatbelts were the various hooks, straps and poles placed about in an arrangement Seven was sure made sense to truckers, but not to a former Elite Guard. They chose the eighteen-wheeler for two reasons. First, the size allowed the Underground to bring a large team, weapons, and computers. Second, in spite of its size, the truck provided camouflage. The outside advertised a grocery store called *Doyle's*. Their driver had been instructed to tell anyone who asked that they were going to pick up food and deliver it back to the Capital.

Their true destination was the Head Church. The name was somewhat of a misnomer. While it was indeed a great and fully functioning cathedral, ordinary people were only allowed to explore the church's famous gardens and snap pictures of its mammoth bell tower. The building was home for the Headmaster and the only people he let in were subordinate clergymen and, Seven assumed, the Saints.

Beside Seven in the truck were Eve, Ana, Shaan, and three other Underground rebels from the Capital that he had just met. They were all dressed in black from head to toe. The newcomers were a merry but rough-looking bunch and seemed eager to fight. One had shown Seven a battle scar earned fighting the Enemy on the coast. He had forgotten the woman's name. To be perfectly honest, he had forgotten all their names.

Luckily, Ana was a natural at that kind of thing and she was going to be in charge of coordinating the B-Team. Seven had to say he was impressed by the way she could grab their attention and clearly lay out what she needed them to do. Even when he was working for the Guard he had always been something of a loner. Eve was the first agent Jonathan Wyle had ever worked alongside. The fact that he ended up proposing to her made him think that team-up didn't really count.

The job of Ana's team was to provide cover for Seven and Eve while they retrieved the Headmaster. Seven hoped they wouldn't need it. In a perfect world, he and Eve would get inside the church and capture the Headmaster with no problems. But deep down he knew that Rodriguez and the Saints would be there waiting for them.

Katie. He was pretty sure the scarred lady's name was Katie.

Shaan called out to Seven. "Hey, I want to say something to you, before we roll the dice on our lives."

He had a tablet in his free hand that Seven could see showed a map of the church grounds. Shaan's role was running communications and providing other technical support. In a way, Seven envied him—he got to stay in the truck. Seven's own job seemed a hell of a lot messier.

They hadn't talked since Shaan stormed off on V-H Day, angry at Seven for his role in Joanna's arrest and execution.

"About the other night–" Shaan began.

"–I'm really sorry," said Seven.

Unexpectedly, a deep laugh erupted from Shaan's belly. "Listen to us, man. If Talia could hear us, she would call us a couple of sissies."

Seven grinned. He could practically envision the look of absolute disgust on her face. Talia had wanted to come, but they agreed she didn't quite have the fighting experience. Anyway,

Danny said he needed her back at the base to help him prepare his upcoming statement to the press.

"No, man," continued Shaan, "I'm the one who needs to apologize. I was in a bad way the other night. I overreacted. Truth is I've known for a long time you were the guy who watched Joanna. I made it my business to know who was watching her."

Seven felt a weight lifting. "I guess that explains what happened in Loganville."

"It might have had something to do with it," Shaan returned with a vicious grin.

"Loganville?" asked Eve.

Shaan explained. "I sort of beat him up."

"Yeah, right before drugging me and tossing me into the trunk of my own minivan."

Eve grimaced. "Ooh…"

The other man cackled again. "No, you know, when you told me the truth, I guess it just caught me off guard. I never thought you would tell me, so I didn't know how to respond. I didn't know the right way to respond. And that night I was depressed and, worse, drinking depressants."

"Talia told me afterward that you had planned to propose on V-H Day," said Seven. "I didn't know."

Shaan waved him off. "Truth is I hated you at first because I knew who you were and what you had done. But since we've known each other, you've done nothing but good for this country. I can see you're a different person, and I hope you see it, too. Don't feel guilty for anything you did in the past." He laughed and in a deep voice boomed, "Jonathan Wyle is dead. Long live Seven!"

The others in the trailer cheered. He looked over at Eve and saw her beaming at him, cheeks flushed red. He thought she looked beautiful.

"Thanks, everyone," Seven said with some embarrassment. "Uh, let's go kick some ass?"

The team roared in approval.

The sky was still black when they reached the Head Church. The truck squeaked to a halt and idled for a few minutes. When the engine finally shut off, all the sound in the world seemed to go out.

Shaan wheeled a chair in front of the computer bolted down at the front of the trailer. He tapped a button and it came to life. There were multiple screens besides the main monitor. One television displayed the view from a hidden camera installed on the side of the truck right in the middle of the "o" in *Doyle's*. The image was muddy so Shaan flipped on the night vision, bathing the scene in neon green.

They could see the Head Church at the north end of a great field, landscaped with round-cut bushes and white marble benches. The building itself was only about two stories high, but a bell tower in the front left corner stretched far past the top of the TV screen. Two long stone paths cut the gardens into four equally sized quadrants, with a large statue of the Headmaster standing in the middle where the paths crossed. The north-south path connected the road where the eighteen-wheeler was standing to the statue, and then to the front entrance of the Head Church.

"Coast looks clear," said Eve.

Shaan tapped at the keyboard and a yellow-on-black map appeared on the screen.

"This is a blueprint of the Head Church." he explained. "Once you get inside, it's a straight shot through the sanctuary to a door behind the altar. The Headmaster will be in one of the two rooms back there. He should either be asleep in his bedroom or awake and heavily caffeinated in his office. But keep your eyes open. I'll be tracking you, so if you get lost or there are any complications I should be able to walk you out of the building."

"Good stuff," said Seven, clapping him on the back. He turned to the rest of the group. "Shall we?"

ATTACK!

In two pairs, Ana and her squad jumped out the back of the truck and spread out across the field, taking cover behind bushes, benches, and other objects. Seven and Eve cut down the center and ducked behind the Headmaster statue.

"Still looking clear," Shaan said over the radio. "Proceed when ready."

Seven looked at Eve to confirm their next move.

"Ready," said a new voice in his ear. One of the new guys?

Eve's face was filled with horror. "Rodriguez," she whispered.

"It came from the tower," exclaimed Shaan. "Oh sh–!"

There was a flash and a loud pop from high above. Seven looked up and saw a small rocket from an RPG screaming over their heads. At first he was confused how it could be so poorly aimed. Was it a warning shot? Then he realized where it was headed.

"Shaan! Get out of there!" Seven yelled into the radio.

The *Doyle's* truck lifted briefly into the air and combusted into flames. Thick steel splinters burst from the exploding vehicle. One shot straight for Seven and he had to fall to all fours to avoid getting hit. The gunfire began while he was laying down there on the grass.

Over the radio, he could hear Ana's panicked voice. "Oh, God, they're everywhere!"

Moving quickly but carefully, Seven tossed himself over a short stone wall surrounding the Headmaster statue. Eve was waiting on the other side.

"Were you hit?" asked Seven, retrieving a semi-automatic pistol from a hip holster.

"Negative. You?"

He breathed a sigh of relief and shook his head. Speaking in the radio, he said, "Ana, pull your team in closer to the church. Rodriguez isn't going to risk blowing up the building."

Next he directed Eve to handle the attackers coming from the west while he took the east. He determined that the Saints could only be coming from those two sides of the grounds.

Except for the bell tower, there was nowhere on the face of the Head Church for someone to fire from. Meanwhile, the eighteen-wheeled fireball across from the church had at least temporarily prevented the attackers' approach from that angle.

He used the stone wall for cover and tracked the Saints by the flash of their guns. He soon fell into a rhythm of ducking and blasting. Once he got a glimpse of the sleek Ana rolling from a bush into cover behind a bench. She popped up, fired a couple shots, and moved on.

Suddenly he saw Katie, the Underground agent he had met earlier. She was shaking on the ground with fresh blood dripping over the old battle scar.

How many Saints were out here? For every ghoul that went down, another seemed to pop up in their place. Seven caught himself at one point worrying that they couldn't be killed, that they were something more than human. But a few well-placed shots helped to chase the irrational thought.

Ana reported in. "Seven, I think my team can hold the rest of them back. You guys should move ahead, continue with the plan."

"You all will burn in the infernal fires of Hell," radioed Rodriguez.

There was another pop from high above.

Seven didn't look. He grabbed Eve and together they hopped the wall and sprinted madly for the Head Church. He felt a boom and a hot rush as the Headmaster statue exploded behind them. The blast sent dust flying into the air, obscuring his vision and making him cough uncontrollably.

"I'm here." Eve's voice was like a guide. "Keep going; the door is straight ahead. They can't fire at us if they can't see us."

She was right. His ears were still ringing from the blast but the staccato bangs had ceased. They rode the brown cloud to the heavy wooden doors of the cathedral. Eve removed a pick from her pocket and went to work on the lock. Seven glanced back to see the dusty blur dissipating and the church grounds coming back into view. On the edge of the field he saw a black-robed man raising a gun in his direction. He was about to yell a warning to Eve when the door opened. They just about fell inside.

Seven pulled the heavy door shut as a bullet ricocheted off the surface. They were standing on a marble floor in a grand foyer, facing a grand and gilded sanctuary. Another hallway ran left to a door labeled, *Stairs to Bell Tower*.

"Turn off your radio," whispered Eve.

When he did, she explained, "I didn't want *him* listening in…"

"Shaan said the Headmaster should be right beyond the sanctuary."

"That's what I wanted to talk to you about. Can you handle the Headmaster by yourself? I think we're going to need to deal with Rodriguez, but we don't want the Headmaster getting away in the meantime."

"If he hasn't gotten away already," sighed Seven. "Okay, I'll get the Headmaster and you take the bell tower. Just…"

She tilted her head in question.

In his head he could see the fire consuming the truck, could hear Shaan's last scream before his voice was silenced forever. God, how was he going to tell Talia about what happened?

"Just be careful," Seven told Eve at last. "I…I love you."

"I love you, too," she purred. She came in close and kissed him long and hard on the mouth. He reached for her cheek and held her face against his as long as he could.

It was over. He watched Eve until she disappeared into the stairwell. With a deep breath, Seven entered the sanctuary. A small surveillance camera just above the door swung clockwise to follow him.

CHAPTER THIRTY-SEVEN
Faith

Eve could hardly see her hands as she climbed the bell tower. The spatter of gunfire continued unabated outside, punctuated every so often by the heavy thunk of Rodriguez's rocket launcher. The steps were tall and their tight spiral path upward was making Eve dizzy, but she refused to pause for even a second. Rodriguez had already killed Shaan, and–unless she stopped him–he was going to kill even more of the people who had unexpectedly become her allies.

That old adage flashed in her mind: *PATRIOTS ARE THE TRUE. HERETICS ARE THE DAMNED.*

And from her temporary imprisonment in Danny Young's basement, Eve recalled the Underground's edit to the expression: *PATRIOTS ARE THE TRUE HERETICS.*

The top of the tower wasn't far now, and Eve had become increasingly aware of the clap of her footsteps against the polished stone steps. Fearing that Rodriquez might hear her coming, she slowed her ascent and took deep, deliberate breaths.

Her mind lingered briefly on Seven and the way he had looked at her before she left him in the foyer. She had seen a love in his eyes that was at once familiar and new. It had been difficult to leave him there, but it had to be done for the sake of the mission. There was too much at stake.

The truth was Eve was relieved to be going after Rodriguez instead of the Headmaster. Not because she didn't want to be with Seven, but because she wasn't sure she could face the leader of the Church. All her life, the Headmaster had seemed more than a man. He was the link between this world and God's kingdom. But the events over the last several weeks had called all of that into question. She could see now that the Headmaster was a fraud, a run-of-the-mill despot who used the name of God for power and control. However, just because he was a bad man, did that mean everything she learned in church was also a lie? She wanted to believe that the Headmaster had exploited a good religion for evil, but a fear filled her that maybe the religion was never good to begin with. Maybe the Headmaster was just the latest product of a manipulative faith. Maybe, there wasn't even a God.

Eve stopped as a terrifying groan reverberated through the tower. It was Rodriguez. It had to be. But what happened? Was he hit? More importantly, was he down?

Eve considered radioing Ana for information but decided it wasn't worth the risk. If Rodriguez was still alive he would likely still be monitoring the radio. Contacting Ana could take away Eve's element of surprise and probably get her killed.

She stood there, thinking and listening, with one foot higher than the other in a frozen climb. The shots outside continued unabated but she didn't hear any more blasts from Rodriguez's RPG launcher. One of the Underground agents could have shot him. It was a tough shot but it was possible. He could be down, but was he down for good? Then again, maybe Rodriguez was quiet because he had heard her coming up the stairs. He could even be on the way down this very instant to intercept her.

"God protect me," whispered Eve, wondering if anyone was listening.

She drew her gun and took the steps two at a time. Up and up she went until finally she could see the dark outline of the church bell against the midnight blue sky. She came out in a square about twenty feet on each side. A still black body lay face up on the floor. As she drew closer, she could see Rodriguez's shaved head. His eyes were closed and he didn't appear to be breathing.

Eve let her gun drop and paced around the floor, thinking. The sides of the tower were largely open except for a railing and the eight tall columns supporting the steeple. Looking up, she could see the inside of that center point about fifteen to eighteen feet above her. Hanging from a heavy wood beam several inches below that was a bell that's mouth consumed nearly a quarter of the room's area. The bronze had greened with age but it still appeared to be in working order.

Eve switched off her radio. She walked toward the ledge nearest Rodriguez and felt a touch of vertigo as she stared down at the gun-blasted gardens below. The Underground agents and the Saints were still engaged in combat. From the tower it looked like a battle of ants.

"Ana," she said over the radio, "I don't know how you did it, but looks like your team got a shot on Rodriguez. He's down."

Ana, sounding out of breath, responded. "What? None of my men reported anything."

With creeping fear, Eve turned back to check on Rodriguez. He was standing inches away with a jagged grin. She saw the knife just as a sharp, cold pain exploded her senses. Eve dropped her gun and fell back onto the cool stone ground.

A gilded altar drew Seven's eyes as he entered the Sanctuary. The gold sparkled beneath the fire of a chandelier of tall red candles. The rest of the room was dark, and gazing at the single light source made the rest of the room seem to grow darker still. He floated down the center aisle like a moth to the flame.

The door slammed behind him. Someone had shut them. Someone was here.

He turned but couldn't see a thing. Listening hard, Seven picked up only the muted pop-pop-pop of the gunfight blazing outside the stone walls.

He held his gun in front of him, ready to shoot the first monster that peeked out of the black. When nothing came, he turned back to the altar. There was a shadowy figure standing with a small flame in his hand. The fire lowered and a candle on the altar burst alive, revealing the gaunt face of the Headmaster.

"Welcome," greeted the high priest, his black eyes searing into Seven's.

"It's over," said Seven. "You're coming with me."

"Go with you?" the Headmaster asked incredulously. The wrinkles on his face grew harder. "I do not think this is God's wish."

Seven trained his gun on the Headmaster. "No, it's mine."

On Seven's left, someone whispered, "Don't."

"We're all around," whispered a voice on the right.

He lowered his gun. There were at least two Saints and they had him surrounded.

The Headmaster cackled, revealing teeth that were yellow and stained with cabernet. "This church is not a place for violence," he said while lifting his arms into the air. "It is a place of *learning*. It is a place of *enlightenment*."

"I assume that's code for brainwashing?"

The Headmaster's arms dropped and he looked patronizingly at Seven. "You believe you are already enlightened. You believe that you have been set free. But you are still Jonathan Wyle and your past will follow for eternity."

With a long and pointed finger, the high priest pressed something on the altar. There was a click and then the walls lit up on all sides with black-and-white projections of men and women. The faces were familiar but Seven couldn't place them. He spent a few seconds on each wall projection, trying to remember.

When Seven saw Joanna, he knew. He had watched all of them. They were faces of the dead.

The images came to life. Tears ran down Joanna's cheeks. Disembodied hands tightened a thick noose around her neck. Her mouth widened into a silent scream and a black bag fell over her head. In ten seconds, she fell off screen. The video repeated. Seven turned sharply and saw the dishonored priest

Paul Roland. His face had no expression as the bag fell over his head. But he shook violently when it did. Roland fell off screen and the video looped back to the beginning.

It was the same everywhere he looked. A familiar face. A horrible grimace. A rope, a black bag, and falling.

The Headmaster provided the soundtrack. "You pretend to be a man without burden. But you can never forget them, can you? They follow you. They haunt your dreams."

Seven's fingers left red marks as they slid tightly down the sides of his face. His mouth gaped and he breathed heavily. He wanted to look away but couldn't. The Headmaster was right. He couldn't escape his past. He…he had killed so many.

"Fifty-seven," stated the Headmaster. "Your arrests led to the executions of fifty-seven. They are all *dead* and *you* killed them. You will carry this burden *as long as you live*."

A whisper came from the left. "As long as you live."

"You will carry this burden *as long as you live*," repeated a low voice to the right.

The Headmaster continued. "You should know that the number doesn't count all the men and women you killed in the line of duty. Nor does it include the ones who died because of you."

Seven closed his eyes to shut out the images, but his mind soon took on the work of the projector. He saw his old friend Adrian standing on the stage. A red dot appeared on his forehead and in the next second he was falling, falling.

Seven was surprised to hear his own panicked voice. "What– what should I do?"

"You must repent," boomed the Headmaster, droning out the whispers. "You must repent!"

"Repent," echoed the whispers. "Repent. Repent. Repent."

"H-how?" he stammered.

"The answer," declared the Headmaster, "is in your hands."

Blankly, Seven looked down at his gun.

The whispers grew louder. "Repent! Repent! Repent! Repent!"

The pain was excruciating and for a few frightening moments Eve thought she was dying. Then her training from the Elite Guard kicked in. She meditated, and in seconds the haze cleared. Now she could see the facts of the situation. One, Rodriguez had cut her arm—she would need to stop the bleeding, but for now it wasn't fatal. Two, she was on her back at the top of the Head Church's bell tower, sprawled out and vulnerable. Three, Rodriguez was standing over her and brandishing a bloody dagger–military grade.

"Eve?" squawked Ana over the radio. "Eve?"

Rodriguez bent over and plucked the device from Eve's ear. He tossed it over her head and over the railing. Grimacing from the throw, Rodriguez shook out his right hand. Eve noticed an awful scar on the back. She felt a small rush of pleasure remembering where he had received it.

"A little stiff?" she asked.

He grabbed her cut arm and squeezed. Eve screamed in agony.

Pleasured by the sound, Rodriguez let go and laughed. "You will experience even more pain before we send you to Hell."

Rodriguez had the knife in his left hand but had thrown with his right. That meant he was likely right-handed but couldn't use it. Still, down on the floor and unarmed, she was still disadvantaged. The gun, she remembered. Where had she dropped her gun?

"Looking for this?" said Rodriguez, pointing to a black object on the ground a few feet from where he was standing. With a grin, he kicked it over to the far end of the tower. She didn't have a hope of reaching it.

If only there was a way to distract Rodriguez, thought Eve, she might be able to get up and knock the knife out of his hand. She looked up past her attacker's head to the mammoth bell hanging from a thick bar of wood over their heads. That might work, she thought, but how would she ring it? She couldn't locate a rope to pull or a button to press. That meant it was either completely automated or the switch was located somewhere else in the church.

"We will be sad to lose you," Rodriguez said with fake regret. "You had a promising career. The Headmaster always thought you could be a Saint. Top-notch record *and* the daughter of a priest. But then you lost your faith. You turned and began walking the trail to Hell. You gave up on God and now He hath given up on you."

The pain in Eve's arm seemed to intensify as he spoke. Was God punishing her? Or was there no God at all? She couldn't decide which was worse.

And then, out of the corner of her eye, Eve thought she saw the bell shift.

There was a deep and bellowing clang from above. Acting on reflex, Rodriguez clapped his hands hard against his ears, pointing the knife behind him. Eve sprung to her feet and charged. The bell rang again as he swung the dagger back around, but the left-handed attack was slow and Eve dodged easily. She caught his wrist and squeezed; the weapon popped out as the bell rang a third time. On the fourth ring, she had him pinned against the railing of the tower, and on the fifth had him bent halfway over the side.

"Heretic!" Rodriguez yelled, but the sixth toll drowned out the cry.

Eve smiled. "Looks like God's still on my side."

Before he could reply, she pushed Rodriguez over the edge and watched him drop.

Eve checked her wristwatch. It had just turned 6:00 a.m. She thought it was a miracle.

Seven held the gun firmly against his head. All he could think about was how many people he had killed; whether it was as Seven or Jonathan made no difference. The Headmaster was right. He was Jonathan Wyle and no amount of rationalization could remove the fact that he had killed so many. He could not say how many had actually been "Heretics," if there even was such a thing. It didn't matter—he knew he had killed innocents, and even if it was just one it was far too many.

The voices chanted. "Repent! Repent! Repent!"

He didn't deserve to live.

"What are you waiting for?" goaded the Headmaster. "You can escape your sins only through death. Pull the trigger. God Himself will illuminate the path to atonement."

As Seven tightened his grip on the pistol, he heard another voice come from deep inside. "Remember your friends."

He thought of Danny Young. Jonathan Wyle's secret mission had resulted in the execution of Danny's father. So why had Danny forgiven Seven? The leader of the Underground trusted him enough to make him his adviser and give him great responsibilities. He actually listened to Seven and respected his opinions. He had sent Seven here tonight to stop the Headmaster and save the nation.

Seven's unwitting mission for the Guard had also gotten Ana arrested and nearly killed. And yet she still wanted to work with him afterward. "No matter who you may have been before, I don't know how I could ever doubt your heart is now with the Underground," she had said.

Then there was Shaan, who somehow found a way past the fact that Jonathan Wyle was responsible for the death of his beloved Joanna. "I can see you're a different person," he said. "Don't feel guilty for anything you did in the past."

Suddenly he heard Talia's voice giving him the straight advice he really needed. "Could you please stop being a stupid idiot?"

He had made it his mission to save the nation from division and self-decay. Together with the Underground he had exposed the government's abuse of power. Now the rebels were on the precipice of taking down the Church. He couldn't give up now. He owed it to his friends and to all the people he had killed to keep going, to stand up and unite the nation once and for all.

As he looked back now at the Headmaster, Seven thought the chandelier hanging over the minister's head looked a bit like a crown of flames. Seven craned his head further back to a glowing ball on the ceiling. It was the machine projecting nightmares in 360 degrees.

In one quick motion, Seven lifted the gun from his temple and targeted the projector. It exploded and in a flash the visions of the dead disappeared from the wall. Bright sparks rained from the ceiling, washing the room with terrific white light. Seven turned left and trained his gun on a Saint entranced by the light show. He squeezed the trigger, ducked, and turned hard to his right to another black-robed soldier. Seven shot first and the Saint collapsed over a pew.

Not detecting any other threats in the room, Seven set his sights on the Headmaster. The pleasure that seconds ago had seemed to ooze from the high priest's every orifice had dried up and been replaced by pure fright. He was crouching by the altar with arms flailing over his head.

As Seven approached, the old man whimpered pathetically. "You can't destroy the Church!" he cried. "You can't! The people won't allow it! The people love me!"

"The people fear you," Seven said, "but they won't fear you anymore."

"Then do it! Kill me for my sins."

Seven took a small loop of rope from his belt and reached for the Headmaster's wrists. "Nah…I think I'd rather you answer for them."

CHAPTER THIRTY-EIGHT
A New Day

Eve was surprised to hear the singing of birds as she pushed open the doors of the Head Church and let the light in. The rising sun cast a pink glow over the torn-up gardens. As her eyes adjusted to the light, she noticed that the statue of the Headmaster was gone, replaced by a crumbled mass of stone. Strewn here and there were the bodies of Underground agents and black-shrouded Saints.

"Eve!" called Ana, running over to her. "Are you all right? You're bleeding."

She had nearly forgotten about her arm but the reminder made her feel all that pain again. Ana helped tear off Eve's sleeve, revealing a dark red cut. With the freshly torn black fabric from Eve's shirt, Ana tied a tourniquet around the wound.

"That should stop the bleeding. You probably don't need to go to the hospital, but if you want to keep the arm you're going to need to disinfect it as soon as possible."

She wasn't worried about that. "Has Seven come out yet?"

Ana took a step back. "I thought he was with you."

Eve was about to bolt back inside when the Headmaster burst through the open gates and fell face-first into the dirt. His hands were tied behind his back and he writhed around the ground like an upturned insect. Seven appeared behind him wearing a half smile. Eve ran to him and let him sweep her into his arms.

Ana chuckled. "You two *are* going to help me move this jackass, right?" she asked, indicating the weeping Headmaster.

"Leave him for now," said a voice Eve did not expect. "I called Danny and reinforcements should be here any minute."

Shaan was alive. His clothing looked singed and his face was smeared with black, but otherwise he looked to be in good health. Eve realized to her chagrin that this was the second time she had been convinced that the former special-effects engineer was dead. This instance had not been a setup. She saw the eighteen-wheeler truck explode with her own eyes. There was nothing fake about that.

"I know what you're thinking," said Shaan, "but I saw that asshole with the rocket launcher a few seconds before he fired. I guess I got the hell out of that truck just in time. It's a damned shame, though–we lost some good equipment."

Ana ran over to hug him. "Hey, we're just glad you're okay," she said.

He shrugged. "Just please tell me someone provided that idiot with a long and painful death."

Eve considered Rodriguez's fall from the top of the tower. "Oh, it was long."

"Well, that does make me feel a little better," he said. "Guess I'm glad we had you on our side."

A distant hum grew into the roar of many engines as a line of Guard police cars and other vehicles pulled up to the Head Church. Seven's blue roadster parked alongside the gardens not far from where they were standing. The door swung open and Haru stepped out.

"How long have you been in town?" exclaimed Ana. "We could have used your help!"

"You know I don't have the balls for shit like this. I'm on the Council; Danny called all of us to headquarters last night. I drove Seven's car over as a favor to Danny."

He turned to Seven.

"It's a super sweet ride, by the way. You must get all the girls."

Seven grinned. "Just one."

A NEW DAY

Eve felt herself turning red as he picked up her hand and led her to the vehicle.

Haru raised his eyebrows and clucked his tongue. "Very well, then. See you back at HQ, sometime? No hurry, yeah?"

As they sped away, Seven felt himself still buzzing from the night's events. He knew he should be tired but he was going to try and maintain this high as long as possible. They had defeated the Headmaster and Danny Young's victory in the election seemed all but assured. He was back with Eve and it felt right. There would be a lot of talking ahead for the two of them, but for now all he wanted to do was take her back to his place by the ocean.

He worried about the wound on Eve's arm, wished he could have done something to stop her from getting hurt. But he was proud of her for facing up to Rodriguez, and he knew she could take the pain. Eve was a survivor.

Peripherally, he saw her looking at him. When he turned to catch her, Eve's eyes floated back to the road. But she couldn't hide the happiness on her face as she guiltily bit her bottom lip.

"We should probably listen to the news," he suggested.

Eve turned on the radio.

"...new evidence that the tape of the Enemy was created out of whole cloth by the Headmaster and his closest followers. It's just another stunning new development in our story. We are hearing now from Susan Levi's camp that she plans to concede the election to Daniel Alexander Young. Levi is expected to make the announcement at a press conference starting within the hour. We expect Young to speak shortly after that. Unknown at this point is what the Headmaster's response will be to the allegations against him..."

"I suppose they haven't heard yet," Eve said lightly.

"Guess not."

She turned down the volume. When he looked over, her face had fallen into dark despair.

"Hey, you all right?"

"Seven…I love you, and you don't know how happy it makes me to think we're going to be together again, but I need you to be absolutely sure you *want* to be with me."

"I'm sure," he protested.

"That's not what I mean. It's just…I don't think we can just fall back into our old patterns like nothing ever happened between us. I don't think we should be planning a wedding. I don't think we should even live together, at least not right way."

"You mean you want to start over?"

She nodded. "I don't want you to be Jon Wyle anymore, but I need to be sure I'm falling in love with Seven. This can't work otherwise."

He thought about what she said for a long time. If he was being honest with himself, Seven decided he couldn't be sure whether he loved her because of Jon's memories or his own. He felt attracted to her; there was no denying that. But maybe Eve was right that it would be a mistake to jump into anything.

"Well," he said eventually, "would you maybe want to go out sometime?"

Eve's features brightened. "Like on a date?"

"Yeah. Maybe some pizza and a show?"

He dropped his hand lightly to the platform between their seats. She reached out and held it. Her palm was soft and warm.

"I'd like that," she said with a yawn. "But maybe…maybe we could have a nap first?"

She was asleep in seconds. Seven clicked off the radio and drove Eve home.

EPILOGUE
Ever After

From the grassy cliffs of the Luna Coast, Seven looked over the edge of the world. It was about an hour before sunset, but already he could feel the slight chill in the air that always came before the fall of night. The lighthouse behind his back was covered with scaffolding, and the last of the workers had just gone home for the day.

The ocean was a vast and empty slate. The Enemy's war boats had long since left the horizon. Whether they would return was a continuing subject of debate. Seven assumed the Enemy would try to strike again, but he wasn't worried. The Guard would be ready this time. Since taking power three months ago, President Young had worked tirelessly to patch the divisions lingering from the old regime. It would take more time still to eliminate all of the prejudice, but the new government was making a difference. Young had even begun to organize talks with the Enemy. Maybe there would be peace after all.

Seven's phone beeped in his hand. He was relieved to see it was just a text message from Talia.

Don't fail

The device beeped again.

Seriously, good luck.

He smiled. She had come a long way since they had met, and he honestly didn't know what he'd do without her as a friend.

Sometimes he wondered what life would have been like if he had taken up Danny's offer to lead and reform the Guard. But Seven was glad he chose to stay behind and take over Young's duties as chairman on the Underground's council. While Shaan and Ana went to work for the Guard, Talia stayed to help Seven write a new charter for the group. The Underground no longer had to fight the government, but it could act as a check against abuse by anyone in a position of power.

The new Underground would operate within the laws of the land–at least mostly–but at the same time answer to no one but themselves. They could not be directly funded by Young, since that could have been seen as a conflict of interest. Fortunately, someone had managed to convince the estate of former President Drake to write them a hefty check.

So far the work was not nearly as glamorous as what had come before. But Seven considered that good news, and he did feel like they were making a difference. They didn't hide from the public eye. He was particularly proud of their campaign to reduce the number of cameras hidden around the city. Tapping into social networks, Talia helped get a huge number of people excited about the issue. Already President Young was responding. Just yesterday he had announced plans to review and scale back the level of surveillance within the Capital and around the nation.

Seven felt good about the work, but it was Eve who he lived for. When Seven turned down Danny's offer to lead the Guard, he recommended Eve for the job. It was a perfect fit. Eve took great pride reshaping the Guard's mission into a force for uniting the people. Her first order of business was to wipe clean the country's internal Watched list and eliminate the labels Patriot and Heretic. The Guard's new, singular mission was to serve and protect the public.

While their schedules often clashed, Seven tried to see Eve every chance he got. He felt they were growing closer than ever, including back when he still went by the name Jonathan Wyle. They had even begun to joke about their strange history.

"Don't forget about our date," Eve said recently.

"Or what?" returned Seven. "You'll cut open my head?"

They were kind of weird. But Seven never felt happier.

A sudden crunch of gravel shifted Seven's attention to the

parking lot. Eve honked her horn as she pulled in. He waved back. Lightly patting his jeans pocket, he walked out to meet her.

Eve stepped out of the car and jaunted toward him. Her golden hair lifted in the wind and Seven felt himself falling into her ocean-blue eyes.

As they embraced, he took a small, round object from his pocket.

"Guess what?" she burst before he could say anything. "I finally got Shaan to tell me how he did it."

Seven closed his fist around the item in his hand. "How he did what?"

"How he faked his death!"

He recalled that Shaan had done it here on the Luna Coast. The guy drove his motorcycle straight off the cliff and into the ocean. Looking over the cliff now, Seven couldn't see any way he could have survived. It was too high. "How?"

"No one saw him do it in person," she said breathlessly. "All we had was a video recording from a single CCTV camera on the lighthouse. Shaan knew where the camera was. He sent his bike off the cliff at *just* the right angle so that we could only see his back."

"You mean it wasn't him? Who was riding the bike?"

"Apparently it was some prosthetic dummy he'd rigged for an action movie a while back."

Seven laughed. He was impressed. "I guess we were the real dummies."

She gave a wide-eyed smile. "Uh, yeah! Good thing he works for me now."

"Eve, there's something I need to ask you." He knew it wasn't an elegant transition, but he was acutely aware of the sun beginning its descent.

She looked concerned. "What is it?"

He got on his knees and held out his hand.

Eve gasped. "You…you kept it."

The ring felt cold against his palm as he asked. The diamond flickered orange when she answered.

The End

WE, THE WATCHED

Watch the beginnings of Seven's fight against the Guard in *We, The Watched*, the prequel to *Divided We Fall*.

After waking with no memory of his past, Seven struggles to conform to a society that accepts invasive surveillance by the government and forced uniformity by the church as necessary safeguards for protecting national security. But will the fresh perspective from his rebirth be a blessing or a curse?

"There's action, romance, and social commentary woven into a brilliant story with an amazing plot twist near the end," writes David Broughton in the *American Chronicle*. "It's science fiction in the way that Orwell's *1984* or *Fahrenheit 451* by Ray Bradbury dystopian novels are considered science fiction … The writing is nearly on par with these geniuses of the written word."

"The dialog was excellent and the situations seemed driven by curiosity, which is a great way to pull you into an adventure," said Elizabeth M. for *Readers' Favorite*. "The author captures the imagination of the reader."

For more information, visit WeTheWatched.com.

ABOUT THE AUTHOR

ADAM BENDER writes speculative fiction that explores modern-day political fears with a balance of action and romance.

Adam self-published his first two novels, *We, The Watched* and *Divided We Fall*. He was a quarterfinalist in the 2013 Amazon Breakthrough Novel Awards, in which *Divided We Fall* was selected as one of the top 100 novels in the sci-fi category. Adam has also written several short stories.

A journalist by day, Adam has reported extensively on technology and the international debate between personal privacy and national security. He is a senior journalist for *Computerworld*, *Techworld* and *CIO* in Sydney, Australia. He previously covered US politics on Capitol Hill for the esteemed Washington trade journal, *Communications Daily*. He has won journalism awards from the Society of Professional Journalists (SPJ) and the Specialized Information Publishers Association.

Adam maintains an active social media presence on Twitter (@WatchAdam) and Facebook (facebook.com/wethewatched). He also has a website and blog located at adambenderwrites.com.

He lives with his wife in Sydney.

Made in the USA
Columbia, SC
21 November 2017